A HOT FAKE-RELATIONSHIP ROMANCE

SARA WHITNEY

THE CINNAMON ROLL ALPHAS SERIES

Tempting Lies

Cinnamon Roll Alphas

Copyright © Sara Whitney 2020

Published by LoveSpark Press, Peoria, IL

Developmental Editor: Sue Brown-Moore
Editor: Victory Editing

Ebook ISBN: 978-1-953565-04-4
Print ISBN: 978-1-953565-03-7

First Edition: September 2020
v. 1.7

To Skye Malone,
an outstanding author and an even better friend

He's out to prove he can do more than swing a hammer.

Thea Blackwell never commits to anything. Not jobs. Not hairstyles. Not men. Yet here she is dreaming about setting down roots by buying a house and having it renovated by the town playboy who never spared her a second glance.

Aiden Murdoch's sick of his wild reputation following him everywhere he goes. Then his childhood friend Thea shows him her money pit of a fixer-upper, and he stumbles on the perfect solution: he'll provide the labor, and she'll make him look happily domesticated to shut down the town gossip.

What should be a simple arrangement gets complicated fast when fake kisses turn into real feelings. With forever on the line, will Thea and Aiden be brave enough to tear down the lies they've told each other—and themselves?

Keep in touch!

Subscribe to Sara's newsletter to stay up on new releases, sales, and giveaways!
sarawhitney.com/newsletter

CONTENTS

Chapter 1	1
Chapter 2	13
Chapter 3	23
Chapter 4	35
Chapter 5	47
Chapter 6	59
Chapter 7	73
Chapter 8	83
Chapter 9	95
Chapter 10	107
Chapter 11	117
Chapter 12	131
Chapter 13	145
Chapter 14	155
Chapter 15	167
Chapter 16	179
Chapter 17	189
Chapter 18	197
Chapter 19	211
Chapter 20	223
Chapter 21	233
Chapter 22	243
Chapter 23	257
Chapter 24	267
Chapter 25	275
Chapter 26	285
Chapter 27	297
Chapter 28	305
Epilogue	315

Author's Note   319
Also by Sara Whitney   321
About the Author   325

ONE

Thea Blackwell wasn't going to let herself cry.

For one thing, she didn't have any Kleenex on her.

For another thing, it was so cold that any tears would probably freeze and scratch her eyeballs.

And for *another* other thing, crying wouldn't make her tire any less flat or the parking lot any less empty or the night any less dark.

"Sh-sh-shit."

The word shuddered from her rapidly numbing lips as a tremor wracked her body. Two minutes in the frigid February air had been enough to leave her fingers stiff and her skin raw. Why the hell hadn't she worn her coat to the bar tonight? Peter was right; her vanity really *would* be the death of her.

Forcing herself into motion under the halo of the buzzing lights attached to the outside of the bar, she fumbled with her keys and popped open the hatchback on Juniper to shove the big box of radio-station swag inside. Then she hustled to the front and slid into the driver's seat. There was no point in turning on the ignition;

Juniper's crappy heater took at least ten minutes to produce any noticeable warmth, at which point she'd be tucked into a Lyft and on her way home.

The thought had her reaching for the phone, but when her stiff fingers finally managed to pull up the app, she whimpered. Not a single car was available. And why would they be? It was an hour past last call for the bars in Beaucoeur, which meant all the party people were off the streets for the night. She'd changed out a flat before, but never in pitch-black subzero weather, and the idea held no appeal.

At that moment, the bar lights shut off for the night, plunging her into total darkness.

"Shit!" She thrust aside the thread of fear curling through her chest and shoved her hands under her armpits for warmth as she considered her from-bad-to-worse options. Call Faith, who might not have her phone on silent and would probably come and rescue her. Or call her mom, who absolutely *would* have hers on silent thanks to Peter's "no calls after eight p.m." rule and might not come rescue her even if she did answer. Either way, it would set her up for a lecture on the dangers of improper car maintenance on an older vehicle like Juniper.

Death by frostbite might be preferable. Somebody would find her body when the bar reopened for its Saturday patrons, right? That's if she didn't get carried off by a murderer lurking out there in the pitch-black night.

"Shit, shit, shit." She let her head fall forward, punctuating each word with forehead taps to the steering wheel. She was so screwed.

"Hey there. Need help?"

Thea whipped upright with a short, sharp scream and frantically mashed the flashlight app on her phone to illuminate the source of the voice outside her window. Brandishing her phone with trembling fingers, she inhaled in preparation to shriek her head off, but the sound died in her throat at the sight of the man wincing under the laser-beam light.

"Aiden?" For a moment every muscle in her body froze. Not because of the subzero weather this time but because the hottest guy in Beaucoeur was lifting a hand to shield his eyes from her flashlight.

"Yeah, just making sure everything was okay. You're the only other car in the lot."

"Uh, sorry," she said, swinging the beam away from his face. Forcing the biggest smile possible, she popped open the door and stepped back out into the night. The wind sliced right through her T-shirt and skinny jeans, and her tremors started up again. "Flat tire and no Lyfts available."

Aiden Murdoch's brows lifted so far they disappeared under his knit hat. "Also no coats anywhere?"

Another tremor, stronger this time. "D-didn't wear one. It's always hot inside the bar."

Without a word, he unzipped his Murdoch Construction coat and handed it to her. "Here."

"No, I couldn't." But even as she objected, she slid it around her shoulders, wrapping her hands around the collar and burrowing into its warmth.

"Oh please," Aiden said as he pulled off his hat and plopped it on her head. "Like I'm gonna let you freeze. Come on. I'm parked over there." He jerked his head to the right, and this time Thea's smile wasn't forced.

"My hero!"

Normally she hated trucks that were so far off the ground she had to make a running jump to get inside, but tonight she gratefully heaved herself onto the plush bench seat with all the grace of a whale beaching itself. Aiden managed to climb in far more smoothly, but his legs were almost as long as her whole body, so it's not like it was a fair comparison.

"So warm," she moaned, holding the icicles that were her fingers up to the heat blasting from the vent.

"That's nothing." Aiden flicked a grin at her and tapped a button on the console.

Almost immediately, her backside started to heat up. She gave a delighted wiggle despite the late hour and the overall crappy circumstances. Heated seats were one of her bucket list items.

Aiden put the car into drive. "Where to?"

"The Mayflower Apartments." She slid her arms into his coat, which was eleventy sizes too big and swaddled her like a warm cocoon that smelled vaguely of sawdust and coffee. "Thanks. You may literally have saved my life."

Her childhood neighbor shrugged as he pulled out of the parking lot, his headlights revealing the empty stretch of road in front of them. As they drove, the streetlights pierced the darkness of the truck cab before retreating, each time illuminating another portion of his handsome, all-American face: the stubble on his sharp jaw, the upward tilt of his generous lips, the slightly-too-long brown hair curling around his ear.

"I'm glad I noticed you. What had you there so late?" he asked, jarring her out of her Aiden trance. She'd been staring at him like a weirdo.

And God, it *was* late. A jaw-cracking yawn attacked her. She indulged and then shook her head to stay alert, reaching up to adjust his hat. Not like it'd mess up her hair, which had gone limp and straggly hours ago thanks to the heat in the overcrowded bar. "Cleaning up after the Brick Babes. You?"

"Cleaning up after the Moo Daddies."

Several times a month, the dozen-member Brick Babe team shimmied into their one-size-too-small T-shirts to rep 105.5 the Brick at events around the Beaucoeur area. Tonight's gig was a concert by the Moo Daddies, the popular local cover band that featured Aiden on drums.

He slid a glance her way as they drove. "If we're on cleanup, does that make us the responsible ones?"

"Scary thought." She gave an exaggerated grimace, yet it wasn't too far from the truth.

The Moo Daddies always drew huge music-loving crowds, so she'd spent her night laughing and flirting and ordering drinks while the band rocked out. And those were all things she was good at. Enjoyed, even. Except tonight, when the responsibility for the girls and the shirts and the bumper stickers had left her feeling annoyed and put-upon.

She sighed and lifted her hands to the heating vent again. "Somehow I've become their den mother. 'Sure, Thea'll take care of the boxes of swag at the end of the night. It's not like she was busy keeping Kimmie's hair from falling into the toilet while she puked up those last four shots of tequila.'" She shuddered at the memory of wrestling the overly apologetic drunk girl away from the water as she flopped around like a fish. "By the time I sent her home with Bex, everybody else had cleared out, so I had to pack it all up on my own."

Oh Lordy, she was babbling. She crammed her still-chilly fingers under her thighs and ordered her motor-mouth to slow its roll. Nervous chatter was her default setting even around gorgeous guys she'd known her whole life. Maybe *especially* around gorgeous guys she'd known her whole life.

This particular gorgeous guy's lips twitched into a smile. "They could have a worse den mother."

"Why do I have to be *anybody's* mother?" she grumbled. "It's not like I'm that much older than them. No more than five years." Actually, Bex was all of twenty-one, which made Thea eight years older. But she didn't offer that factoid up to Aiden. "So how'd you get to be the den father for the band?"

"Drums take the longest to pack up." He tapped his fingers on the top of the steering wheel in time to the Liz Phair song on the radio. "And I've got the most space."

"Makes sense." She cast a teasing glance at the truck bed. "Got the lucky lady of the night stashed back there too?"

As she turned back around, she caught sight of the smile slipping off his face. "Nothing there but my kit."

Huh. The tightness of his voice surprised her, as did his answer. "No girl?"

Aiden *always* ended the night with a woman—not that she'd ever experienced that for herself, although several of her girlfriends had.

"No girl," he said shortly.

She watched his fingers tense and then release around the steering wheel, but before she could pursue it further —and oh, she would *definitely* love to pursue it further— her phone buzzed in her jeans pocket. She did a little dance to slide it out from under the coat and seat belt.

"Ooooh." Her pulse kicked up at the notification box, and she tapped to open the new screen. *"Oooooohhhh."*

"What's got you so excited?" Aiden inclined his chin

toward her phone as they idled at a stoplight regulating an empty intersection.

"Porn," she said absently. But he looked so startled that she immediately let him off the hook. "Real estate porn."

His shoulders relaxed and he grinned. "Whew, kid. You scared me for a second."

Kid? Her eyes narrowed. "For actual porn, I prefer man-on-man. Twice the beautiful bodies to ogle."

"Jesus," he muttered, eyes snapping forward. The light turned green, and he hit the accelerator with enough force that she rocked back against the seat.

"Serves you right. I'm not the little girl next door anymore." But her attention was already back on her phone as she swiped through photos. Despite the Midwest cold pressing against the window, heat ignited in her chest. It was *perfect*.

"So tell me about this real estate porn."

She hadn't expected Aiden to be interested. Then again, construction was his family business.

"It's my house." She clasped the phone to her heart where it was going *pitter-pat* under the thick layer of his coat. "The house I've wanted to buy my whole life."

"Oh yeah? Which number?"

His question confused her until she realized he'd pulled into her apartment complex. "Oh, building two."

He pulled his truck around and slid it into the available guest slot in front of the glass entrance door before notching the gear into park. "And the house?"

She looked down at her phone and bit her lip, already feeling a little silly for bringing it up. Still, how often was she sitting next to a certified expert? "Okay, I know it's late, but can you tell me if I'm an idiot for thinking about buying this?" She handed her phone over.

After a moment, recognition spread across his face. "This is one of the houses off Prospect Point."

She nodded. "One of the smaller ones, yeah." She kept talking as he swiped through the listing photos. "The only reason I could come close to affording anything on that street is because it needs so much work. What I don't know is if it maybe needs too much work for me to afford."

His large hand dwarfed her phone as he pinched and zoomed, the glow from the screen illuminating his furrowed brow. "It's tough to tell just from the pictures. Considering the age of the house and some of these photos, I'm guessing it's full of lead paint and outdated heating and cooling. Oh, and the basement probably floods."

Her heart dropped. "You're right. It was stupid to even think about buying it." She inhaled hard against the sharp swell of disappointment and reached for her phone.

He refused to relinquish it, instead flashing that irresistible grin. "Are you kidding me? This is one of my favorite houses on the Point. All that Tudor architecture and brickwork. And look at the ceiling in the master bedroom here. It's just begging for a skylight, don't you think?" He tapped the photo in question with one long finger. "You should at least get someone with some expertise to walk through it with you."

"Good idea. Do you know anybody?" she chirped, and as she hoped, it made him laugh.

"Sixteen years of construction experience at your service." He waved a hand down his body with a flourish.

"Are you serious?" She held her breath, expecting him

to brush her off. After all, he was *Aiden freaking Murdoch*, every woman's fantasy fling and one of the busiest contractors in town. Why would he take the time to help her? They were friendly, but they weren't exactly friends.

Then he almost killed her by flashing that smile and crinkling the corners of those hazel eyes. "If I wasn't serious, I wouldn't have offered."

Her heart hammered at this unexpected turn. "Okay then. Would... would you be willing to walk through it with me sometime this coming week? Because I really love this house and I've been waiting for it to go on the market forever, and my Realtor friend told me to keep my eye out, and the listing just popped up, and I don't want to wait." More word babble, but Aiden just rolled with it.

"Sure. Make an appointment and I'll be there. Here." He tapped in a number on her phone, and a moment later an electric ringing sounded from his pocket. He hit End on the call and held her phone out for her.

His fingers brushed against hers as she reached for it, and she barely suppressed a nervous giggle at the zing of pleasure she got from the contact. Was she really ending her shit night by collecting Aiden's digits? Most of the single ladies in Beaucoeur would slap their grandmas to get their hands on that. Although they'd known each other for two and a half decades, they'd never had a single reason to exchange phone numbers before, and for some reason this felt more intimate than knowing she could reach him through whatever social media accounts they were connected on. Then again, this was for work purposes, and he wasn't exactly angling to come upstairs with her tonight, was he? Not that she'd say yes if he was.

Probably.

Her eyes cut over to the strong lines of his face, and she shifted at the thought of what bringing Aiden up to her apartment would actually be like. Then something sharp jabbed her in the butt. "Ow!"

She arced off the seat and groped around until she found the culprit: an earring.

"Um. Yours?" She held it out to him, all dangle and sparkles in the watery light of the parking lot, and he had the good grace to look chagrined.

"Yeah, no." He plucked it from her palm and dropped it into the cup holder. "Sorry about that."

The physical reminder of Aiden's playboy ways was what she needed to get her sorry self out of the truck. This night would *definitely* not end with him following her up to the fifth floor. She sighed and started to shrug out of his jacket.

"Give it back on the house tour." He reached for his seat belt. "I'll walk you up."

"No!" He'd called her *kid* not ten minutes ago. No need for another reminder that their night would end with nothing more heart-racing than a platonic hand-shake. "It's eight feet to the entrance, and you can see the elevator from here. Thanks though."

He shrugged and tapped the steering wheel, and she slid out of the truck, praying that she'd stick the landing.

"Okay, thanks again!"

"Night," he said. Then, "Hey!"

She turned quickly, heart in her throat and hoping for... What? That he'd invite himself up?

"You got a tire guy?" he asked. "For your car?"

She blinked. Right. Her car. "Uh, no."

He nodded. "I'll text you my guy's number. Tell him I sent you."

"Oh. Thanks. Again. Um, good night." With an awkward final smile, she slammed the door shut and hustled inside, grateful for the warmth of his coat and the brightness of his headlights until she was safely on the elevator. As soon as the doors dinged shut, she dropped her perky-girl act and sagged against the wall.

For better or for worse, she was the one woman in Beaucoeur that Aiden Murdoch never even considered going home with.

TWO

Aiden Murdoch woke up on Saturday morning, alone in his bed and with a clear head.

Still a little weird, but it was all part of the plan.

He rolled over and blinked up at the ceiling, frowning when he noticed a crack that had appeared in the far corner near the wall. The heir to Beaucoeur's premiere construction and renovation business couldn't possibly let that stand.

He added it to the day's mental to-do list, then rolled out of bed and headed for the bathroom. The mirror over the sink confirmed that the tan he'd picked up on his beach vacation last month had mostly vanished under his usual February-in-Illinois pallor. Unlike most Saturday mornings over the past several years, his eyes weren't bloodshot and he hadn't kicked aside a used condom wrapper on his way across the room, but his expression was grim, and his hair was shaggy and in need of a cut.

"You're killing it," he muttered at his reflection before turning away from the mirror.

He snapped on the shower and contemplated stepping under the icy water before it'd warmed up, just to shock the self-pity out of his system, but steam obscured the gray-and-black-tiles almost immediately thanks to his beast of a water heater. Masochistic shower foiled by good home maintenance. He stepped under the spray and let the hot water drum away every other thought for a few minutes before he soaped up, rinsed off, and toweled dry, glad he'd dropped the money to install heaters in the new bathroom flooring. No one living in Beaucoeur would regret warm tiles under their cold, wet feet in February.

Twenty minutes later, he was dressed and behind the wheel of his truck, on his way to his buddy Dave's with a travel mug of coffee riding shotgun. His phone dinged with an incoming email alert, and he immediately turned it to silent. Not even weekends were safe from some new work crisis. A promise his dad had made to a client but forgotten to tell him about or some new backhanded dig from his perpetually pissed-off brother. It would all be there waiting for him on Monday.

When he arrived at the Chiltons' two-story brick house, Dave opened the door before Aiden had a chance to knock. His friend resettled his glasses on his long nose. "Rough night?"

"Late night." Aiden stepped inside and shrugged off his jacket. It was the one with the varnish stain on the sleeve since Thea had his good one. He'd basically had a whole conversation with her eyebrows last night because the rest of her face had been swaddled in his far-too-big coat.

"Late night, huh?"

Dave's speculative tone made him bristle. "Nothing like that. Thea Blackwell had a flat, so I helped her out."

"A flat in that cold last night? Poor kid."

Unexpected heat twisted in Aiden's stomach. "I wouldn't call her 'kid' to her face."

Knowing Thea's porn preferences shouldn't be that weird. Knowing that she watched porn *at all* shouldn't be that weird. She wasn't the eight-year-old living across the street anymore. Still, the thought of Thea, all wholesome pink cheeks and perky smiles, typing in search terms and hitting Play on a video while her hand crept down to her—

"You with me, dude?"

Dave's words jolted him back to reality, and he self-consciously cleared his throat. "Yeah. Yep. Let's hit that last wall."

This was his third weekend in a row helping Dave finish his basement to turn it into a playroom for his kids, and Aiden took a great deal of professional pride in the fact that the work was right on schedule. The last of the drywall would go up today, they'd spend next weekend painting, and then Dave could move in whatever furniture the kids might want to destroy just in time for his wife to give birth to Chilton Child Number Three.

"Actually," Dave said as he weaved around the toys scattered across the living room on the way to the basement stairs, "I was wondering if we could focus on the bathroom today. Ana's been complaining about how dingy the floor in there is, so I'd love to put down something fresh."

Aiden almost tripped over an abandoned toy fire truck that Dave had neatly sidestepped, and the wail of the little electronic siren followed them as they descended the basement stairs. He could lay tile with his eyes closed, but the timetable he'd built for the project didn't account for bathroom work. Time to treat Dave the way he would a client who made a suggestion that didn't quite fit inside the project parameter: with a winning smile and a polite misdirect.

"How about we finish up the walls today, then I'll take measurements and shoot you some flooring options on Monday for you to consider?"

"Sure thing. You're the expert," Dave said easily.

He started shuffling his schedule around in his head as he and Dave laid out the drywall supplies. If he swung by some night during the week, he could get started on the paint job, which would open up some time next Saturday for the tile while still keeping the end date on track. He was supposed to meet his buddy Daniel at the gym after work on Tuesday, so maybe Wednesday would work to start painting. Yeah, that could be good.

"So you really didn't pick up a girl after the show?"

Aiden's mental schedule rejiggering slammed to a halt. *Christ, this again?*

"Really." His fists clenched around the drywall screws in his palm.

"No offense." Dave gave a typical laid-back shrug. "I just figured if you were going to backslide, it'd happen on a Moo Daddies night."

"That makes two of us," he muttered, snatching the electric drill as he braced for yet another conversation on this godforsaken topic.

Aiden had spun through his twenties on a merry-go-round of women who hopped on and off with ease. But a few months ago he'd shut the carnival down entirely. Not like he was *looking* to settle down, but he'd faced the fact that he needed to stop sleeping around for a bit to focus on the family's construction business. As a bonus, it might make him the subject of a little less gossip around town. But fast, easy, no-strings sex was a hard habit to break, and he'd be lying if he said he hadn't been tempted to go back to his old ways once or twice or ten times.

"No backsliding, no hookups. That's the plan." He said it out loud, more as a reminder to himself than anything else.

Dave smirked as he grabbed the next sheet of drywall. "Your legions of fans will be devastated."

Aiden just grunted and was saved from further conversation on the topic by the arrival of Dave's extremely pregnant wife hauling an overstuffed laundry hamper behind her.

"No, no, I got it," Ana announced as the hamper bumped down each step in her wake. "Really, Aiden, what man leaves his pregnant wife to deal with mounds of their children's laundry all by herself?"

She hit the bottom of the steps and slumped dramatically against the wall, resting a hand possessively on her belly. But her eyes danced as she looked at her husband, and Aiden bounded forward to play his part.

"A monster, that's who." He grabbed the handle of the hamper and dragged it the rest of the way to the washing machine. "Dump him and get with me. I'll carry anything you want. I'm very strong."

"Hear that, husband?" Ana twined a strand of hair around her finger and batted her lashes. "I've got other offers."

Dave pulled her in for a kiss. "Go back upstairs and put your feet up, woman. We've got this." He sent her on her way with a butt pat, and Aiden pointedly focused on placing the next sheet of drywall while Dave started on the laundry.

A hard knot of jealousy lodged in his throat. Not because he was in love with his friend's wife or anything, but they were so... happy. Settled. Comfortable. They were a team, and for all that Aiden had great parents and good friends and an important role in the family business, he'd never had that kind of partnership with someone else, that ease and familiarity.

Staying single was a choice he'd actively made years ago. He'd dutifully majored in construction management at ISU and even dropped his music minor in favor of business, like his dad wanted. He'd started his career at Murdoch Construction the Monday after he'd graduated from college, and he'd never complained that he'd been groomed from day one to take over the business someday. But he'd drawn the line at marrying some nice girl way too young, the way his brother had. Sleeping around and staying unattached was his single act of rebellion, and he didn't regret it. His life was great.

Sometimes though. Sometimes a tiny part of him did wonder if he was missing out. Wondered if he even had it in him to be a boyfriend, husband, father.

"Hey. Lazy ass." Dave's voice snapped him out of his impending spiral. "I'm not paying you zero dollars to stand around daydreaming."

"I'm gonna start charging you by the insult," he warned as he picked up his drill and got back to work. By midafternoon they hit a stopping point, so Aiden packed up his shit, bid farewell to the Chilton family, and headed to the hardware store to grab the joint compound he'd need to fix the crack in his bedroom ceiling. Anything to keep his hands and his mind occupied so he wouldn't be tempted to backslide into "fuck first, ask questions later" territory. Sticking to the plan was easier when he filled his time, which usually wasn't hard. He had Moo Daddies gigs. He met up with his buddies at the Tenth Inning for pizza and beer while they watched whatever sports were in season at the time: Cubs, Bears, Bulls, Blackhawks. Hell, he even kept up his volunteer maintenance work for a handful of nonprofits around the area.

But tonight was wide open, and as he left the hardware store with his purchase, the siren song of the familiar started up in his head. It'd be so easy to head to a bar or call up one of the handful of women in his phone who had no expectations of him. It's how he'd spent his weekends for so long that it felt weird *not* to. He could text Paige, or maybe Jen. One of them might—

His phone buzzed as he slid into his truck.

Thea: *Does the offer still stand?*

For a split second, the question confused him. God, what had he promised her? And then he remembered the run-down house and Thea's nervous face as she asked him about it. Why nervous though? It had bothered him at the time, how tense she was in his car and how reluctant she was to ask for his help. He tapped out an immediate response.

Aiden: *Of course.*

Thea: *Is this afternoon too soon? Like in half an hour?*

Perfect. A house-walk-through distraction would keep him from making bad choices.

Aiden: *Sure. Meet you there.*

He tossed the phone on the seat next to him and started to put his truck in gear, then notched it back into park and reached for his phone.

Aiden: *Did my guy get your tire fixed?*

Jumping dots. No jumping dots. Jumping dots again, and finally a response.

Thea: *Not yet. He had to order a new one.*

His thumbs started to work across the phone, but he abandoned that in favor of just hitting Call.

"Um, hi!" She sounded surprised to hear from him— fair, since he himself was a little surprised to have called her—yet her voice remained as chipper as ever.

"And how are you planning to get to the house if your car's still at Troy's shop?"

"Beaucoeur has Lyfts," she said in the friendliest *duh, idiot* voice he'd ever heard.

"Oh, for..." His eyes rolled skyward, and he put the truck back into gear. "Sit tight. I'll be at your place in ten minutes."

"You don't have to—" she was saying as he disconnected and pulled out of the parking lot.

He found her waiting in the glass entryway of her apartment building, his coat folded over one arm. As soon as he pulled up, she practically skipped out to join him, hauling herself into his truck cab with a tiny bit of thrashing.

"You didn't have to pick me up!" she said by way of greeting, settling the jacket between them and adjusting a fuzzy scarf around her neck.

"Such an imposition. I was all of three miles away. Just a nightmare commute."

She wrinkled her nose at him. "I didn't mean to hijack your whole afternoon."

"I don't mind."

"Really?"

Again the surprise. It rankled. "Really. Why would I mind?"

"I mean, we're not friends." She studied her thumbnail as she said it, not meeting his eyes, which was just as well. It meant she didn't see his chin jerk backward.

"We're not?" He ignored the tiny sting her words caused.

"Come on, not really." She sounded exasperated, which was only slightly preferable to nervous. "We say hi when we bump into each other. We chat when our mutual friends all get together. But we don't do *this*." She gestured around his truck, he guessed to encompass "go places together" or "intentionally hang out."

"I suppose you've got a point."

The smile she gave him was a lot less perky than usual. "We rode bikes together when we were kids. Then..." Her half smile vanished, and she swallowed hard before continuing. "Then Mom and I moved, and I didn't see you again until high school."

He was aware that a chasm of pain lurked beneath the details she'd skipped over, but if she wasn't going to address it, he sure as hell wasn't going there. "You were a freshman when I was a senior. It would've been a little weird if we'd hung out after all that time."

"Well that. And by then you'd turned into—" Rather than finish the thought, she waved a hand in his direction.

"Turned into...?" The smart part of him didn't want her to keep going, but the masochistic part of him was dying to hear her description.

"You know." Her smile was back, tart as ever. "Adonis Aiden."

He groaned as he turned his truck in to Prospect Point. "Don't tell me she got to you too?"

"Who, Mabel? The bestower of great nicknames?" She bounced in her seat. "She sure did, Adonis!"

"Dammit," he muttered but without any heat. Busting-his-chops Thea was preferable to nervous Thea and *far* preferable to sad Thea. He brought the truck to a halt in front of their destination. "Friends or not, we're here."

THREE

She was parked in front of her dream house, but Thea couldn't tear her eyes off the man behind the wheel. Aiden's too-long brown hair curled against his neck, and his cheeks and nose were pink from the cold. With the playful tilt of his lips and the crinkles at the corner of his eyes, he could star in a commercial promoting the healthful benefits of brisk midwestern winters. Women would move here in droves.

She'd been flustered ever since she'd heard his voice on the other end of the phone, so much so that she blurted out all that nonsense about their nonfriendship. Like he cared about any of that. *Get your shit together, Blackwell.* He was just a man, after all. A nice, handsome man with big, capable hands that dwarfed the steering wheel.

Okay, thinking about his hands wasn't helping. And now she'd been sitting there silently for far longer than was normal, and her stupid brain wouldn't cough up a single thing to say that wouldn't make her sound like an idiot.

"Realtor's not here yet." See? Idiot.

Thankfully, the charisma machine next to her just grinned and slouched back in his seat, his eyes traveling past her to 201 Prospect Point with its steep pitched roof and light-colored stone-and-timber exterior. "So talk to me while we wait. Why is this the house for you?"

Here was a topic she could warm up to. "I just... I love it so much." She sighed. "It's like the scrappy kid sister to all the other houses in the neighborhood."

Prospect Point ran along the bluff overlooking the Illinois River, with the city's grandest homes on one side and a glorious view of the river valley on the other. The majority of the houses were either intimidating palaces built a century and a half earlier by the city's founders or they were recently constructed monuments of glass and sharp angles built after the new owners bought the less-desirable homes on the street to knock down.

Not Thea's house though. It was located at the very end of the road and was far more modest than its showy neighbors. In fact, Thea's house could be stowed inside the living rooms of most of the Point houses.

"If you have a house on Prospect, you go all out for the holidays. Everybody spends the weekend after Thanksgiving getting ready for all the traffic that drives by to see the decorations." She pressed her forehead against the cold window glass, imagining twinkle lights lining the picture window and a cascade of pine and mistletoe gracing the front door. "Isn't that nice?"

"It's a Norman Rockwell nightmare."

His reply was unapologetically horrified, and on instinct, she reached out and flicked a finger against his bicep. Even though it would barely have registered through all his winter layers, she froze, a nervous smile fixed on her face. They definitely didn't have a touchy-feely relationship, and she'd probably made it weird.

But he just laughed and wrapped one of those work-man's hands around his upper arm. "Geez, killer. That's some left hook."

The pressure in her chest dissolved at the curl of lazy amusement in his voice. "Ha, sorry," she said weakly. God, she hated when her natural exuberance went to war with her fear of rejection. But his grin assured her she'd worried for nothing yet again. Story of her life. She shrugged and returned to the topic. "After years of apart-ment living, the thought of being part of a community like that is intriguing." Intriguing and a little scary actually. But there was no sense dwelling on whether she was brave enough to commit to a house before knowing if she could even afford the damn thing.

"So if the neighborhood is all about community, what caused *this*?" Aiden gestured toward the property in front of them.

She sighed. Age hadn't been kind to her house. The timber beams badly needed a coat or three of paint, and the gutters sagged drunkenly off the roofline in all direc-tions, soggy leaves and tufts of birds' nests sticking out haphazardly.

"Okay, you know Faith Fox?" Thea asked. "She grad-uated in my year."

"Faith Fox..." He frowned in thought. "Tall, blond hair, blue streaks?"

She nodded, and he shrugged. "Yeah, I've seen her around."

Of course. Good ol' Thea never got a second glance from Aiden in high school or beyond, but he knew exactly what the brash, gorgeous Faith looked like.

"Well." She cleared her throat and pressed forward. "Faith's parents know half the people on the block, and apparently the owner moved into assisted care about fifteen years ago. Mrs. Rebhetz's family tried it as a rental property for a little bit but got tired of the maintenance, so it sat empty until she died last winter."

She fought back a wave of sadness. Doris Rebhetz had loved this house and lavished it with care until she wasn't able to anymore. Now more than anything, Thea wanted to be the person to set the house to rights and make it a beloved home once more, even if it required the biggest commitment she'd ever made.

"That's a shame." Aiden's eyes moved across the bedraggled, overgrown landscape, dressed in the dead brown of winter.

"It is," Thea said fiercely, her anger surging at the thoughtless family who let this beautiful place fall into disrepair. "I guess it took a little while for her estate to settle. I've had my Realtor friend stalking the listings for me, and... here we are."

"What's your renovation budget?" Aiden asked.

"Yeah. Umm, about that."

The only good thing about 201's sad state was that it made the listing price almost—*almost*—within the realm of affordability for her. If it were in even slightly better shape or anywhere approaching the size of its fancy neighbors, it would be comically far out of her price range. She gnawed on her lip for a second, then blurted out the renovation amount she'd calculated based on the house's listed price, the estimated monthly payments, and the lack of zeroes in her bank account.

Aiden grabbed a zippered portfolio from the center console and opened it to jot the figure down. And then because she was still a little nervous and being nervous made her talkative, she filled the truck with more chatter.

"So it's got three bedrooms, which is perfectly cozy, and a master bath with a claw-foot tub. Oh! And there's a breakfast nook and built-in bookshelves, and I know the landscaping's a mess, but I think there's something salvageable in there once summer rolls around. And look! The front door's round on top, like something out of the Shire."

"Bilbo-approved," Aiden said. "What else?"

She cut her eyes to him, searching for sarcasm, but his mouth was curved into a relaxed smile as his gaze traced the steep roofline, so she plowed ahead.

"I know its interior was last updated in like 1973, and since it was built near the turn of the century, I'm sure it has wiring issues and God knows what else, but I don't want somebody to buy this house and tear it down so they can build something bigger and fancier," she said. "Too many people overlook the small and the cute in favor of the extravagant and the obvious, and that's too bad." She blinked and stopped talking.

Aiden had turned in the passenger seat to face her, his eyes alight. "Okay," he said. "I'll give you a fair estimate of how much work it's going to take to make your small little charmer into a habitable home."

Before she started burbling a monologue of gratitude, the Realtor's SUV pulled into the driveway behind them.

"Showtime." Aiden tossed open the door and let a blast of cold air invade the cozy interior.

"Thea!" Melinda May, with her steel-wool hair and her red blazer peeking out from her faux-leopard coat, greeted her with a hug when they reached the round-topped hobbit door. "I didn't know you were bringing your boyfriend."

"Oh, he's not my boyfriend!" Thea exclaimed, and Melinda looked more closely at him once they were inside and out of the cold.

"No, he's definitely not." She inclined her head. "You're Aiden Murdoch."

He returned her nod with a curious lift of his brows, and she explained, "Your company did a remodel on my office building about five years ago. Most of the girls took long lunch breaks when you were there working."

"I had no idea I had fans in the real estate biz." Aiden grinned as he said it, but it didn't look as natural to Thea's eyes as those white flashes of teeth he'd treated her to in the car.

Melinda nudged Thea. "You probably remember. You were answering my phones back then, right?"

"Sure was!" she chirped, glancing nervously at Aiden.

Now his smile was the real thing. "Did you take in the show over lunch, Ms. Blackwell?"

Busted for ogling half a decade later. That had to be some kind of record. She cleared her throat and spun toward the living room. "Smells musty," she said loudly. Anything to get off the topic of the three weeks she'd spent eating turkey wraps and watching Aiden's lean, strong arms flex as he climbed up and down a ladder.

"Not surprising. The grout around the stone at the entrance looks a little patchy. Water might've gotten in." He'd jumped into all-work mode too, thank God. "You'll want the home inspector to make sure it's not a major leak or hiding a bunch of mold. It's fixable but could be pricey."

He brushed against her in the narrow entryway on his

way to the living room, and she briefly imagined that she could feel the heat of his body through their thick winter coats.

"So are you still at the dentist's office? That's who you left me for, as I recall."

Melinda's words pulled Thea back. "Hmm? Oh no. That was"—she studied the ceiling as she counted back—"maybe four jobs ago?"

"Weren't you working customer relations at the Beaucoeur zoo?" Aiden's question came from the far end of the room, where he had his pen tucked behind his ear as he stretched a tape measure across the front window.

How the hell did he know about that? It had been her shortest employment stint to date, at least until her ill-fated radio career. "Yep," she said brightly. "After the dentist but before the bakery."

He gave a hum of acknowledgment and went back to measuring, although Thea could feel the unspoken questions from both of them pressing against her: *What is this chick's problem with work?*

God, if they only knew the half of it.

"Kitchen's through that door." Melinda took control of the walk-through again. "And it flows into the dining room, then the hallway leading to an office, a bathroom, and the stairs to the second floor."

Aiden fiddled with the light switch on the wall. "Knob and tube wiring?"

"Used to be," Melinda said. "They replaced it in the seventies."

He nodded and scrawled another note as she herded them along. Thea ran a hand along the faded rose-patterned wallpaper in the hall on the way to the kitchen, stopping short in the doorway. *"Wow."*

Aiden whistled long and low. "You can say that again."

"Okay. *Wooooow.*" They stood side by side in silence, taking in the fussy, dark-stained cabinets with gaudy curlicue handles. The countertops were avocado, the worn linoleum had flecks of orange and green, and the crowning glory was the ancient harvest-gold refrigerator.

"Yes. It needs a little work," Melinda acknowledged before she moved on to the dining room.

"'A little' is an understatement," Aiden whispered.

She wrinkled her nose and whispered back, "Isn't it awful?" Then she looked around again and pictured it when it was shiny and new. "I bet Doris was so excited when she picked it all out."

"Nice thought." He ran a finger through the dust that had accumulated on the kitchen windowsill. "It goes on the list. At least I don't see any signs of busted pipes or vermin."

"Vermin?" Thea glanced up at him sharply. "What kind?"

"Termites, spiders, sometimes rats."

She took a nervous step toward him. "Rats?"

He slung an arm around her shoulder and gave her a quick squeeze. "Don't worry. I'll fend 'em off."

She shuddered and allowed herself to shrink into his side for one brief, heady moment before pulling away to follow Melinda through the dining room and up the stairs to the second floor. She was intensely aware of Aiden right behind her on the steps, no doubt eye level with her butt. Not that he'd be tempted to take a peek.

The second floor was a little smaller than the first floor, with two bedrooms facing the street and the master suite facing the river. The ceiling in the bedroom was low enough that Aiden barely had to stretch to poke at the drop ceiling.

"Whatever's under here has to be better than this." He nudged her and gestured upward. "What do think? Skylight potential?" Before she could answer, he'd turned to Melinda. "What's under this carpet?"

"Let's find out." She carefully knelt in her suit skirt and pried up a corner of the dusty shag carpeting, revealing scuffed wooden boards. "The original flooring was oak all through the house, I believe."

"It's hard to say what shape it's in now," Aiden said, more to himself than either of the women. "Might be nice if it's refinished. Might be a disaster if it's got too much damage though."

He knelt to look more closely at the exposed bit of floor, adding more notes to his book. Thea had been nervous about spending so much time with him this afternoon, but his laid-back questions about the house had eased her jitters. Plus she really *had* worried for nothing after she'd swatted his arm in the truck. Aiden was a toucher—not inappropriately, but he didn't hesitate to put a hand on her back to guide her toward the stairs or bump her shoulder to point out the glass-front, built-in bookcases along one wall in the bedroom. It chased away the last of her self-consciousness so much that when he came to stand next to her as she looked out of the sliding door that opened onto a balcony off the bedroom, she spoke without thinking.

"My dad loved this house." The words were out before she could call them back, and Aiden tipped his head toward her as he listened. "Doris hired him every summer to maintain the landscaping, so he spent a lot of hours here. He always said it would be the perfect fairytale cottage for his princess." Her eyes stung at the memory.

"I noticed the rosebushes outside. Do you think he planted those?" Aiden asked.

She'd seen the overgrown bushes too. "I do. As far as I know, nobody touched the landscaping after she moved out." She couldn't speak for a long moment as she battled back emotions at the thought of buying a house with roses that her father had selected and placed in the ground.

"Your dad's the one who taught me how to prune rosebushes."

She looked at him in surprise. "Did he? I didn't know that."

"Yeah. I was ten or so, and he joked that the Murdochs worked on the inside of houses and the Black-wells worked on the outside of houses." He shifted from foot to foot. "That was just before he..."

"Yeah." Before the cancer burned through him. Lee Blackwell died three months after his diagnosis, and Thea's life changed overnight. A hot lump rose in her throat and she swallowed hard, relieved that Melinda had descended to the first floor and was out of earshot.

"Anyway." She cleared her throat and willed away her melancholy. "I've been waiting my whole life for this house to go on the market, and now here we are."

"Here we are," he repeated, and together they turned back to the view of the river from the master bedroom. "Nice. I'm starting to think I should bid against you for this place. It's got potential."

She wheeled to face him, mouth open in horror. Then she saw his lips twitch. "Funny guy." She jabbed her elbow into his ribs, no longer afraid of overstepping now that she knew how tactile he was. "Back off. I saw it first."

He laughed and rubbed his side. "My God but you're pointy, woman."

They descended the stairs together, and Melinda busied herself in the front of the house, leaving the two of them alone in the glassed-in sunroom that ran the length of the house on the main floor. It had a spectacular view of the backyard and the bluff as it fell away to the river. At this time of day in February, the water caught the ruddy orange glow of the setting sun. They stood in the center of the empty room, the air turning their breath visible as they exhaled. They were silent for a few beats before Aiden spoke.

"I get why you want to bring this place back to life."

It thrilled her that he saw the beauty of the house too. "What do you think? Is it hopeless?"

He squinted as he flipped through the notes he'd taken on the tour. The dying daylight painted him in stripes of orange and pink, and the thick eyelashes resting on his cheeks briefly distracted her from her worry that she'd never be able to afford the repairs. Then he tapped his pen on the paper in a quick little rhythm, drawing her attention away from his face.

"It's not hopeless. The wiring's old but in decent shape. The bathrooms look okay. Some of the problems are cosmetic, like the shag carpeting and the drop ceiling. Others are more serious. That kitchen's a mess, and the exterior needs a whole overhaul. Oh, and I wouldn't walk out on that balcony until a structural engineer examines it more closely."

His pen never stopped moving as he spoke. "Of course, you'll need an actual home inspection prior to purchase; that'll tell you what shape the roof's in. But here's what I'm thinking."

He pushed the pad under her nose, and she saw a circled dollar amount that brought tears to her eyes.

"This is only a rough estimate," he said. "I'll need to draw up an official bid back at the office..."

His voice trailed off at Thea's shaky exhale.

"That's... There's no way I can afford that. Not along with actually buying the house." Even with the money from her dad's life insurance sitting in her account, she couldn't make it stretch that far. The knowledge settled heavy on her heart, and she stared at the reflection of the setting sun in the slow-moving river in front of them, blinking rapidly to keep the tears at bay.

Her dad had been wrong. She wasn't a princess, and this wasn't the house for her after all.

FOUR

Aiden parked in front of his parents' white-shuttered ranch house but didn't make a move to leave the cab of his truck. His was the third company vehicle on the property: his truck, license plate Murdoch 2, was on the street because Trip's Murdoch 3 was already parked next to his dad's Murdoch 1 in the driveway. Seeing the two trucks side by side ratcheted up his anxiety, as did the crooked mailbox at the edge of the property. It looked like someone had backed into it and hadn't bothered to secure it to its base again, which was an unsettling departure in form for his persnickety father.

The slam of his parents' front door pulled his attention to the porch where Trip stood waiting, arms crossed forbiddingly over his chest. Fuck, he hated this. He was built for chatting people up and organizing schedules, not fighting the people he loved over every decision. But judging by his brother's scowl, not fighting wasn't going to be in the cards today. Great.

He turned off the ignition and stepped outside, welcoming the cold bite of the metal on his skin when he pushed the door shut. He paused before walking up the sidewalk to face Trip and whatever was waiting for him at Sunday family dinner. Instead, he turned to the house across the street where grayish clumps of snow dotted the front yard. His gaze kept traveling until it landed on the wide driveway, and he was smacked by the memory of a knock-kneed little girl wobbling by on her first bicycle. Thea'd been the neighborhood socialite, always stopping to say hello to every neighbor she met and chattering away about school or unicorns or whatever it was that little girls were into.

And then her dad had died, and he hadn't seen her again until his senior year of high school. He'd figured she had enough sadness in her life by then, so he and his newly forming player reputation had steered clear of her. And that's how it'd been ever since. Casual *hi, how are you*s were the extent of their interaction over the past decade or so. Regret swirled in his stomach. He should've talked to her sooner, *really* talked to her, as someone who knew her full history.

"Dickhead! Let's go!"

The barked command had Aiden shutting his eyes and desperately trying to remember the serenity prayer. *Lord, grant me the wisdom to not murder my fucking brother over the mashed potatoes. Amen.*

He headed up the driveway and joined Trip on the porch. "Hey. I'm glad you're out here." He wasn't, but why be truthful? "We need to talk about Dad's—"

"Are you fucking kidding me?"

His brother's snarled words caught him off guard. "What's the problem?" He kept his voice even, but it was hard, particularly since Trip had blown up at him in front of their employees twice last week.

Trip brandished a handful of crumpled sheets of paper. "What the hell kind of estimate is this? Are we just doing work for free these days?"

Ah. The proposed contract for Thea's house, the one that cut every possible cost to the bone. He opened his mouth to defend himself, then snapped it shut. Admitting he'd guessed what Trip meant would be the same as admitting that he knew the estimate was abnormally low. So he played dumb. "I have no idea what you're talking about, man."

Trip flung the printout at him, but the pages just fluttered to the all-weather carpet under their feet, coming nowhere close to actually hitting him. "What's this bullshit?" Trip's thick finger stabbed downward at the scattered pages. "That's underbid by at least forty percent."

Aiden counted to five before speaking. He seemed to always be counting to five around his family. Every conversation he had with them these days felt like he was on *Sesame Street*. "Forty percent? Hardly." He bent and calmly collected the sheets. "It includes material at cost and a slightly reduced amount for labor if she's willing to let us do the work during our slow days."

Trip's gaze sharpened on Aiden's face. "*She?*"

Fuck. "Just a friend."

"A friend you're banging. Got it."

Yeah, that was about enough. Aiden's fist clenched around the papers and he hardened his voice, hating that everything with his brother was a battle these days. "She's a friend. That's all. I was just playing around with numbers for the job."

Trip's broad face twisted into a sneer. "Gotta use company perks to score a little pussy these days?"

"You jealous?" Aiden lifted his chin and regarded his

brother with smug pity. "Almost sounds like you wish *you* were the single one." He felt sick the instant he said it; his sister-in-law was great, and as far as he knew, she and Trip were happy. He dropped the asshole expression immediately. "Hey, I'm sorry—"

But Trip cut off his apology with a snarl. "Fuck you, *Adonis*. Like you know shit about commitment. I'd love to see you get a girl to stick around long enough to actually renovate her house."

The words arrowed straight to the center of his chest, and Aiden's hands curled into fists. But a rap on the front door interrupted the escalating fight, and they both turned to see their father's scowling face through the front-door glass. Trip turned on his heel and stormed inside, with Aiden following at a slower pace.

"About time," Rudy Murdoch grumbled after he stepped over the threshold.

"Thanks, Dad. Nice to see you too."

He harrumphed at Aiden's aggressively good-natured response. "Lunch is ready."

Aiden watched in consternation as Rudy shuffled into the dining room. When had his dad's mobility gotten so bad? That was an alarming development for a sixty-eight-year-old who refused to even consider slowing down on the job.

His mom planted a kiss on his cheek. "Perfect timing, sweetie. I just pulled the roast out of the oven."

"Of course you did," he said. Gloria Murdoch had some kind of second sense for the precise moment her offspring would be arriving and had always just pulled something out of the oven for them. Thanks to her gift of maternal foresight, he and Trip had been blessed with a childhood of still-warm cookies after school and an adulthood of home-cooked Sunday meals still sizzling in the pan.

He slipped into his usual spot at the table next to his mom and across from Trip and Ashley, who gave him a cheerful "hi!" Guilt swamped him again; the cute blonde didn't deserve to be pulled into his ongoing war with Trip. But his brother's face was carefully neutral, so hopefully the scene on the porch was the end of the ugliness for the day.

"Did Dale Deavers finalize the paint colors for his new garage interior?" Trip passed the bread basket to Ashley and looked to their dad for an answer, but Rudy didn't respond as he bit into his roast.

"Yes," Aiden said after a moment. "It's in your email. He wants Desert Sand."

Trip's eyes cut to him, then back to Rudy. "Okay. I can start tomorrow."

"You can have this whole conversation tomorrow at work. We're having a nice family dinner right now." As always, their mother sounded exasperated at the business talk around the table, and as always the Murdoch men ignored her.

"It's the only time all three of us are in the same place, Ma," Aiden said as he reached for a bowl of carrots swimming in gingery butter.

Her cheeks plumped in a smile, and she patted his hand where it rested on the table next to her. "Okay then."

Gloria Murdoch was petite and pleasant and entirely huggable. She was the patient center of the masculine storm that was the Murdoch household, keeping order at the family construction business as the office manager and making a warm and loving home even when her sons had been teenagers prone to thundering through the house and bellowing rather than speaking or when her husband got a little too rowdy while watching the Bears play.

"We're behind on the McClarens. They should've been done a week ago," Rudy announced. He'd missed a spot of gravy with his napkin, and it glistened on his chin.

Trip met Aiden's eye, and they shared a frown. They might not be able to hold a civil conversation these days, but they were both worried about their dad. "We finished that, remember?" Aiden said slowly, dread building in his gut. "Last Friday."

"No." Rudy's tone turned belligerent. "I left instructions for Trip and his crew—"

"We handled it," Trip said. "It's done."

"No, I..." Rudy's thick brows snapped together, and he shook his head like a bull about to charge. "I... okay. If you say it's done, then it's done. What's next?"

He and Trip exchanged another look, and he knew his brother was fighting back the same fear. Rudy's memory problems were getting worse. Aiden knew it. Trip knew it. All the Murdoch Construction guys working jobs around town knew it. The big question was how many of their clients knew it and whether the Murdoch brothers could agree on what to do about it.

"We should finish up the Riverside Grill job this week," Trip said. "Next up is Santiago Pharmacy. They're ready to go on the reno for their new location in the Heights."

Aiden grunted. "City permits got held up. We can't start yet. I'll talk to the Santiagos."

"No," Rudy said sharply, swiping his sleeve across his chin. "I'll do it."

Across the table, anticipation flashed in Trip's eyes,

which made no sense. Aiden was the one who worked with local governments to secure permits.

"I'll call Tony Santiago first thing tomorrow to—"

"Goddammit, I *said* I'd handle it." Rudy slammed his fist down and rattled every drinking glass and piece of silverware on the table. His dad could be firm, but that level of vehemence shocked the whole table into silence for a moment. Gloria pressed her hands to her lips as Ashley stared wide-eyed at Rudy. Trip even lost his smirk.

"Okay," Aiden finally said, keeping his voice level. "Okay." He rested his hand on his mother's shoulder when she turned to look at him with bleak, pleading eyes. "Maybe Mom's right. We should scrap the shop talk and just enjoy lunch."

As if anybody was enjoying anything around that table. His appetite was gone, Rudy had retreated into himself, and Ash looked like she wanted to be anywhere else.

"So. Aiden," Gloria said briskly. "Have you met any nice girls recently?"

Trip's scornful snort would've chafed if it wasn't part of the Sunday lunch ritual. His mother was the last person on earth who held out hope that Aiden had the capacity to settle down someday. Every week his mother asked this question with hope in her voice, and every week he quashed that little spark while Trip made barely audible comments about man-whoring.

"I know lots of nice girls," he said. Then he reconsidered his usual answer. "Actually, I spent some time with Thea Blackwell this weekend. Remember Thea?"

Gloria's smile faded. "Yes. That poor girl, losing her dad so young."

"I helped her out with a flat tire after the show on

Friday."

"'*Helped her out,*'" Trip muttered. Ashley frowned and nudged him, but it didn't stop his derisive snickering.

Aiden leaned back in his chair to study his brother. "Got something to say to me? Or something to say about Thea?" His smile was casual, but his voice carried a warning that Trip actually heeded. He crammed a forkful of pot roast into his mouth and let the subject drop, thank Christ. Because really, sleeping with Thea? Ridiculous. It wasn't just that she was slender in all the places he was used to finding curves, but she was clearly a "marry me" girl. He didn't mess with that type, and doubly not when it was someone who'd proudly shown him her tooth fairy haul when she was a kid.

Sleeping with Thea. *Ha.*

But then he tipped his head back and thought about standing on the back porch of the house she desperately wanted to make her own. The setting sun had limned her sharp cheekbones and soft mouth with an orange glow. She'd turned to him with those huge brown eyes, crushed when his estimate came in too high, and that sad, hopeful expression was what had driven him to write up a contract that underbid the job.

So no, he wasn't sleeping with Thea. But he did want to find some way to help her afford her princess house. Not that he'd waste his breath explaining that to his asshole brother.

"When's your next Moo Daddies show?"

He smiled at Ashley, grateful her question had shifted the subject. "The weekend after the home expo. We don't usually do them so close together, but we're fitting in one last one before we go on hiatus for Dave's paternity leave."

"Fun!" Ash said, patting Trip's forearm. "We should go, babe. Do something different for a change."

"Pass." Trip leaned back in his chair but kept his eyes on his empty plate. "Not my kind of music."

Everybody around the table recognized that as bull-shit; his brother had gone to plenty of Moo Daddies shows early on. This animosity now was yet another frustrating piece of the Trip puzzle these days. Thankfully they managed to finish lunch without further incident, and Gloria herded Trip and Ashley into the kitchen for dish duty while Aiden joined Rudy in the study to discuss the job assignments for the week.

"First thing," Aiden said, "what happened to your mailbox?"

Rudy just looked blankly at him, so he dropped it and made a mental note to fix it himself before he left for the day. Then he turned his attention to filling out the company assignment grid. "That shipment of doors we're waiting on for the new office park is late."

"Goddammit." Rudy wasn't a big guy, but he carried himself like one, and until recently his lean, ropy strength could put the younger workers in his employ to shame. Aiden was alarmed to see a lurch in his step as he walked an agitated circle around the room, puffing out his chest and squawking like a bantam rooster. "We need to fix it."

"The blizzard out East held up the door shipment. Nothing we can do there." Moving on. "Did the lumber supplies get ordered for the Johnson job? You said you'd handle it."

His father's pale blue eyes shifted from side to side. "Don't know," he finally muttered, crossing his arms over his chest.

"Okay, that's no problem." He kept his voice easy. "I'll

look into it. Anything else I need to take care of?"

Rudy's shoulders drooped under his Murdoch Construction sweatshirt, and he slumped into a chair. "Don't know," he said. "Check with your mother."

"Okay," Aiden said again, sinking into the chair opposite his father and resting his head in his hands.

This was bad. And it wasn't going to get better. Rudy had founded the company close to forty years ago and had always managed every single project on the books with seemingly nothing more than his memory and a collection of Post-its he kept scattered around his truck and office. But these lapses were happening all the time now. How was he supposed to convince his proud, tough father that he couldn't keep running the business he'd built from the ground up because his memory problems were getting worse, along with his temper?

Shit. He didn't even know how to begin to have that conversation. Instead, he focused on one project he might be able to help with. "Listen, Dad, I really think I should come with you to talk to the Santiagos."

"God, don't you get it?" Trip's voice came from the doorway. "You fucked their daughter and never called her again. They don't want you anywhere near their project."

"I'm sorry, what?" A bolt of alarm raced down Aiden's spine.

"Looks like you won't be the big boss on *that* project," Trip said. Aiden looked at Rudy for clarification, but Trip was the one who spoke. "They told Dad that if you come near the project, they'll take their business elsewhere."

Aiden plunged a hand into his hair as he processed this revelation. "Wait, so I take Millie Santiago home one night a few years ago, and now I have to make myself scarce on our biggest job of the season?"

His eyes bounced between the two men. One looked delighted and one looked regretful, and neither looked like they were joking. That explained Trip's glee at the dinner table at least.

"Unbelievable." This time it was Aiden who stood to pace the room. "Why the hell would Millie even tell her parents about..."

In truth, it had been so long ago that Aiden barely remembered the hookup. He'd thought Millie was fine with it too. Anytime he took a woman home, he made sure never to mislead them about what the encounter meant, and he sent them on their way with plenty of orgasms to show for it. Where was the fucking harm in any of that?

"Your wild ways." Rudy spat out the words, and Aiden's already battered psyche sank even further at the venom in his father's voice.

"Have I ever once, one single time, not done my job well?" he asked tightly.

Rudy leaned forward, his eyes sharp and his expression engaged for the first time all day. "Not once have you disappointed me. But the Santiagos like that Trip's married and settled. Said they trust him to see the job through without getting distracted. Fucking puritans."

Ah. A little of that panicky pain eased. His father wasn't upset with him but with the client. Still, this was a problem. Part of the reason he'd hit pause on his hookups was so he had the focus to take on more responsibility at work. But what was the point of completely recalibrating that part of his life if their clients still didn't trust him with their money or their property?

His brother's thinly veiled delight bubbled to the surface again. "They're not the only ones. Why do you think I've been running point on the Baker kitchen remodel and the garage construction out in Spring Ridge?" Trip was a hair shorter than Aiden but thicker through the middle, and he used every bit of his former high school football-player bulk to look intimidating now. Christ, Trip was fucking *loving* this, seeing his big brother ejected from job sites.

Aiden's heart pounded in his ears. It wasn't fair. He'd been sick of his reputation even before it had started affecting his job, and now he wanted to scream about the injustice of it all.

"All I've done," he said numbly. "All I've done since college is try to help the business."

"And fuck everything that moves," Trip muttered.

"Boys!" Their father's voice cracked through the room. "I'm sorry, son." The regret in Rudy's eyes almost knocked Aiden off his feet. He sounded like the father from his childhood, the one who taught him how to hold a hammer and select a drill bit and tie a tie. And now he was stuck delivering the last news Aiden wanted to hear. "You know I trust you with the business. You're my right hand. But if our clients think you're risky, well..."

Rudy didn't have to finish the thought. The client got what the client wanted. And the clients wanted the increasingly forgetful Rudy and the surly, short-tempered Trip.

Wasn't that a kick in the teeth.

"Okay," he finally said. "Okay. So I'll focus on the Johnson remodel this week and leave the Santiagos to you and Trip."

Rudy blinked, frowned. "Johnson? We're not doing any work for the Johnsons, are we?"

Fuck. They were all so screwed.

FIVE

Thea stared at the paper in front of her until her eyes unfocused and the black digits blurred into ants crawling across the page. No matter how many times she ran the numbers, they didn't work. She slapped her hand on the center of the page, shifting her gaze to her ruby-red nails. She couldn't afford a house, but she *could* afford a manicure. Time to try out a new color. Beige, maybe. Pale pink. Something safe and soothing.

The chirp of the phone jolted her out of her nail-care fugue, and she tapped her Bluetooth earpiece. "105.5 FM, how may I direct your call?

"You may direct yourself to the buzzer because I'm pulling in with your Monday pick-me-up lunch."

Thea's stomach growled in response. She hadn't stopped for breakfast that morning, so Faith's timing was perfect. "On it."

"See you in three minutes."

She yanked off the earpiece and dropped it next to the phone, setting the calls to go to voice mail for the next thirty minutes. When Faith Fox's tall form appeared on the security-camera feed, Thea held down the button that unlocked the door and allowed her friend to push it open with her shoulder. She hurried around the reception desk to grab one of the carryout bags and peeked inside. "Soup. Oh my God *yes*."

"Bread too. Can't have soup without fresh bread. Conference room?"

Thea nodded and led the way down the hall, stopping to snag the paperwork sitting on her desk. She and Faith settled into one corner of the long, glossy table and unpacked their lunches.

"Thanks again for the delivery." She talked around a mouthful of minestrone. "We should do this more often."

Faith grimaced. "I wish we could. But no offense, babe, more time for lunch means things at work are slow. I love you, but I'd rather be too busy to leave the office."

Faith nibbled at the edge of her baguette, expression tense. She worked at an educational nonprofit that was always on the brink of running out of funding, so busy was better in terms of keeping the lights on.

"How 'bout that state funding?" Thea hadn't seen her friend for almost a month while Faith had been wrestling with Beaucoeur BUILD's budgetary needs.

"Still writing letters to our rep." Faith dropped the bread onto her napkin as if it had offended her.

"You'll figure it out. You always do."

"I do, don't I?" She gave a breezy toss of her blue-streaked white-blond hair, and they both laughed.

Thea had been Faith's biggest fan since they'd been paired up during the dissection unit in sophomore biology class. Back then, Faith was the prototype rich girl, polite and preppy and tightly wound. But just before college, she'd told her overbearing parents to go to hell, ditched her country club wardrobe, and started carving out her own path. Thea still admired the hell out of her for that bravery.

Faith tapped a finger on the printout resting between them. "What's this?"

"Oh, nothing. Just the *death of my dreams*."

Faith gave her a "lower it a notch, drama queen" look and picked up the proposed budget. "Ah. The princess house."

"The princess house." Thea propped her chin on her hand and watched as Faith's eyes skimmed down the rows of numbers. Her friend was the only person in the world who knew why she wanted that house so badly; she hadn't even discussed it with her mom. Every time she visited, her stepdad was hanging around, badgering her about one life shortcoming or another, which wasn't exactly conducive to sharing childhood real estate fantasies. And she wasn't even sure her mom wanted to hear them in the first place. The laughing Carly who'd been married to Lee Blackwell was night-and-day different from Peter Johnson's brittle, agreeable wife, and it left Thea feeling like the only person on earth who remembered her dad.

Actually, that wasn't true. Aiden remembered him. His generous mouth had curved in sympathy when she'd told him about the fairy tales her dad had spun for her, and he'd shared a memory himself, giving her a piece of her dad that she hadn't had before. Emotion caught in her throat, and she swallowed hard.

"Hey, ladies. Can I crash?" Mabel Bowen, the station's morning-show cohost, stood in the doorway with a lunch sack and a big smile.

"Sure!" Anything to chase away her melancholy.

Amazing what a powerful bite grief had, even decades after her father's death.

"No boyfriends allowed." Faith lifted a brow. "It's girl time."

Thea's smile froze on her face. Her oldest friend and her newest one didn't know each other well, but when they were together, it always felt a little like letting a pair of alpha dogs sniff it out. They were each gorgeous and confident in their own way, leaving her feeling like the nervous diplomat between two nuclear powers.

Mabel floated into the room, unconcerned. "Jake got stuck on a conference call with some kind of numbers emergency, so it's a man-free zone today."

She claimed the seat on the other side of Thea, who was now surrounded by blond glamazons. She bet their feet always touched the ground no matter how tall the chairs were. Lucky bitches.

"We were just figuring out how Thea can afford her dream house." Faith slid the sheets across to Mabel, who set her partially unwrapped sandwich back down.

"Ooooh, real estate listings. Excellent."

Thea slurped her soup as Mabel's eyes flicked over the numbers that told Thea what she already knew: even with a reduced labor cost, even if she was willing to be patient with the renovations, even if she put off work that could be delayed, she couldn't afford it. A howl built in her chest, but she pushed it down. "You know, Faithy, if you'd come to yoga with us, we could hang out like this every Sunday."

Faith gave an elegant shudder. "I don't do yoga."

Mabel snorted. "You are aware that ninety percent of the time we skip it and get donuts and coffee, right?"

Another twitch of Faith's shoulders. "I also don't do Sunday mornings."

"Your loss." Thea grabbed the budget sheets and folded them once, then twice, hiding that crushing total from sight.

"So." Mabel picked a piece of lettuce off her sandwich. "Aiden, huh?"

"Yeah." Thea cast her a sharp look, not sure what that tone meant. "Is that weird for you?"

Mabel gave an epic eye roll. "For the last time, we've always been just friends. He's a great guy. He was just never going to be *my* great guy because I'd already *met* my great guy—I just hadn't accepted that my great guy was actually my great guy yet."

Faith raised her brows at Mabel's tortured explanation.

"You missed out on so much relationship drama with those two," Thea explained before turning back to Mabel. "And Aiden's not the great guy for me either. He's just my contractor. Or he would be if I could afford any of this. Which I can't." Another pang as her dream slipped further from her fingers.

"Ah, but he could be so much more though," Mabel said smugly.

That pulled her mind off her house disappointment. "So much more *what*?"

"I may have been half-dead from misery at the time, but I saw the way you looked at him in Jamaica."

"Oooh, how?" Faith leaned forward in interest.

Mabel looked past Thea to address Faith. "Like he was the jelly-filled donut in the middle of a box of glazed."

"I prefer glazed," Thea muttered, tossing her crumpled napkin into her empty bowl and intentionally missing Mabel's point.

"Nobody prefers glazed, and you're intentionally missing my point," Mabel said. "You think he's attractive."

"Empirically, he *is* attractive." Thea threw up her hands. "There are eighty-year-old nuns who consider tossing their wimples at him when he shows up to do repairs at Saint Mark's."

Mabel blinked. "He told you about his volunteer work?"

"He must've mentioned it at some point, yeah." She shifted in her chair. "I mean, we've known each other forever."

Mabel leaned back in her chair, eyeing Thea speculatively. "Hmm."

"Oh stop." She turned to Faith, who'd been suspiciously quiet during all this. "And what about you? Any weirdness from you?"

"Why, Thea Blackwell, are you asking if I've ever hooked up with Aiden?" Faith smiled a Mona Lisa smile and brushed her mass of wavy hair back from her face.

Blood rushed to Thea's cheeks because yes, that's exactly what she'd been asking. Aiden hadn't given any indication that he'd slept with her best friend when she brought up Faith's name the previous weekend, but then again he wasn't known for bragging about his hookups. And if Faith actually *had* slept with Aiden, that would definitely put a crimp in all her daydreams. But Faith just shrugged.

"It's wild, but somehow I managed to resist the allure of the Murdoch cock. He's all yours." Faith serenely returned to her soup while a bolt of heat shot through Thea's belly. "Anyway, one hookup with Aiden Murdoch hardly qualifies a girl to feel proprietary. If that was the case, half the female population of this town would be at war with the other half."

"Gee, thanks," she managed. "I'll let him know he's cleared to date me. I'm sure that's the only thing stopping him."

"Why shouldn't he? You're hot, babes." Faith was the one who said it, but Mabel nodded along enthusiastically, bless them both.

"I mean, obviously I know I'm adorable," Thea said matter-of-factly. "But I think he still sees me as the kid he had to rescue from the neighbor's big scary dog when it got off the leash and started chasing people."

"When was this?" Mabel asked in amusement.

"When I was five. In his eyes, I'm pretty sure I'm *still* five," she said. "And okay, let's say hypothetically I manage to buy the house and Faith throws me the house-warming party that I know she's dying to plan—"

"It'll be glorious," Faith said. "No male strippers, I promise. Just lots of booze and dancing. Something tasteful."

Thea ignored her and continued. "So let's say Aiden miraculously decides to come to this stripper-free house-warming party, and while he's there suffers a head injury of some sort that makes him think that he'd be interested in dating me. Can you even picture us together?"

Thea held her arms out wide and dramatically gazed down at herself. When she looked up, the glamazons were frowning in confusion.

"Not really getting your point," Faith said.

"Look at me! And look at you two! You're the women he goes home with. You're both blond and your tits are magnificent—"

Mabel sputtered. "I'm sorry, have you been possessed by a thirteen-year-old boy?"

"Meanwhile," she continued as if she hadn't been interrupted, "Aiden has his pick of women in town while I'm just hanging out over here alone. Good ol' Thea. Amazing personality, always smells nice, but no boobs to speak of. Ever wonder what Aiden looks for in his hookups? Here's your answer: not these."

She'd stood and slapped her hands against her chest to emphasize just how flat she was compared to the bombshells on either side of her, squeezing her slightly-larger-than-A cups for emphasis, when a fourth voice joined the conversation.

"I'm pretty sure I'm paying some of you to at least *pretend* to work, no?"

She froze as Brandon Lowell, the station owner, propped a shoulder in the doorway and tipped his head to study the three of them curiously. An excruciating few seconds ticked by before her brain sent the command to her hands: let go of the ladies. Face burning, she plopped into her seat and tucked her fingers under her thighs.

"We're at lunch," Mabel snapped. "Women only."

Thea winced at the other woman's sharp tone; Mabel had taken a dislike to Brandon from their first meeting and hadn't seen any reason to change her mind since. But he was barely a blip on the scale of bad bosses Thea had experienced in her colorful work history, so he'd never bothered her much.

Not much bothered him either, and that included Mabel's out-and-out rudeness. "Oh, I clearly interrupted *some* kind of female-empowerment session." He turned to Faith with his toothiest smile. "Apologies if it was your turn next. I don't think we've met. Brandon Lowell."

"Faith Fox," she said coolly, lifting her chin to study the blond man in front of her and somehow managing to look self-possessed and in command from her seated position. "I've heard... *things* about you."

He didn't even flinch. "Hope it was from this one"—he pointed to Thea—"and not that one." His finger moved to Mabel, who narrowed her eyes.

"If I promise to cut that new Abrams Motor commercial this afternoon, will you leave?" she asked.

Brandon pressed a hand to the expensive suit covering his chest. "Why Mabel, I'm overjoyed to hear that you plan to do your job. Thea, let me know when that fax comes in from corporate. Delighted to make your acquaintance, Ms. Fox." With one last smarmy smile, he disappeared.

"He's the worst," Mabel seethed.

"He's not so bad," Thea chided her.

"He still gets faxes?" Faith asked.

"I don't even know why he's here so often on site visits. *Your actual office is in Detroit,*" Mabel called to the empty door. Then she brushed her hands together as if she were knocking off the Brandon dust. "Anyway, I want to get back to your weird Aiden issues."

"Agreed," Faith said. "So you're on the slender side. Audrey Hepburn was slender. Lots of guys dig that."

"Not Aiden." Thea crossed her arms over her chest. "He always goes home with the Marilyns."

"Since when are you an Aiden stalker?"

She dropped her head into her hands at Mabel's questions. "I'm not! He's just always *around*, you know? Everywhere I go in town, he's there with his"—she waved a hand helplessly—"with his smile and his tallness and his charisma." God, she wasn't doing justice to the overwhelming hotness of Aiden Murdoch. "It's hard to miss where he goes and who he's with."

"Aww, kitten, I'm sorry he never took you home for a night of mediocre sex before forgetting to call you," Faith crooned, stroking a hand down Thea's back. "I know how special that is for a girl."

"Oh, shut it," Thea snapped. "And anyway, it doesn't matter. I've got to go send an email explaining that I can't afford his services, so it's all moot. I'll go back to being that girl he sees around town sometimes and stops to chat with when he's got nothing better to do."

With that, she turned her attention to the rest of their woman-only lunch, or tried to at least. But the drumbeat at the base of her skull refused to let up: No house. No hookups. No changes to her life.

"Maybe I should get a dog." The instant she blurted out the nonsense idea, it took hold of her brain, but Faith and Mabel merely stared at her with identical looks of confusion. "No really, should I get a dog?"

Mabel spoke first. "You know dogs are a lot of responsibility, right? Walking. Feeding. Walking again."

"I'm not a child." She heard the snap in her voice, but she was incapable of controlling her tone at the moment. If she couldn't have her dream house, then maybe she could have a small furry animal to love.

"Obviously you're not," Faith said levelly. "But you are the person who broke up with her last boyfriend for being too clingy."

"Well, he was!"

"He asked you to put his keys and sunglasses in your purse at the movies."

She humphed and took a swig of her Diet Coke. "I'm not a pack mule."

"Mmm-hmm. And you're not great at sticking with things," Faith said. "A dog would stick with you."

"Ah, but a dog's not a person." And a dog wouldn't ask her to change anything about herself other than maybe an increased tolerance for shedding. Then the reality of her situation hit her, and she deflated. "It doesn't matter. I'm not getting my house, and my apartment's no place for a dog."

The urge to put her head down on the conference table and weep overwhelmed her, but this wasn't her first go-round with disappointment. She'd learn to live with it eventually, and until then she'd lift her chin and smile and never let on that another little crack had appeared on her heart.

SIX

"What's the problem?"

Kimmie's shove to Thea's shoulder wasn't enough to move her out of the packed aisle of the Baker Center Arena. They were standing in front of the correct row, and their two empty seats were waiting for them. But sprawled in the chair next to their spots was a walking reminder of Thea's latest heartbreak.

"What is he *doing* here?" she hissed.

Kimmie looked over Thea's head—not hard; Kimmie was another tall, leggy type—and gasped in excitement. "Aiden Murdoch!"

Thea turned and shot her an exasperated *shut it* look, but it was too late. The guy who wasn't destined to be her contractor smiled and lifted his hand in greeting.

"Go! We're gonna get trampled!" This time Kimmie's shove set her in motion, and Thea clambered awkwardly past the already seated Brick Babes and radio-station guests.

"Trade you?" Kimmie asked hopefully, again peering over her head at Aiden.

"Not on your life." She'd rather be reminded of her lost princess house for three excruciating periods of Beaucoeur Anchors hockey than spend that time watching Kimmie giggle with Aiden.

"Hey, ladies." The man in question leaned forward with a warm grin. "Repping the Brick tonight, I see. And in a coat this time."

That last bit was said in an undertone for her benefit only, and she had to suppress a full-body shiver at being part of an inside joke with Aiden.

"I do learn eventually." She shrugged out of her North Face and adjusted her oversized Brick T-shirt, tied at the back in a knot to pull it tight against her torso. Once she was settled into her seat, she leaned forward to greet Dave Chilton, who was seated on the other side of Aiden. "Hey, pal. Flying solo tonight?"

"Brought this guy as my date since Ana opted to be pregnant at home instead of pregnant in an arena full of maniacs." Dave tilted his head toward Aiden, although his gaze didn't budge from the Zamboni making its final pass around the ice before the game got underway.

"Just because you bought my beer doesn't mean I'm putting out." Aiden took a sip from his foamy plastic cup.

"Damn," Dave said mildly, as always a master of comedic timing. Thea had admired the hilarity he and Mabel brought to their morning show for years and still couldn't believe that she'd been able to keep up with him as his replacement cohost for a few months while the station was experimenting with some new programming. But wow, those early-morning hours hadn't been for her. Neither was answering phones at the station, come to think of it, but it was fine for now. She'd move on sooner or later.

Okay, probably sooner.

Her arm brushed Aiden's as she fidgeted in her seat, and she resigned herself to spending all night in close contact with the soft fabric of his sweater, which skimmed his body like a second skin. Might as well get this over with.

"Thanks again for trying to fit my pathetic budget." She leaned close enough that they could have a semiprivate conversation. "I guess it wasn't meant to be." For a horrifying moment, she feared that lame cliché would make her burst into tears, but she managed to push her crushing disappointment down, down, down where she stored all life's hurts both big and small.

He shifted his attention to her as if they weren't in the middle of a rowdy crowd of hockey fans. "I'm sorry we couldn't make it work. I really did want to help you get your princess house."

Dammit. He was being so nice she *was* going to cry. Then she was saved by a wail of distress from Dave, who was scrambling for a napkin to blot at a splotch of nuclear-orange liquid cheese that had dripped from his nachos onto his Rolling Stones 1972 North American Tour T-shirt. "Dammit!"

"No worries. I gotcha." She pawed through her purse until she produced a stain stick. "Four months as a nanny after college taught me to never leave home without this. God forbid your favorite tour shirt gets ruined."

She handed it over, and Dave went to town on the stain. "You're a lifesaver."

"I know, but honestly too few people are brave enough to say it out loud." She lifted her shoulders in a faux-modest shrug, and because they were sharing an armrest, she felt Aiden's body shake with a quick laugh.

Before she could mentally high-five herself for amusing him, a man toting one of the civic center's video cameras on his shoulder moved in front of their section while a headset-wearing producer stood behind him barking orders.

Thea sprang into motion. "Ladies! Camera! Everybody look thrilled to be here!" Her command was directed at the Brick Babes scattered throughout the station's VIP seating area, and the dozen women all exploded into cheers and shimmies, and within seconds, their antics were projected on the massive four-sided display hanging over the ice. Thea smiled and hollered and bounced on her toes with the rest of them, but once their faces were replaced with player stats on the big screen, she dropped into her seat with a sigh.

"I'm too old for this," she muttered to Aiden.

His only response was an exaggerated rubbing of his ears, a wordless commentary on the high-pitched squeals he'd just been subjected to, and she felt compelled to let him know what he was in for. "Be warned: Brandon worked it out with the production crews to have us featured on the big screen a few times tonight. There's going to be more screaming."

"Oh shit."

She looked at him in surprise. He sounded alarmed, and as far as she knew, Aiden didn't *do* alarm. He ambled through the world on a cloud of laid-back cool that Thea had never once been able to muster for herself.

"You okay?"

"Yeah. It's just..." He was staring at the blond producer in the headset as she guided the cameraman to another section of the jersey-clad Anchor fans. "That's Bree Wilkie. She hates me."

She looked back at the producer. "You pissed off the woman who controls the civic center video feed?"

"What makes you think I'm the bad guy?" His hazel gaze moved to Thea, and she opened her mouth before she could think better of it.

"I mean, it's *you*. Didja maybe sleep with her and then blow her off the next day?" She regretted her flippant words when his jaw bunched.

"Actually, she's pissed that I *didn't* sleep with her."

She took a closer look at Bree, who was whispering in the ear of her cameraman and staring at... *Yikes*, she seemed to be staring right at her and Aiden.

"Really." Her voice came out flatter than she intended, and if anything, Aiden's whole body tensed even more.

"Look, I'm not a fuckboy," he said in a low voice. "I may joke with Dave, but I don't go home with just anybody on command."

A wisp of shame curled through her at her assumptions. "Ah."

"Yeah, *ah*."

Now he sounded pissed, which in turn made her a little panicky. *Damn*. She hadn't meant to offend him. She inhaled hard and forced herself to brazen through it. Smile, joke, move on before anybody got hurt. She gave a breezy grin and patted his knee, trying not to dwell on the hard muscle shifting beneath the denim. "Sorry. Didn't mean to make you feel like a himbo."

"Hmm. Thanks." He relaxed back into his seat, although his posture lacked the lazy sprawl from earlier. "I'm more than a pretty face, you know."

"If you say so, Adonis." She held her breath, unsure if that last barb was a step too far. But when he rolled his head to look at her, her chest eased to see amusement in his eyes instead of irritation.

"Smartass," he drawled, and before she could reply, the nine thousand fans in the Baker Center Arena surged to their feet in an explosion of shouts and wild cheers as the Beaucoeur Anchors took to the ice. The cacophony popped their strange circle of intimacy like a soap bubble, and they stood and joined the other fans in their section in rooting on the Anchors to continue their at-home winning streak.

Soon enough, Thea got sucked into the Brick Babe whirl, taking selfies with the girls and chatting with the fans who wandered by their section, sharing everything to the station's social media pages. As always, the vibe was "boy, don't you wish you were here?" and as the game wore on, she more and more wished she wasn't. The Brick Babes were fun, but the Brick Babes were also exhausting.

And then the kiss cam came around.

By the break between the second and third period, she'd reached the end of her second beer. It was enough to put a glint in her eye and an extra oomph to her laughter as she chattered with the other Babes. Then "Kiss Me" started booming through the arena as the half dozen camera operators spread out and highlighted one couple at a time on the big screen over the ice. Each time, the happy duos laughed in surprise as they saw themselves projected on the enormous four-sided display, then obliged the crowd with a kiss amid good-natured catcalling from the fans in the arena.

Riding high on fermented hops and a little too much sass, she nudged Aiden. "So I guess I don't get to joke about how many former hookups you've seen on the kiss cam tonight, huh?"

His lips quirked. "Two, actually."

Her jaw dropped. "I was kidding!"

"I was too. Maybe." He grinned at her, that irresistible smile that lured in women of all ages, colors, and creeds, and she was helpless not to grin right back.

Suddenly everyone around them started shrieking in excitement, and when Kimmie jabbed her in the spine, Thea looked around in confusion. "Wha—"

Producer Bree was standing a few feet away with a smirk on her face and her trusty cameraman right next to her. And Thea just *knew*.

She forced her eyes upward with trepidation, and there she was, sharing the big screen with *Aiden freaking Murdoch* as Sixpence None the Richer echoed through the vast arena.

The smile froze on her face as embarrassed heat started to pour off her. "Umm..."

She glanced over at Aiden, who looked as startled as she did. His eyes cut to Bree and narrowed for a millisecond before bouncing up to the screen, where their image seemed to be getting bigger the longer they were front and center. God, why wasn't the camera cutting away? She and Aiden clearly weren't together. But if anything, the camera zoomed in even tighter, and she didn't know where to look. At the screen? At Aiden? At Bree, who was *absolutely* doing this on purpose?

Without warning, Aiden's hand snaked around the back of her neck, and he turned her face toward him. Her eyes popped at the proprietary gesture and widened even more when he leaned forward, his mouth a fraction of an inch away from her ear.

"This all right?" he whispered.

"Y-yes," she managed, and before she could draw a

second breath, he pressed his lips to hers. At first she froze, paralyzed by shock, but a moment later his mouth softened against hers, and the movement shot heat through her body. Without intending it, she started kissing him back, dimly aware that the arena had erupted into cheers even more raucous than the ones that had accompanied the Anchors' only goal that night.

She barely noticed. She was too focused on the press of Aiden's fingers against her neck and the gentle pressure of his tongue as it met hers. Heat coursed through her as her hands crept up to clutch the front of his shirt. He slid his fingers into her hair, angling her head to give him better access to scrape his teeth across her bottom lip, and she moaned at the sharp little dart of pleasurable pain.

The horn that called the players to the ice for the final period penetrated her brain, which probably meant that the camera was no longer on them and she should really let go. But she was reluctant to break their contact, and the tug of his fingers on her hair made her wonder if he might feel similarly.

Then she realized where they were—sitting in full view of an arena of people, for God's sake—and she yanked her hands away. Aiden's fingers disentangled themselves more slowly, but his eyes didn't move from her face. She stared right back, unsure what she was seeing in his expression. Was it an apology? Embarrassment? What was causing his breath to hitch and his pulse to jump at the base of his throat? When she reached up to brush the tips of her fingers across her lips, he opened his mouth and then shut it just as suddenly.

His gaze flicked to the screen, which now showed the action on the ice, before he finally spoke. "I'm so sorry. I just figured she wouldn't move on until we—"

"I get it." Her blood thundered in her ears, but she kept her voice chipper and her smile bright while she groped for an escape. "Um, I'm going to..." She jabbed a thumb over her shoulder. "I think I'm going to call it a night."

Aiden frowned but nodded. "Okay. Good night?"

His words came out like a question, but it didn't matter because she was already out of her seat and scampering up the stairs. Her steps slowed when she reached the main floor, and she stopped in the middle of the hallway, almost getting knocked to her knees when two drunk guys spilled out of the men's room and clipped her on the shoulder.

Aiden had *kissed* her. Aiden had kissed *her*.

The bottom dropped out of her stomach. The hottest guy she'd ever seen had leaned over and put his lips on hers. He'd put his *tongue in her mouth*. In *public*. She sagged against the brick wall of the arena as people streamed past, trying to calm her racing heart.

He'd kissed her out of practicality, obviously. Never ever *ever* did she expect to actually know what Aiden's lips on hers would feel like. Full and soft and warm, as it turned out. Tentative at first, then commanding but not overbearing. Nice. Her lips tingled as she relived the heat and hardness of his chest when she clutched his shirt to bring him closer to her. She'd wanted his mouth to stay moving over hers forever.

And he's probably already forgotten it. Shuddered and laughed it off with Dave. It'd be best if she did the same thing.

Then her phone buzzed with a text from Faith: *What the hell did I just watch??*

A moment later, a video popped up. Faith had used

her phone to record fifteen seconds of the local access channel's broadcast of the Anchors game, and there was her face smack in the center of the screen. She hit Play and watched the kiss unfold. That sneaky snake Bree hadn't even cut away before it ended. No, she'd lingered to catch the moment after they'd pulled back, both breathing heavily and looking dazed. Their gazes had remained locked for an eternal, suspended moment before the video cut out.

"Oh God," she whispered, scrubbing back to the beginning of the clip to watch it again. The second time showed nothing different. Neither did the third time. Her lips met his, and afterward she was nothing but pink cheeks and dreamy eyes.

Had she really tugged on his collar to pull him closer?

She had. Those were her fingers clutching his shirt.

And had he really positioned her head to gain better access to her mouth?

He had. Those were his fingers clutching her hair.

"Heyyyyy! You're totally famous!"

Thea's head snapped up as a woman tottered over in skyscraper heels. She draped her skinny arms around Thea's neck and pressed her sweaty cheek into Thea's, the smell of stadium beer assaulting her nose. "You are so awesome, do you know that? That guy was *hot*. Where'd he go?" She scanned the mostly empty hallway hungrily.

"He's where all the hot guys go," she said flatly, disentangling herself from the stranger's hug. "Not coming home with me."

FOR APPROXIMATELY SIXTY seconds after Thea's hasty departure, Dave didn't say anything, instead pulling his glasses off his face to polish them with a handkerchief he produced from his back pocket. When he'd finished and settled them back on his nose, he asked, "You running a kissing booth now?"

The disbelief in his friend's voice told Aiden just how shocking what he'd done was. "Shut the fuck up, man." He ran a hand through his hair. "I had to do it. It wasn't going to end otherwise."

"Right, right," Dave said placidly. "Then again, you could've left your tongue in your own mouth."

"And you can keep your teeth in your own mouth if you drop it right now." Because yes, he could have, and he didn't appreciate Dave pointing it out.

Dave just shrugged, clearly aware that the threat lacked any intent. "All I'm saying is, this may be the best hockey game I've ever been to." He leaned back in his seat and turned his full attention back to the ice.

Aiden drained his beer and willed his blood to cool down. Goddamn Bree. What a petty way to get revenge on him for not taking her up on her offer to end a show night at her place maybe six months ago. He vaguely recalled the event, but he'd been exhausted from a long day on a job site after his dad had forgotten to tell him the client expected the work done by the end of the week, and he'd just wanted to pack up his kit and get home. Apparently being rejected by the town player was a personal slight. And God, poor Thea getting dragged into all that. What was he going to say to her the next time he saw her? *Sorry I had to kiss you to get our faces off the big screen. I think they would've paused the game until we made out in public.*

An apology then, after which they'd never talk about it again. Except kissing Thea had been... *fun*. She'd tasted good, and the skin at the nape of her neck was soft. So was her hair. So were her lips.

The crowd erupted as the Anchors scored again, and Aiden willed himself to believe that the goal was responsible for his kicked-up heart rate. But that was a lie. His brain wouldn't stop replaying that moment when she'd sighed and tugged him closer to give him full access to her mouth. He couldn't remember the last kiss that woke him up this much.

Which was ridiculous. This was *Thea*. The little girl next door who lost her dad but carried on without losing her sparkle. He was just suffering from a couple of months without sex, that was all. He drained the rest of his beer and crumpled the empty plastic cup, slowly becoming aware of the curious stares from the Brick Babes section. When he finally glanced over, the redhead who'd been sitting next to Thea sent him a knowing wink. What the hell did that even *mean*? Did they really think that kiss-cam display had meant something? He sent her a carefully calibrated smile: friendly, self-deprecating, not at all a come-on. He didn't need any other pissed-off women lurking in the vicinity right now.

Mercifully, the clock eventually counted down to zero on that last eternal period, the Anchors skated to a 2–0 victory, and Aiden was free to leave the stadium. He pulled on his coat and followed Dave up the stairs to join the throngs of people packed together like sardines as they shuffled for the exits. He kept his head down to avoid any additional speculative looks but managed to collect three separate slaps on the back from random dudes passing by before he and Dave made it to the safety of the car.

"Jesus, has nobody in this town ever seen a kiss cam before?" He slammed his seat belt into place, cursing when he caught the web of his left hand in the buckle.

Dave flipped on his headlights and inched his van into the massive line of vehicles waiting to leave the lot. "*I* knew it was all fake, but you still almost had me convinced." He slammed on the brakes to avoid the tail-lights of the suddenly stopped car in front of them.

Aiden groaned and flopped back against the bucket seat, rubbing his thumb over the pinched skin. "I don't care how cold it is, I can walk home."

"Your call," Dave said. "I'm not the one who basically announced his engagement to the whole town."

He straightened in alarm. "Come on, nobody thinks that."

"That Aiden Murdoch was on a date with a woman he willingly kissed in public?" Dave shrugged and yawned, it being ten p.m. and miles past his bedtime. "You might as well have."

"Shit. You don't think Thea thinks…" He pulled out his phone and stared at it, not sure how to even craft a text that covered what he needed to cover. What did you say to the woman who managed to turn you on in the middle of a hockey arena? He tucked his phone back into his pocket with a growl.

Yeah. Definitely *definitely* never talking about it again.

SEVEN

On Monday, the kiss-cam incident was all anybody wanted to talk about.

The morning started off normally enough. Aiden met his attorney friend Daniel Walden at the gym as soon as its doors opened at six a.m. As usual, their conversation was sparse as they warmed up and worked their way to heavier and heavier weights on their bench press. But Daniel took him by surprise while Aiden was gasping for breath on the bench between sets.

"So who's the lucky girl?"

"What...," he wheezed, "the hell... do you mean?"

"The girl at the hockey game." Daniel smiled smugly at him and added another plate on each side of the bar while Aiden gaped at him. "Shove over."

He pulled himself to his feet and moved on autopilot to the other side of the bench to spot his friend. Possibly his *former* friend, depending on how this conversation went. "It was nothing."

"That's not what Tessa heard from a friend of a friend

who was there." As he spoke, he hefted the weight up and down with no visible effort while Aiden ground his teeth at the mention of Daniel's just-the-facts girlfriend. If that's what she was telling people, it must've passed her rigorous truth test.

"Jesus," he groaned.

"I'm hurt, man." Daniel racked the weight and popped right up. "Thought I'd be one of the first people you'd tell when you fell in love." Aiden's only answer was a growl, and Daniel took a laughing step back with his hands raised. "Hey, I'm not the one who goes on and on about domesticity being a trap."

"Because it is," Aiden shot back, although his response was more a habit at this point than actual strong feelings. He'd been railing against settling down for so long that this jokey anticommitment patter was part of his repertoire. "Thea's just an old friend."

He glared at Daniel, who shrugged and grabbed a towel to wipe down the bench. "If you say so. I'll tell Tessa she got it wrong." He glanced at his phone. "Gotta run. See you tomorrow after work for cardio?"

Aiden grumbled his assent and wrapped up his own workout shortly afterward. He raced through his post-workout cleanup so he was able to stroll into the Murdoch Construction break room at seven thirty a.m. on the dot, where the dozen employees gathered to guzzle coffee and wait for the day's work assignments all burst into hoots and kissy noises.

"Hey, lover boy!" one of them shouted.

Aiden looked incredulously around the group. "How the *hell* do you all know about that?"

Painter Ben Mendez stepped forward with a shit-eating grin on his face. "My daughter sent me the video."

"And?" Aiden asked slowly.

"And I forwarded it to all the guys!"

Aiden ran his tongue along the inside of his lower lip as he glanced around at the laughing faces of guys he'd worked with for years. A decade, some of them. "It's not a big deal."

They responded with increased hilarity that Aiden tolerated for a few seconds before he slapped his binder against his leg and hollered, "Okay then! How about some hard labor, gentlemen?"

The group shifted to good-natured groans as he called out the work teams for the day and rattled off the list of supplies each job site would need. They cleared out in groups of two and three until it was only him and Gene Fitzsimmons, one of the old-timers who'd been with the company practically from the day his old man had founded it. His quiet word carried weight with the other workers.

"It's good of you to put up with their teasing." Fitz finished pouring coffee into his oversized travel mug as he spoke.

"They're worse than a knitting circle," Aiden muttered.

Fitz slapped a massive hand on the lid. "Naw. They're excited for you."

"Come on." He shrugged uncomfortably. "They're excited because I got tricked into kissing a woman at a hockey game?"

"Tricked?" His gray caterpillar brows inched up his forehead.

A hasty yes danced on the tip of his tongue, but if he was being totally honest, he hadn't been *tricked*. He'd been the one to reach for Thea, to ask if it was okay with her. It hadn't been his choice, but it had been his idea.

It had been a fucking great idea. Until the aftermath anyway.

God, that didn't even make sense. He scrubbed a hand through his hair in frustration, and when he looked over at Fitz, he was chagrined to see the older man chuckling softly. "That's how it starts, young man."

"How what starts?"

Those brows gyrated again. "Ah, it's more fun if you find out for yourself." Without another word, he snatched up his coffee and left the room. Grumbling, Aiden retreated to his office to review the permits he needed to submit to the city that week and return client email with links to products and design inspirations for their renovations. The morning flowed in a productive blur until three quick raps on his door pulled his attention from his laptop.

Aiden smiled at the sound. "Come in, Mom. You don't have to knock, you know."

"I don't want to just barge in." She bustled into the room and set a container on his desk. "I brought you some lunch. You never stop for lunch."

He glanced at the clock on the wall and saw that it was after noon. He and his dad were supposed to meet with the Sappersteins at two thirty, so he had plenty of time to eat and chat.

He pried the top off the container and moaned when the scent hit him. "Chicken and dumplings? You're the greatest."

She just dimpled and handed him a fork. As a kid, he believed his mother was a sorceress who could conjure any item that the men in her life requested. As an adult, he wasn't totally convinced that this wasn't still the case.

As he demolished the food, his mother folded her hands in her lap and announced, "I was hoping to talk with you."

He swallowed his mouthful and bit back a groan, readying himself to launch into another round of "that thing with Thea isn't what it looked like." But instead, she said something much worse.

"It's your dad."

Appetite gone. He should've recognized the home-made dumplings for what they were: a ploy to soften a hard blow. His mom had made the same meal after his grandma's funeral and when he'd been home with a broken arm when he was supposed to be at baseball camp for a week.

"I know you've seen it too," she said gently. "His memory, his temper. He's not himself at work, and he's not himself at home."

"Home too?"

She nodded once and pressed her lips together, and he moved to sit next to her so there wasn't a desk between them. His mom rarely got upset, so this was worrisome.

"I came into the kitchen the other night and found a pot of water boiling on the stove. We'd already had dinner, and when I found your dad in the bedroom, he had no idea what I was asking about. But there was an unopened box of macaroni and cheese on the dresser."

He rocked back in the chair, taking in what she was saying.

"Nothing was damaged, but it could've been..."

"It could've been bad." Aiden grimly finished her thought.

"It's been getting worse for months," she said, voice tired. Suddenly she looked less like the robust mother he'd always known and more like a scared sixty-six-year-old, pale and drawn and worried about her forgetful husband.

Dammit. He'd thrown himself into keeping the business flowing smoothly, but he'd been so focused on the work end of things that the true severity of his father's condition had escaped him. Worse, his mother had been left to deal that aspect on her own. What a shitty son.

"What do we need to do now?" he asked.

"Actually, I took him to the doctor yesterday."

His eyes widened. "Dad agreed to a doctor visit?"

"Believe me, it was a fight."

They exchanged sad smiles. Of course it was. Rudy had nearly severed his thumb in a band saw accident a few years ago, and Aiden had to physically force him into the car to get him to the ER.

"Maybe it's not as bad as we think," he said, desperation coloring his tone.

For a moment it looked like she was going to offer him the kind of warm reassurances she'd given him his whole life. Instead, she knuckled away a tear. "It's dementia. And it's progressed beyond what any of us really knew. He was so good at hiding the signs, but..."

Sorrow gripped him, followed closely by fear. Fear for his dad. His mom. The business. His whole life, Rudy was the brash, cantankerous center of everything, and Aiden didn't know what their family looked like without him.

"So what now?" he asked raggedly.

His mom nodded and swung into office-manager mode, all practical efficiency. "Now we get him into a clinical trial. There's a great one in Chicago that looks promising."

He frowned. "Except it's in Chicago."

"Which is three hours away. Not *that* far," she said. "If he's accepted, I'll go with him. Find a little apartment. I have to stay with him."

"Of course." Forty-two years of marriage and never more than one night apart. It was a point of pride for them, so of course she'd go with her husband on this next step.

Her face crumpled, and Aiden wondered if she was thinking the same thing. He shifted closer to pull her into a hug, and she turned her face to his chest with a sob. But she pulled herself together almost immediately, turning to root through her purse for a tissue while he leaned back in his chair.

"Okay." He exhaled hard. "Okay. You go with him to Chicago, and Trip and I will handle things here until you sort it out. Maybe he'll be back in a month better than new, right?"

Her mouth formed something approximating a smile if you didn't know what her usual expression looked like. "Of course, sweetie. We'll get through it as a family." She patted his cheek. "My handsome boy. We'll need you to step up and run the business. And keep an eye on your brother even if it's hard. I hate to see you two fight. You used to be friends."

"Yeah, we did." The memory of their last family lunch resurfaced, and he shifted in his chair, hating to bring this subject up with his mother. "Then again, I may not be the best choice to run the business right now."

That engaged her inner mama bear, and she leaned

forward, eyes fierce. "That person those people think you are? That's not you. You just need to show them that you're as steady and reliable as your dad. Even steadier. I've never once heard you raise your voice with our employees." She placed her hand over his. "You'll figure it out. But right now I need to get back home and keep making phone calls about our Chicago move."

After one more pat of his hand, she stood and left his office, and he squeezed his eyes shut and dug his thumbs into either side of the bridge of his nose. Once he'd composed himself, he walked back to his desk chair and on autopilot reviewed the notes he'd made for the Sapper-steins. He had a schedule to stick to. If the company rested on his shoulders now, he wouldn't let it fall.

He greeted Fred and Elena Sapperstein in the lobby later that afternoon and took them through the lobby to the consultation room in the back.

"How's that new addition treating you folks?" he asked as they took their seats. Murdoch Construction had built an all-season room for them last year, and since they were back to discuss a master bathroom reno, it was a rela-tively safe assumption that they were pleased. But it never hurt to ask.

"Oh, it's perfect. A lovely reading spot." The silver-haired woman waved her hand dismissively and leaned forward. "Now tell me about that beautiful girl we saw you kissing at the hockey game on Saturday."

His pleasant salesman's mask froze on his face. "You saw that?"

Her cheeks plumped into a smile. "We never miss a game. Isn't that right, Frank?" Frank bobbed his head and gazed adoringly at his wife, who barreled on. "You two were the cutest couple of the night. How long have you been seeing her?"

He blinked and looked desperately at the tile samples on the table in front of him as if they'd help him out of the endless conversational loop that fucking kiss had dropped him into. "Oh, I'm not—"

"Young love. Isn't it wonderful, Frank?"

The man's bald pate flashed under the fluorescents as he nodded affably. "Is she a good cook? Does she treat you right?"

"She, uh—"

"That's how I won him over." Elena nodded at her husband. "My apple pie."

"She makes the best apple pie." Frank patted his belly and smiled the smile of a man who knows the pleasure of a good fruit-and-pastry combination.

Jesus. Time to get this under control. "Thea's never made me apple pie actually." That was honest at least.

"Just ask her nicely. I'm sure she'll be happy to. We all saw how she looked at you." Elena sighed dreamily. "After all the stories we've heard, it's just nice to see you settling down."

For God's sake, he'd just become responsible for the bulk of the activities that kept the family business solvent, but apparently it took publicly linking himself with a woman to be seen as a trustworthy adult. It rankled, and his jaw hurt from the effort of keeping his smile on his face and his thoughts to himself.

"Leave him be, Lena," the pie-loving Frank finally said. "Let the poor boy show us the bathroom of our dreams."

Yes. Fixtures and mirror and vanity options. Safe

ground. But as he discussed the benefits of the various tile brands, a plan began to germinate.

A terrible plan. Risky and dumb. Harebrained, even. But it was an idea that could change everything for him right now, when he needed it the most. And he was pretty sure he knew how to get Thea on board.

EIGHT

Thea perched on the edge of her couch and glanced at her phone one more time.

The text was still there. She hadn't imagined it.

Can I swing by your place tonight?

"Gah!" She tossed the phone on the couch and looked around her apartment one more time with dismay. Aiden was coming here? *Why?* And where would she even put him? Her furniture was girl-sized. How would his tall, cool, sex-god vibe even fit in with her flower-patterned love seats and squashy velvet ottoman? Even her clothes were wrong. She usually felt supercute in these skinny jeans and soft, slouchy top, but tonight they managed to make her feel both sloppy and fussy at the same time.

God, he was coming here to tell her in person that Saturday night was all for show, wasn't he? He was so worried about poor sad Thea showing up and tossing her panties at him on a job site that he was driving to her apartment to tell her to her face that they were only pals. It was almost like he knew how many times she'd watched that video that Faith had sent of their kiss.

Their unimportant, not meaningful, totally forget-table kiss.

"Oh God." Her self-pitying moan was interrupted by the screech of her intercom, and she bolted from the couch to buzz open the entrance and meet her fate. Two minutes later, a strong pair of knuckles collided with her door in a self-assured knock that had her shivering. Even his *knock* was sexy.

"Get it together," she whispered, tugging at the hem of her shirt once more before swinging open the door with the biggest welcome smile she could muster. "Hiya!"

"Hey." He propped one shoulder against her door-frame and smiled back, all slow and lazy, and she flut-tered. Every last part of her sat up and fluttered.

Crap.

Pushing aside her nerves, she stepped back and flung an arm out to encompass her cozy little living space. "Come on in! Toss your coat anywhere."

"Thanks." He slid out of his jacket and hung it on the coatrack next to the door with a raised brow.

"Right. Ha. Use the thing intended for coats." And just like that, the tension drained from her body. Why was she so nervous? She knew why he was here, so she might as well calm down so he could get on with it. She shook out her hands in an attempt to get rid of her fidgets. "Want something to drink?"

"Beer?"

"Something cheap and domestic coming up." She headed toward the fridge. "Have a seat."

She fetched the beverages and joined him in the living room, where he was nestled among the upholstery flowers, legs looking longer than ever. She bit back a smile at the mismatch as she handed him a cool bottle.

"Thanks." He wrapped his fingers around it but didn't drink until she'd settled herself onto the sofa opposite him with her glass of moscato.

Now that her muscles weren't performing a full-body clench, she had a little more focus to spare for her guest, and to her surprise, *he* looked nervous. His smile was gone, and the corners of his eyes were taut. After one sip, he set his beer down on the coffee table. He used the coaster of course; a guy who worked on houses knew how to treat stained wood.

"So I'm guessing I know why you're here." She took a long swallow of the crisp, sweet wine and prepared herself for minor humiliation. At least they weren't in public.

"I'm guessing you don't." Aiden leaned forward to study her, elbows on his knees. His gaze was intense, like he was really seeing her for the first time, and she squirmed a little. "I've got a proposal for you."

"A proposal?" That was... unexpected.

"Here's the thing." He smiled, but again she caught a hint of nerves lurking under that gorgeous stretch of lips. "Everybody I talked to today saw the kiss cam or heard about it. And they all wanted to know how long we've been dating."

"Oh no," she breathed, covering her face with the hand not gripping her wine. "I'm so sorry. Did you tell them it was just a dumb thing we got forced into?"

"I didn't actually." His thick brows met over the bridge of his nose as he frowned. "And that's my proposal."

"What is?"

"That we not tell them that it was fake."

He fell silent and studied her, as if waiting for

comprehension to cross her face, but she just tilted her head far enough to the side that her hair slithered over her shoulder. "I don't get it."

He tossed himself back against her love seat with a groan, plunging a hand into his hair as he stared up at her ceiling. After a beat, he looked down and met her eyes again. No nerves, only a glittering intensity that made her sit up straight.

"My dad's been diagnosed with dementia." He stopped talking and swallowed hard before continuing. "He can't keep running the business the way he has been. He just... can't."

"Oh, Aiden. I'm sorry." She was the one leaning forward now, reaching across the space between them to rest her hand on his knee. Despite how little time they'd spent together over the past decade, that comforting touch felt like the right thing to do.

"Thanks." His smile was small but sincere, and she pulled her hand back so she wouldn't be too distracted to hear him out. "I need to step up at work, but the thing is..." He stopped speaking again, but this time it was embarrassment, not pain, that marched across his face. He scratched his neck and continued. "The thing is, my reputation isn't great."

"You don't say," she said drily.

"Smartass." It was the second time he'd called her that, and she loved the way it sounded like a compliment when it crossed his lips. "But all day today, people were excited to talk to me about our relationship. They think I'm finally getting serious with someone. Making a commitment. And I'm starting to think our clients will trust a one-woman man with their business far more than they'll trust the guy who..."

When he didn't finish the thought, she took a stab herself. "The guy who's out getting his dick wet with someone new every night?" Blood rushed to her cheeks at the crude phrasing, but it was worth it to see his eyes widen.

"Christ, woman, the mouth on you." He snatched up his beer and took a long swallow, and the shake of his head was almost admiring as he set it back down. "Anyway, yeah, that's basically the gist. You apparently make me look like a responsible adult, and I need to be a responsible adult now more than ever to keep the company together."

"Ooookay," she said. "So you want me to..." Surely she was misunderstanding. It was too ludicrous for her to say out loud.

Then he went and said it for her.

"I want you to pretend to be my girlfriend." Those eyes were hot on her again. Hot and a little desperate. A shiver traveled down her spine. "And in exchange, I'll renovate your house within your budget."

Now she gasped. Opened her mouth. Closed it. Brought her glass to her lips and drained the contents in an effort to seek clarity or completely obscure it. Once she'd guzzled her wine, she swiped a hand over the back of her mouth and asked, "Why me?"

Another frown crossed his face, and then he said simply, "I trust you." When she opened her mouth, he pointed an accusing finger at her. "And don't give me that 'we're not friends' garbage. I was the cashier at your lemonade stand."

"When I was six!" She jumped up and practically sprinted to the kitchen to pour herself another glass. "Any girl in town would do this for you. I don't understand why you'd bother with me."

His face twisted. "You're overestimating my appeal. I'm no different than any other guys you've dated."

Her hand halted dead with the glass halfway to her lips, and she broke into a peal of laughter. "Ha! Wrong." The past few guys she'd dated had been nice. Cute enough. Okay in bed. But not a single one of them had Aiden's magnetic pull, that gorgeous-guy self-confidence that was bone deep and somehow effortless.

She looked at him now as he watched her steadily from her fancy floral couch. Their eyes locked, and she realized with a start that he was utterly serious. Any sign of the relaxed, teasing guy she usually saw around town was gone, replaced by a furrowed brow and an almost pleading expression.

"Okay." She walked back over and collapsed onto the velvet ottoman sitting next to the arm of the floral couch. "So what you're saying is that I pretend to be your girlfriend so you can take over your family's business, and you'll fix up my princess house."

"Exactly." He straightened, excitement stamped across his features at her willingness to keep discussing this insane proposal. He probably looked like that when he was upselling rich customers on the name-brand countertops too.

"Well, that's hardly a fair trade." Her brain spun. "I get all that free labor. What do you get out of it?"

He lifted his hands in a *stop right there* gesture. "Jesus, not *that*. I would never make that part of—"

"*Oh my God,* obviously I didn't mean *sex*!" She practically shouted in her haste to wipe the horrified look from his face.

"Phew." He exhaled and comically wiped his brow while she dropped her head to her knees, holding her wine aloft so she wouldn't spill it.

Could the floor please open up and swallow her right now? She was clearly not going to barter sex for renovations, but geez, did he have to sound so horrified by the idea? It left her feeling about as sexy as a bridge-dwelling troll.

While she'd been spiraling into self-doubt, he'd reached into his pocket and produced a folded sheet of paper. "Here's a revised budget. I got the home inspector report you sent me, and it knocked some of the items off my list. The roof's in good shape, and there're no signs of water damage in the basement or on the front of the house. The heating-and-cooling system works, but I bet it'll need to be replaced within the next five or ten years."

Her eyes dropped to the bottom of the page where he'd bolded a figure. It was a much smaller dollar amount, and hope sprouted a tender little shoot in her heart. She took another fortifying sip of wine, then set the glass on the floor next to her to take the paper in both hands.

"If you're willing to let me do most of the one-man jobs at night or on the weekends and are flexible about when my crew can take care of the bigger stuff, I can get it done at your drop-dead price point."

Her heart lubbed hard. The princess house could be hers. The house her dad had dreamed of for her. The one that still had the rosebushes he'd planted for Doris Rebhetz before his death. She could have that glorious river view and put down roots and be part of the neighborhood holiday decorations. All she had to do was pretend that she'd somehow captured the heart of Beaucoeur's most notorious womanizer.

Disappointment clouded her vision. "Nobody's going to buy it. Us as a couple?"

His frown was back. "Why not?"

"Because... because!" She sputtered and waved her arms through the air. "Because you're you and I'm me!"

"And?"

"And you've never looked twice at me before! Nobody will believe I'm the person who finally hog-tied you." Her exasperation made her shrill, and she hated it.

Aiden didn't seem to care. Instead, the tip of his tongue peeked out to wet the corner of his upper lip as he studied her with an over-the-top smoldering gaze. "Or maybe it's *because* of your hog-tying skills that I finally settled down, hot stuff." He winked broadly before dropping the seductive act with a shrug. "Everybody watching the kiss cam seemed convinced anyway."

Oh! Her cheeks flamed, and she slapped her palms over them to keep the glow from giving her away. "Stop! It's ridiculous!"

"It's really not." His smile this time was genuine, not his salesman smirk or his lady-killer grin. "I have it on good authority that we gave off a strong couple vibe."

Her hands fell to her lap. He wasn't wrong, was he? She'd seen the dazed expression on her own face for herself, and she'd seen the unsteadiness of his breathing when they'd pulled apart. They'd looked like two people who really enjoyed kissing each other.

"Besides," he said quietly, "I fell for that house too, and I'd like to make sure you're its owner. You just might have to live with a really ugly kitchen for longer than you imagined."

Now that the offer was out, he relaxed back onto her flowery couch and snagged his beer, taking a sip as she worked through this insane proposal. She followed suit and picked up her wineglass from the floor, draining the rest of its contents.

"Okay. *If* we agree to this, then no fooling around with anybody else."

"Obviously not," he said immediately. "And that goes for you too."

"Sure." She rolled her eyes. She hadn't been in the same zip code of fooling around with anybody in too long to remember, so that wasn't exactly a sacrifice. "And it's not like anybody's falling in love with anyone else because..."

She gestured between the two of them, and a shadow darkened his face before vanishing. "Yeah. The whole world knows I'm the guy who doesn't do relationships."

"It's basically your brand," she said, although in truth she'd been referring to herself as well. She wasn't exactly known for her successful romantic track record. Still... "When the time comes for us to break up, how do we do it?"

"Mutual and respectful," he said. "Nobody gets the blame. We decide we're better off as friends."

Friends. Which is what they were, even if his presence in her apartment did make her... flutter.

She'd seriously have to get over that.

"So we have a deal?"

Why was she even hesitating? This was her dream come true. It was almost *two* dreams come true if she was being honest: the dream house *and* the hot guy, even if one was only temporary. "I... yes. I guess we do."

"Excellent." He polished off his beer and stood, unfurling his lean, muscular body to its full height and making her immediately second-guess her ability to carry this off.

Then he reached down and pulled her into a standing position beside him, and she did something she'd never dreamed she'd be able to do: she reached out and hugged Aiden Murdoch. Arms around his waist. Cheek against his chest. Torsos smashed together.

"Thank you," she whispered. "For helping me get my house."

After a pause, his arms wrapped around her shoulders. "Happy to," he murmured back, arms briefly tightening around her before she pulled away, cheeks flushed yet again. Their eyes caught and held, and for a split second, he leaned toward her. Was he going to kiss her again? Seal their wild, ridiculous bargain with another tangle of mouths and tongues that would give her a second dose of fantasy fodder?

But he didn't close the distance between them, and self-consciousness creeped in. She stepped away and said brightly, "I've gotta call Melinda right now. Tell her to put in an offer."

It broke the spell, and Aiden moved to snag his coat from the rack. "Do you want my advice on negotiating, or are you good?"

"Yes, please! You're the house expert." She whipped out her phone and opened her notes app to take down whatever information he was willing to impart.

He spoke as he pulled on his coat. "I think you ought to offer $5,000 less than the asking price. Make sure Melinda tells the sellers that the kitchen's gonna be a real bitch for your hardworking and immensely talented contractor."

Excitement swelled in her chest and almost drowned

out the Aiden flutters. Almost. Then he went and winked at her, and it was all over. "The trick'll be putting up with me for that long. Before this is over, I'll know how you take your coffee in the mornings and what side of the bed you sleep on."

His casual mention of her bed knocked the air from her lungs. "The bed?" She was amazed she'd been able to get the words out without hyperventilating. Even if it was all going to be pretend, the very idea of her and Aiden and a bed left her breathless.

But he replied innocently, "If you decide to add that skylight in the bedroom, I need to know where you'll be sleeping so I can position it perfectly."

Oh. The skylight. Of course. "If I can afford a skylight. And if I even get the house." She bit her lip. "That's a lot of ifs."

"I have faith in you." He lifted his hand to her face and brushed his thumb gently over her cheek, eyes fixed on hers. Then the intensity in his expression vanished, replaced by his usual laid-back hot-guy vibe. "Go get 'em, killer." He was gone with a final flash of white teeth, leaving her to sag against the wall as her knees threatened to give out.

That night Thea learned that making an offer on your first home is a piece of cake when your brain is buzzing about the fact that a handsome man asked for your hand in fake girlfriend-dom.

NINE

"You coming in?"

Thea's voice beckoned from the master bath, and the splashing sounds clued him in on what to expect. He closed his laptop and set it on the bedside table, then walked directly into the adjacent room, his dick already hardening.

She was in the enormous tub, wearing nothing but a smile. Fluffy mounds of fragrant bubbles covered her to her shoulders, but the long expanse of neck he could see was flushed pink with the heat of the water, and her dark hair curled at her temples in the humidity. With an inviting flash of her eyes, she slowly lifted one foot out of the water and pressed a button with her toe. The jets of the whirlpool tub kicked on, and she gave a little shiver.

"Oooh, that's nice." Her teeth sank into her lower lip. "Not as nice as your tongue though. Get in."

A frantic bolt of lust raced through him at her words, at the command in her voice, and touching her warm, wet skin became the only thing in the world that mattered. Yet his chest rose and fell as he stood frozen in the doorway, struck by the tableau: Thea in the bathroom he'd renovated with his own hands, waiting for him to strip and join her.

When he didn't move, she frowned and leaned back against the far slope of the tub, the bubbles shifting to give him tantalizing peeks at a curve of a breast here, a dusky nipple there.

"What's the matter? I'm not a little kid anymore."

He sucked in a deep breath before he finally found his voice. "Don't I fucking know it." He reached for the button on his jeans and yanked it free, desperate to join her in the—

"Hi! Trip said I could find you here."

The fantasy shattered, leaving Aiden with an erection in his jeans and his new fake girlfriend in his office.

"You okay?" Thea frowned at him. "I can come back."

He ran a hand through his hair as he brought his breathing under control. Had his wild and unexpected daydream conjured her somehow? This Thea wasn't warm and wet and covered in bubbles though; she was zipped into a puffy coat and holding a striped knit hat in her hands, the tip of her nose red from the cold.

"No! Please stay." He shot to his feet, then sat right back down again. His body needed a little more time to chill the fuck out. "I was just reviewing whirlpool tub options for some clients."

True. He'd been looking at suggestions for the Sappersteins, but his mind had galloped away from him, and what the hell was that all about anyway? The bargain they'd struck last night hadn't changed anything between them, just like that damn hockey-game kiss hadn't changed anything.

Means to an end. His end was a thriving family business. Hers was a house she could call home. Out-of-left-field hot tub fantasies had absolutely no place in his plan to deal with the woman he'd known his whole life. The same woman who'd looked ready to puke when she thought he was including sexual favors in their bargain.

That same woman was currently staring at him like he'd suddenly sprouted antennae.

Good thing she had no idea what head actually *was* growing; she'd probably run screaming out of the building and never look back. Time to get this under control. "What brings you here?" He gestured to a guest chair. "Can I get you some coffee?"

She unzipped her jacket and flopped down, grinning at him. "I got the house!"

He slapped his palms down on his desk. "You got the house!"

"They didn't even try to negotiate," she announced proudly.

"Guess they knew you meant business."

"Damn straight." She lifted her chin, looking every inch the confident negotiator, and he was hit with another wave of heat. She didn't need to be wet and naked to be breathtaking; she carried it off just fine in jeans and a Brick T-shirt.

"Now, let's talk timelines." She folded her hands on her lap and neatly crossed one leg over the other, adopting an all-business tone. "I close in three weeks. Will I be okay to move in right away?"

Business. Yes. Good thing one of them was focused. He pulled up the project outline on his laptop. "We've got paint and gutters and grout and steps on the exterior. Tear out the shag carpet and refinish the floors. Destroy that drop ceiling. Strip the old wallpaper and paint every-thing. Let me add that skylight." He grinned at her as he tapped his pen on his desk, mindlessly banging out the drumbeat for "Mr. Blue Sky." "And of course there's that kitchen. But if you're okay living with dust and chaos for a while, you can move in the instant they hand you the keys."

"Yay!" She gave a little bounce in her chair.

"Well. We're talking weeks and weeks of me and my crew underfoot. That's a lot of clutter to live with." The last thing he needed was her getting fed up and ending their agreement when the equilibrium of the business was still off.

"I'm highly adaptable, and besides, you're doing *me* the favor." The corners of her mouth tipped down. "Are you sure this is a fair price for your work though?"

He waved a hand dismissively. "It's a mutual favor, and you're still paying for materials and some labor." Weird to think about faking feelings as a mutual favor, but this was a weird situation.

"Thank you." She met his eyes with her serious brown ones. "Truly, I wouldn't have been able to make this leap without you."

"It's my pleasure." He reached forward and squeezed her hand, pleased to be playing a role in bringing her dream to life. She jumped a little at the contact, and he couldn't pass up the chance to tease her a tiny bit. "Gonna have to get used to having my hands all over you."

Pink flooded her cheeks, and she looked down. "You're really sure you want to do this? With me, I mean?"

Had any woman underestimated her charm more than Thea? "We already covered this."

But the fantasy of a bubble-covered Thea surged in

his mind again, and for a moment he *wasn't* sure this was a good idea. One of the biggest reasons he'd suggested this agreement was because she was a safe choice. They'd known each other forever, and neither of them was interested in the other one like that. His brain just needed to get with the program and stop picturing her tits.

It was probably just that he hadn't slept with anyone in way too long. Celibacy was messing with his focus.

"Hey, how's your dad?"

Her soft voice was a bucket of cold water on his wayward libido. "He's... well, he's pissed. He doesn't understand why he's not allowed to drive anymore, why we're not letting him come into work. Good news is, he got accepted into a clinical trial in Chicago."

"That's great!"

If only her optimism was contagious. "Yeah, but the bad news is he and my mom are moving up there while it's ongoing. So now we're losing our office queen too."

"Office queen?"

"Mom says it sounds better than office manager."

Thea grinned. "Cool. Does it come with a crown?"

"Don't give her any ideas."

Losing his dad in the business was one thing, but their mom was an equally important lynchpin keeping the company running. She kept track of bookings and inventory, sweet-talked angry clients, and generally solved problems and offered a listening ear for every person who came through the doors. His dad was the growl, but his mom was the purr. You needed both to keep things afloat, and Aiden was worried. Trip was taking control of the office-manager portion of the business right now, but it wasn't sustainable. How long did they have before his brother pissed off some important customer? Aiden pressed the heel of his hand to his forehead where a stress headache threatened to form.

"So do we need a signed contract or anything?"

Her question stopped him cold. "I'm not sure that's smart."

"Not about the..." She circled her hand between the two of them. "But for the house stuff. Not that I don't trust you."

"But it's still a business thing. I get it." As he spoke, he hit print on the most recent paperwork he'd presented her and pulled the pages off the printer on the credenza behind him. "Here."

He slid it across the desk to her, and her eyes skimmed over the line before she fished a pen with a unicorn topper out of her purse and signed her name. "Your turn."

She'd signed in bright pink ink, which made him smile as he reached for his own blue ballpoint. "Unicorn writing utensils. Stain sticks. What else you got in there?"

She primly clutched the red leather bag to her chest. "Wouldn't you like to know." She hopped up and grabbed her coat. "I'll leave you to it. Thanks again."

She turned to leave, but some instinct propelled him up and around his desk. He caught her by a belt loop as she headed for the door.

"Wait just a second."

She turned in surprise, her mouth forming a little pink O.

"Let me walk you out."

He held out his hand palm up, and she stared at it but didn't make a move to place her hand in his.

"We should be touchy in public. Unless I disgust you

that much?" He kept his tone light, but a small part of him wondered what caused her hesitation.

Thankfully, she wasted no time smacking her palm against his and lacing their fingers together.

"Disgust? Hardly." She tossed her hair. "I just find exceptionally handsome men a little intimidating. I'll get over it."

She met his eyes as if daring him to challenge her, and after a long moment, he drawled, "Well, well. *Exceptionally* handsome, am I?"

Her fierce expression dissolved into an eye roll. "You're so irritating."

She tugged on his arm to get him to move toward the exit, but he planted his feet and squeezed her hand. "Give me a second. It's not every day I get called handsome *and* irritating. Would you say I'm *exceptionally* irritating?"

"Right now, yes," she grumbled.

"Excellent." He nudged her toward the door. "Let's go, *babe*."

"Irritating!"

"Irritatingly handsome," he batted back. A glow bloomed deep in his chest at the revelation that she found him handsome. *Exceptionally* handsome. And she hadn't even watched him swing a hammer yet.

Hand in hand, they left his office and headed down the hall to the open room that served as a lobby and display area for their selection of drawer pulls and tile and granite samples. Loud chatter drifted from the spacious work area in the back, and he paused at the opportunity to execute Stage One of his reputation rehabilitation plan.

"Are you okay talking to some of the guys?" He squeezed her hand, letting her know the true meaning of his question: *Are you okay starting our charade right now?*

"Sure." She batted her lashes up at him. "Anything for you, *sugar lump.*"

He groaned. "That one's terrible." But they'd entered the lion's den, where half a dozen of the nosiest guys on the Murdoch payroll were eyeballing the two of them. "Guys, this is Thea Blackwell. Thea, this is a pack of reprobates who hopefully know enough to behave themselves in front of my lady."

His unsubtle hint didn't work in the least, and the guys all broke into whistles and catcalls. "Oooh, your lady!" one hooted while another coughed out something that sounded like "ball and chain."

"Hi, everybody." Thea gave a sunny smile and did a little bounce and wave before elbowing him in the side. "Geez, if this is the company you were keeping before, no wonder you came knocking on my door, Adonis."

The laughs around the room were even louder this time, along with a chorus of "Adonis!" Aiden closed his eyes as the knowledge that this was the only name he'd be called at work for the rest of his life seeped into his bones. But when he opened them again, Thea's flushed face and delighted grin took away the sting of that new nickname. She looked so proud to have won the approval of a room full of rowdy guys that he wasn't even mad. Instead, he lifted their linked hands and pressed a kiss to her knuckles. Her flush deepened as their eyes caught and held.

"Get a room!"

Of course fucking Ben Mendez was the guy who'd take it a step too far. Thea blinked and broke their stare with a short, embarrassed laugh, and Aiden let their hands drop. "Actually, you guys are supposed to be *building* a room, aren't you? Schedule says you've got three days left."

"Three days for what?" Thea asked, eyes bright as she took in the partially assembled kitchen island in the middle of the open space.

"Our display for the Beaucoeur Home Expo," he said. "We're building a whole kitchen at our booth to showcase some of the newest products we're using these days."

"Oh right! I can't believe I forgot that was this weekend." Her lips twitched, and he knew she was internally celebrating her smooth cover-up of the fact that they'd never actually discussed the expo even though it was one of the company's biggest promotional events of the year. "I've never been before. As a renter, I didn't think I was allowed on the premises."

"You're with me now, hot stuff. I'll get you in."

That prompted another round of teasing commentary from the Murdoch crew, but Aiden didn't care. Hadn't he been wondering for the past few months what a real relationship would be like? This weird little trial run with Thea was turning out to be kind of fun. She knew the score and had zero expectations of him, so he could relax into this new role of boyfriend and try it on for size. Domesticity cosplay for the player.

"Okay, back to work. I'm walking this one out, and then I'll be back to help troubleshoot the backsplash placement."

He slung an arm around Thea's shoulders and steered her out of the room. They passed Trip on their way out, hunched and scowling at the central command desk as he dealt with whoever was on the other end of the phone. Letting him fill in for their mom was definitely not a long-term solution. Trip gave Thea a jerky chin nod as they passed, his brows lowering when he noticed Aiden's arm around her.

Great. Another thing for his brother to be pissy about later.

At the entrance, Thea stopped and slid on her coat.

He grabbed her hat from the pocket and plopped it onto her head, where it perched at a drunken angle. "Can't have my lady getting cold."

"You have to stop calling me 'your lady.'" She adjusted the hat so it sat squarely over her brown hair. "It's weird."

"Okay, *baby girl*."

He held open the door for her, but she stabbed a finger in his face. *"Absolutely not."*

He just laughed and guided her out with a hand on the small of her back. She'd parked on the street directly in front of the shop, and the frigid wind blasted them as soon as they stepped outside. Rather than jog back to his office to grab his coat, he crammed his hands in his pockets and hunched his shoulders to protect his ears, planning on a quick goodbye. "Will you need help with your move? I've got my truck, and we can dig up some boxes from the warehouse."

She leaned against the side of her car and wrapped her arms around her torso. "You'd do that?" She tipped her chin up as he stepped closer to block the wind.

"Of course." He reached out and zipped her coat the last three inches so it nestled under her chin. He could survive the cold, but he hated the thought of the chill touching her skin. "Anything for my new fake girlfriend."

Her eyes drifted over his shoulder. "We have an audience."

The family business was located in Beaucoeur's riverfront warehouse district in an old distillery that had gone out of business during Prohibition. About thirty years ago, his dad had bought it on the cheap and renovated the massive space for the company's needs. Normally Aiden appreciated the floor-to-ceiling display windows that showcased a selection of the company's bathroom and kitchen fixtures to everyone who drove by. Today though, it provided the perfect vantage point for half a dozen nosy men to stampede from the work area in back to spy on his and Thea's goodbye.

He sighed, his breath a visible cloud swirling between them in the cold. "I swear to God, carpenters, plumbers, and painters are the source of eighty percent of the rumors in this town." He reached for her hand again. "I'm gonna kiss you goodbye now, okay?"

Her eyes widened a tick but she nodded, so he bent his head and closed the distance between the two of them.

Before his lips touched hers, he offered a final warning. "Gotta be convincing."

Her eyes sparked as she whispered back, "Better make it good." Then she shocked the hell out of him by twining her fingers around his neck and pulling his face down to meet hers.

When their lips met, two things became apparent: their kiss at the hockey game hadn't been a fluke, and his out-of-the-blue bathtub fantasy from earlier wasn't so out of the blue after all. Because kissing Thea was incredible. He wasn't trying to move past this stage or thinking ahead to how he wanted to touch her next. Instead, he just focused on the press and slide of her lips against his and on the clean scent of her skin and the intimacy of sharing breath with another person. The February cold receded, and his plans for a quick goodbye fled as her tongue met his and her fingers tugged at his hair. When she tilted her head to give him better access to the heat of her mouth, he groaned and shifted closer, pressing his leg between hers and pinning her to the side of her car. She shivered and rocked against him, and *Jesus fuck*, were they dry-humping on the street in front of his place of business in the middle of the day?

He tore himself away but didn't drop his hands where they cupped her face. Instead, he ran his thumbs over the crest of her cheeks, and a bolt of heat raced straight to his dick when her eyes fluttered shut and she turned to press a kiss into his palm. For a heady moment, he wanted to hustle her into the back seat of her car and pull off her clothes one by one to see if she went all warm and melty everywhere he kissed.

Then the sound of a hand banging on the display window brought him back to reality. For a moment he resented the audience that he knew had their noses pressed against the glass, but a split second later he said a silent prayer of thanks. Dealing with his hard-on wasn't what Thea had signed up to do, and those idiots inside had given him a necessary reminder.

He took a step back, hoping the February air would do its job and cool his overheated body down.

But it didn't help when Thea smiled up at him and said almost wistfully, "Hand-holding, pet names, goodbye kisses. We can survive a couple of months of this, right?"

He shifted to make room in his suddenly tight jeans. "Beats digging ditches." By a lot. Kissing Thea beat digging ditches by a *lot*.

She laughed a little nervously and fumbled her keys into the lock. "Okay, um. Thanks."

"*Thanks?*" he said out loud to himself as she pulled away.

What the hell had he gotten himself into?

TEN

"Next time you want a coffee girl, call somebody else."

Thea looked up from her precariously balanced cardboard coffee-cup holder to find Faith's identical carrier about to implode under the weight of the full take-out cups.

"Suck it up!" she chirped. "We're spreading joy."

Her friend glanced down at her pearly white jacket. "We're spreading coffee stains."

"Grump. One of those cups is for you, you know."

Faith leaned over the cups and inhaled. "It's the least you can do."

By now they'd reached the exhibit building in the Cavelier County fairgrounds, where Beaucoeur's massive home expo was underway. It was only twenty minutes away from the official throwing open of the doors for the crowds to float from booth to booth, picking up ideas for spring home-improvement projects from the eighty-some vendors inside.

At the entrance, a bored-looking security guy stopped them. "It's not open yet."

Thea lifted her chin toward their ready-to-topple coffee deliveries. "Right, of course. But can we maybe deliver these to the Murdoch booth and then come back out to wait for the official start?"

The guard's face lit up. "Oh, you're with the Murdoch team! Sorry about that. Go right ahead."

And like that, they gained entrance to downstate Illinois's premiere home renovation destination.

"Wow," Faith said as they weaved through the displays to the Murdoch kitchen in the back corner. "Is that what it's like to be treated like royalty?"

"You tell me. You're the daughter of the Fox empire."

Faith shuddered, risking more coffee to the torso. "I renounced that filthy money years ago."

Thea's joking tone fell away at her friend's genuine disgust. "Yeah, I know."

Part of Faith's post high school emancipation had involved walking away from a sizable trust fund after her overprotective parents sabotaged her relationship with the love of her life. She'd cried for weeks afterward, and Thea knew not a single tear had been over that money. They'd all been about the boy.

"So we're both nobodies here to check out what's new in residential siding. What a time to be alive!" Thea gripped her coffee and spun in a circle, giddily happy to be out with her friend at an event she'd never been to before. And truth be told, she was giddily happy to be walking in the direction of her fake boyfriend.

When they were a few feet from the booth, Thea said quietly, "Remember, you're the only other person who knows about the..."

"The ridiculous scheme that will absolutely blow up

in your faces?" Faith asked. "Yeah, got it. Not a word until I can say 'I told you so.'"

"Thanks for the support!" Thea singsonged her response to cover her nerves. Aiden had just caught sight of her and waved in welcome, and damn, but he was nice to look at in his company polo and worn-in jeans.

"Morning." He ambled over and plucked the tray from her hands, giving her a quick kiss that set her heart pumping harder.

This kiss didn't come close to the one that threatened to scorch the paint off the side of Juniper on Tuesday, which was probably for the best. If they went around kissing like that whenever anybody needed to be reminded about their relationship, she was going to combust. His pheromones were off the charts, and she wasn't going to survive if he kept turning them on and then switching them off again once the show was over.

Brain-scrambling kisses or no, it was time to be her breeziest, best-girlfriend-iest self. "I figured you'd appreciate some caffeine. We brought enough for an army." She gestured to where Faith was handing out cups to the workers putting finishing touches on the under-cabinet lighting.

Aiden draped an arm around her and dropped a kiss on her temple. "This is really public. You good?"

His whisper stirred the hair next to her ear, and she whispered back, "I appreciate you always checking in with me, but I agreed to this. You don't have to ask. You can just *do*."

When his brows arched in amusement, she flushed as she replayed her words. She'd basically just given him *carte blanche* to do, well, *anything*, and she'd bet the title to Juniper that whatever he'd do to her would be better than anything she'd experienced with any of her actual boyfriends.

But this line of thinking wasn't going to help her keep her cool around him, so with a short clearing of her throat, she gestured to the tray he was effortlessly balancing in one hand. "Make sure to grab one for yourself."

"So thoughtful, *honey bear*." He set his tray next to Faith's empty one on the marble-topped island in the center of the Murdoch display and snagged a cup. When one of his workers called him over with a question, Thea took the chance to lean an elbow on the countertop and simply watch him as he listened to his guy and drank his coffee. At one point he tipped his head to down a long swallow, and her gaze zeroed in on the strong column of his throat.

Lickable, it was. Suckable. Bitable, even.

"Good morning, dear."

Thea spun around and cursed her wicked thoughts when she found herself nose to nose with Aiden's sweet-faced mother. "H-hi, Mrs. Murdoch."

She was immediately enveloped in a soft, floral-perfumy hug.

"It's been too long. And call me Gloria please."

"Oh sure. Sure." After an initial hesitation, she hugged Gloria right back, surprised by the warm welcome. "Would you like some coffee? I brought enough for the group."

"Well, aren't you sweet. But no, thanks. No caffeine for me these days."

"Aiden told me about Mr. Murdoch. I'm so sorry. When do you leave for Chicago? Can I help with anything?"

Gloria's smile dimmed, but she said quietly, "We

leave on Wednesday, and it would be a huge relief if you"
—her eyes cut over to her son, who was now frowning and
gesturing at the display sink—"well, if you'd look out for
Aiden. Make sure he's all right. Make sure he's not
lonely."

Damn. Being dishonest to this kind woman who was
worried about her son felt all kinds of wrong. Then again,
she was going to be spending time with Aiden, so it wasn't
quite a lie.

"It'll be my pleasure." She made the promise and then
immediately flushed. Did that make her sound pervy?
Because there was pleasure and then there was *pleasure*,
and Gloria didn't know that she wasn't referring to the
second kind.

A clatter interrupted her frantic musings, and they
both turned to see the large vinyl banner with the
company logo tumble to the floor in a heap.

"Well, darn." Gloria bustled over to it. "I bought a
new stand for this, but nobody can get the silly thing to
stay upright."

Thea was already digging into her purse. "Hang on. I
can help." After a moment, she produced a binder clip
and a hair tie and picked up the crumpled display. "If we
loop this through the top and slide it over the pole, then
clip it to the top of the banner, it should be good." She
spoke as she worked and quickly had the display securely
fastened to the stand. "It'd take a tornado to knock it over
now."

Gloria clapped her hands. "Amazing! How'd you do
that so quickly?"

Thea shrugged. "I was an admissions rep for Barton
College a few years ago. I got really good at setting up and
taking down displays at high school job fairs." And while

she was at it, she might as well straighten the brochures piled on the island. She slapped them into a tidy stack and then fanned them out like a Vegas croupier as Gloria watched in delight.

"We need to get you a Murdoch Construction shirt!" she exclaimed before leveling another look at Thea. "Oh, I like you for Aiden very much."

Her anxiety ratcheted up. "Um, thanks?" Could Gloria not see the flashing neon sign over her head declaring YOUR SON AND I ARE IN A FAKE RELATION- SHIP? Apparently not; the other woman settled a hand over her heart and beamed.

"Now tell me how you ended up reconnecting with my boy after all this time."

"*Mom.*" Aiden joined the conversation with a groan. "Don't harass her."

Gloria turned dancing eyes on him. "I'm not allowed to be curious? You know as well as I do that you've never brought a girl around before."

Thea tried not to inject herself into this family dynamic, but then again she didn't try *that* hard. "Wait, he's never brought someone home to meet you? Like, ever?"

Gloria dropped her chin as she prepared to spill her firstborn's secrets. "Never once. Not even in high school. It's enough to break a mother's heart."

"Okay," Aiden said loudly. "That's enough of that. We're on business time, not bust-Aiden's-balls time."

"Language!"

"Sorry, Ma."

Thea watched the interplay like she was watching a tennis match. Aiden didn't look terribly sorry, but Gloria didn't look offended in the least. If anything, she looked happy to be teasing her big handsome son.

"I think we've got things under control here," Aiden told his mom. "Do you want to do a quick circuit? See what King Construction thinks they're going to show us up with this year?"

"Oh, the *Kings.*" Gloria all but hissed the name, and Thea blinked at the competitive venom on her kind face. "I'll find them and report back."

With that, she zipped off into the crowd in her sensible white tennis shoes, leaving Thea alone with her fake boyfriend.

"She was seconds away from ordering you a company license plate," he said, sounding surprisingly unbothered by the idea. He held out a cup of coffee with his winningest smile. "We had one left over. Can I offer you coffee that you brought yourself?"

She accepted it gratefully, biting back a yawn. "Such a gentleman."

"Such a morning person."

"Definitely not. My morning-show stint with Dave was torture." She sipped and looked around. "Where'd Faith go?"

She followed Aiden behind the kitchen island, where he opened and closed one drawer after another.

"She said she wanted to check out what's new in toilets, but I think she wanted to get away from Devon. He kept asking if he could touch the blue streaks in her hair."

She wrinkled her nose. "Devon's lucky she didn't snap his wrist like a twig."

"It might come to that if he's still here when she gets back." He slammed the last cabinet door shut. "Damn."

"What are you looking for?"

"I wanted to hang a curtain in the window, but nobody remembered to bring a tension rod, and I'm worried nails will split the wood."

The aggravation in his voice was at odds with such a seemingly small oversight, but when she looked at the empty window frame above the sink, she could see why. They'd done all this work to build a whole dang kitchen in the expo building, and the window now provided a picturesque view of the men's restroom entrance.

"Yeah, you probably want to cover that up." She grabbed the lightweight material lying on the counter. "Do you care what happens to this after the show?"

"Nope," he said.

She tapped a finger to her lips in thought. "Do you have painter's tape and a hot-glue gun, perchance?"

He opened the door under the sink and produced a thick blue roll of tape. "I think we've got Gorilla Glue someplace. Hang on."

He disappeared behind the display where they'd stashed their assembly supplies, and by the time he was back, Thea had clambered up onto the sink and was unrolling a length of tape along the top of the window casing.

"Hey, careful." Without any warning, strong hands grabbed either side of her waist. She'd been steady before, but the heat of his hands through her shirt made her wobble, and his grip tightened. "Got it?"

"Yeah, I'm good." She forced herself to ignore his touch and finished securing the tape to the window. "Glue?"

He set the tube on her palm, and she squirted a

healthy amount across the tape, then quickly pressed the top of the curtain to it.

"If this was any heavier, it probably wouldn't hold. But it'll work for today at least." She glanced over her shoulder to find him hovering close enough that she'd squash him if she fell off the sink. "Okay, that ought to do it."

She capped the glue and tossed it on the counter. Then she straightened the gauzy white curtain, which now successfully hid the activity in the men's room. She started to clamber down, but before she could make any progress, Aiden's hands were back on her waist, and he swung her off the edge of the sink and onto the floor. The movement ended with her back against the countertop and Aiden's front pressing into hers. Neither of them moved.

"Thanks." She almost didn't breathe for fear of breaking the spell.

He looked down at her for a moment before he glanced over her head at her handiwork. "How on earth did you know how to do that? Wait, don't tell me." His hands were back on her waist again even though she was no longer in danger of toppling over. "You spent a month as an interior decorator. Or you majored in textile design. Or"—he leaned down so his mouth brushed her ear—"you're a King Construction spy, sent to steal our secrets."

Did she think she wasn't in danger of toppling over? Because right then, with the smell of coffee mixing with the woodsy scent of his aftershave, her knees went weak.

"Actually," she whispered back, "I had a stepdad who didn't like holes in the walls of his house, and this let me hang up tapestries without damaging anything."

He stepped back with a frown. "Really?"

She laughed lightly. "And look at what great life skills it taught me!"

His mouth worked as if he might say something else, but the sounds of people approaching penetrated their bubble. They broke away to find a middle-aged couple studying a brochure. And just like that, it was sales time.

"Hi, folks. I'm Aiden Murdoch, and this is Thea. What questions can I answer for you today?"

She stepped forward, absurdly pleased at being included in his introduction, and watched as he answered every one of their renovation queries with succinct yet enticing answers. The encounter ended with them tucking away his business card and wandering off with a promise to call on Monday.

"Wow. Now *I* kind of want a Cambria countertop."

"Nah," he said immediately. "I've already got big ideas for your kitchen."

And before she could press him for more details, another potential customer approached, and Thea settled in to watch him work.

It was her pleasure, truly.

ELEVEN

"Hello?" Aiden pushed open the front door and stepped over the threshold of the house on Prospect Point. "Is there a homeowner on the premises?"

"In the back!"

He weaved through the stack of boxes piled against the wall in the hallway and headed for the sunroom. As he moved through the house, he squinted up at the low-wattage fixture struggling to illuminate the hallway. One more thing for his list of items in need of the Murdoch touch. When he reached the all-glass room, the lady of the house was sprawled on one of the three colorful striped lounge chairs lined up and facing the Illinois River.

"The queen's in her castle, I see."

Thea stretched like a lazy cat, grinning up at him. "She is. She's quite content, despite the shag carpet and the ugly kitchen and the drop ceiling."

He settled into the lounge chair positioned next to hers. "Nice view you've got here, Ms. Blackwell."

She sighed dreamily. "It is, isn't it? And it's all mine."

"Yes it is. Happy closing day." He'd stopped by her brand-new home toward the end of his workday, and the sun hung low in the sky, painting the river, bluffs, and bare trees with its dying rays. Since it was March, everything would be greening up soon enough, but for now it was a black-and-orange landscape.

"Honestly, you could touch not a single thing in this house, and I think I'd be perfectly happy with just this view."

"It is gorgeous." But he wasn't looking at the river. Thea's hair was pulled into two braids, and she'd shut her eyes again, the tiniest smile ghosting across her pink lips. In that moment, he believed that she'd live with the shag and the dim lighting and all of it, and she wouldn't complain once.

"Does that mean I'm off the hook on refinishing those floors?"

"Nice try." She cracked open one eye. "You can't dump me that easily, *huggy bear*."

"I wouldn't dream of it. My guys love you."

She rolled to her side to face him. "Well, that's good. I tend to be a love-me-or-hate-me kind of person."

"Who could possibly hate you?" The very idea baffled him.

"You'd be surprised." She spoke lightly, but the question took root in his brain. In the month since the offer on her house had been accepted, they'd spent major chunks of time together making renovation plans, and he'd become a fan of her bouncy good cheer. They'd turned into regulars at the hardware stores around town as they looked at options for lights and fixtures and flooring, and every single Murdoch employee knew her by name at this point because everywhere she went, she was unfailingly friendly and upbeat. Amazingly competent too. The woman never met a situation she couldn't fix or improve in some way.

Speaking of.

"New purchase?" He patted the metal frame of his chair.

"First thing I bought for the house. Two for down here and one for the balcony off the master bedroom."

"What, you didn't walk out there, did you?" He lifted his head in alarm. "I know the home inspector said it was safe, but some of those support beams look water damaged. I'm going to—"

"Yeah, yeah." She waved him off. "You're going to replace some sketchy wood with your magical tools to make the balcony safe and sound, and I'm forbidden out there until you do."

"Okay." He settled back again and crossed one ankle over the other. "So you've officially owned this place for three hours. Do you want to go over the renovation schedule now?"

"Honestly, I kind of want to chill and enjoy the moment."

"Yeah, I get it." Then he frowned. "Oh, do you mean you want to enjoy it alone? I didn't mean to intrude."

She lazily swatted at his arm. "Don't be weird. I'm glad you're here."

He was too, and they lapsed into contented silence as the sun finally vanished behind the horizon and the stars poked through the darkening sky one by one.

He let his imagination wander to what this place

would be like once he'd made it worthy of her. Pictured her neatly made bed nestled against the wall in the upstairs room with exposed ceiling beams and a new skylight letting in the warm morning sun. Pictured her sipping coffee in the breakfast nook on Saturday morning, that dark, shiny hair mussed from sleep. Pictured her ending every night in the lounger on the balcony, watching the sun set over the river.

"This is a great setup," he finally said.

"Mmmm. Stargazing for two." Her voice was dreamy, and an unexpected bolt of jealousy gripped him. She was dreaming about whatever guy she was planning on sharing this setup with once he was gone.

For the first time it occurred to him that he was renovating the house where she'd fall in love and raise a family. She'd share that bed with someone, drink coffee with him in the breakfast nook, cuddle with him on the balcony at the end of the night. For some reason all his mental pictures had been of just her, with no guy in sight. Weird that it bothered him a little now.

"I'm scared shitless."

Her words knocked him right out of his head, but he managed to volley back a joke. "I told you I'm gonna make that balcony perfectly safe for you, *schmoopie*."

"I don't know how, but your nicknames are getting worse." She sat up and swung her feet to the side of the lounger. "Just... roots. A mortgage. Permanence. Not things I'm particularly known for."

He sat up too. "Hey, you got this."

"Thanks." She looked down as she played with the end of a braid. "Should I get a dog?"

Not what he was expecting, but okay. "This house has

a great backyard for a dog. Lots of nice areas for walks too."

"Right, but should *I* get a dog?"

The question seemed to matter to her, although he had no idea why. "Sure. I bet you love animals. And it'd be something else for you to talk to." He grinned at the picture of Thea keeping up a running conversation with her dog at all hours of the day. When she didn't smile back at him, he nudged her foot with his. "Seriously, I think you'd love a dog. And your dog would love you." All that warmth and affection? Hugs and pets and kisses? He was almost ready to switch places with the hypothetical canine.

"Well." She slapped her hands on her thighs and said crisply, "since that's not happening anytime soon, I guess we'd better go over the schedule for the next few weeks." She stood, and Aiden joined her.

As they moved through the house, they flipped on lights to ward off the darkness pressing against the windows.

"Sorry I can't offer you anywhere to sit or anything to drink but water," she said when they reached the counter separating the kitchen from the dining room. "Also, I haven't moved my drinking glasses in yet, so it'll have to be straight from the tap."

"Horrible hospitality." He set his binder on the ugly countertop as Thea's gaze drifted back to the dark shimmer of the Illinois River.

"It looks so different at night."

"Yeah, you'd almost think it was safe to swim in."

"Ew." She wrinkled her nose. "That poor river."

"It may be brown and sludgy, but it's great for summertime boating."

"I'll take your word on that." She leaned her elbows on the counter as he pulled out the schedule for them to review.

"Not a boating fan?"

"Never really tried it."

"You're missing out. Trip's got a boat, and you haven't lived until you've spent an afternoon drinking beer in the sun on the river."

Maybe not this summer though. Not with Trip's attitude. A shame too; some of his favorite memories were family time on the boat. He clenched and released his fingers to banish the memories, spreading them flat on the printed sheets in front of him. When he looked up, Thea was staring at his hand where the tips pressed so hard into the countertop that his nails turned white.

"There any shade on that boat?"

His tension vanished at her question, which was obviously designed to distract him. And damn if it didn't work. "Of course. We've got a canopy. We're not animals." He smiled at her in gratitude; she had a deft way of pulling him back from the brink.

"I guess that doesn't sound too bad then."

"You'll love it. Just wait until it warms up and I'll take you out." If Trip didn't come around, he'd just have to rent a boat. But now *she* was the one frowning. "What's wrong?"

Her gaze returned to the river. "I mean... summer's months away. And we're not gonna be together that long."

Apparently he wasn't the only one already thinking about life after their agreement was over. "Yeah, but we're staying friends when we break up, remember?" He stretched his pinky across the space to brush against hers. "Friends can go boating together."

Just like that, her perkiness was back. "Damn straight. Okay, what've you got? Is that a *blueprint*?" She snatched up one of the sheets he'd spread across her counter and held it out accusingly.

"More like a sketch."

"A whole damn blueprint of my little kitchen!" she hooted.

He leaned his elbow on the counter and propped his head on his fist, content to watch her study the printout like it was some kind of holy text. "Do you want your pretty new cabinets to fit perfectly, or do you want me to just toss them up there randomly?"

"Everything I do is a wee bit haphazard." She peered at him over the edge of the paper. "It's a trip being around someone this organized."

"I'm a contractor," he pointed out. "Organization is basically prereq number one."

"I guess this explains the itemized, day-by-day schedule of work to be done." She pointed accusingly at his Excel printout.

"Listen, lady, if we don't have a plan and stick to it, this whole project could fall into chaos and anarchy."

"Chaos *and* anarchy?" She gasped. "My God. Fill me on this schedule then."

They'd just turned their attention to the grid he'd filled out of which jobs would be performed when, based on the availability of his workers and his own nights-and-weekend plans, when the doorbell *bing-bonged* through the house.

"Expecting someone?"

"Nope."

She walked toward the front door, and he followed in her wake, glad he was with her so she wasn't alone when she greeted whoever was knocking after dark in a new neighborhood. She threw open the round-top front door, and he was standing close enough to feel her whole body stiffen as she took in the three people on her front step.

"Mom!" With a jolt, she moved forward to hug the woman standing in front. "What are you guys doing here?"

"Happy housewarming, sweetie!"

Aiden stepped back to let the group inside. Thea's mom entered first, followed by a teenage girl and a balding man holding a large potted plant. The furrows etched into the man's forehead deepened when he greeted Thea.

"You're still driving that death trap? It's a wonder it gets you to work in the mornings. You need a good American car!" He shifted the pot to the crook of his left elbow as his attention turned to the wallpaper in the hallway. He ran a finger over one peeling seam and announced, "Your daughter's going to have her work cut out for her, Carly."

"I think it's got potential," Carly said, turning to Thea. "It's going to be beautiful, honey."

"Thanks." Thea's voice sounded flatter than he'd ever heard it, but when she turned toward the teenager, she bounced back to chipper. "Good to see you, Belly."

"You too," the girl said. "I love your front door."

"Isn't it cute?" Thea squealed, and they exchanged identical one-side-kicked-up smiles.

And that's when Aiden realized he was looking at Thea's half sister, the surprisingly tall product of her mom's marriage to the sweaty man currently shoving the plant into Thea's hands.

"Here. Let's see how long you can keep this one alive." Then he turned and steamrolled his way down the hall. "Jesus, would you look at this?" His voice drifted from the kitchen, but Aiden couldn't tell if he was complimenting the view or complaining about the decor.

"Let's just... let him explore," Carly said. Then she noticed the stranger lurking in the entrance. "And who's this?"

Oh shit. They hadn't discussed what to tell Thea's family. Did they know about their deal, or was he playing the dutiful boyfriend? The uncertainty left him frozen in the hallway with a half smile glued to his face.

"Mom, that's Aiden Murdoch." The teenager didn't roll her eyes, but it was heavily implied in her tone.

Thea glanced sharply at her. "How do you know Aiden?"

The girl shrugged and pulled out her phone. "Moo Daddies," she said as if that explained everything.

"Aiden!" Carly exclaimed. "I haven't seen you since..." The short silence stretched awkwardly until she said, "Well, you've certainly gotten taller."

"Twenty-odd years can change a man," he said easily. Of course, two decades ago Carly's hair was as brown as Thea's and her smile had radiated the same level of warmth and humor. Now she was blond and a little sharp around the edges, so much so that he almost hadn't recognized her.

"Aiden, this is Annabelle. She's a senior at Beaucoeur High," Thea said, and the teenager's eyes flicked up from her phone in acknowledgment. "And that's Peter passing judgment on the house. He'll be along in a second to tell me everything that's wrong with it."

"Oh, honey, that's not fair," Carly said softly. "He just wants to help. You know insurance is his thing."

"Health insurance, not home insurance," Thea grumbled. Her brown eyes found his through the foliage bursting from the terra-cotta pot, and he wondered what the hell family dynamic he'd just walked into.

At that moment, Peter came stalking back into the entryway. "I wish you'd called me to come check this place out before you put any money down. What were you thinking?"

"I was thinking it's the house I've always wanted to own." She spoke evenly and without an ounce of her usual enthusiasm.

"In this neighborhood?" He waved his stubby arms. "With these property taxes?"

For a moment Aiden worried that Thea was going to chuck the plant at ol' Pete's head, but Carly stepped up and put a hand on her husband's back. "You know Thea, hon. She's always got things figured out. Our little Miss Independent."

If anything, Thea's fingers clenched even tighter around the plant pot, but when she spoke, her tone was amiable. "I handled it. Your buddy Gil got me a good homeowner's policy, and I used Dad's life insurance money for the down payment."

She lifted her chin as she said it while everybody else in the hallway stiffened, including Aiden. His fake girlfriend had just tossed Lee Blackwell's name into the middle of the group as if it were a grenade.

"Oh, sweetie, that's..." Carly's voice trailed off.

"Smart," Peter said decisively before extending his elbow to his wife. "Come on, dear. You've got to check out this view."

The two of them walked away, leaving Thea holding the plant and gritting her teeth.

"I wanna be you when I grow up."

They both looked at Annabelle in surprise, and Thea laughed weakly. "God, don't say that." Then she brightened. "Want to check out the master bedroom? It has the grossest shag carpet you've ever seen."

"Sure." The girl pocketed her phone and headed down the hall as Thea grilled her about a recent varsity volleyball game, which explained what Annabelle did with all that height.

When Peter and Carly followed them up to the second floor, Aiden melted into the background to give them privacy, although he couldn't stop himself from calling after them, "Everybody stay off the balcony!"

He wandered into the living room while Thea did the tour guide thing, and when he heard their feet on the stairs heading back down, he joined them in the front hallway, still not sure if he was a friend, a boyfriend, or the contractor in this scenario.

"Sorry, did you say why Aiden's here?" Carly asked as she buttoned up her coat.

"Oh, um." Thea tangled her fingers together, clearly feeling the same level of uncertainty he did about what story to tell her family.

Fuck that. Acting on a protective instinct that he didn't know he had in him, he wrapped his arms around her sternum and hauled her against his chest. Her small frame relaxed against him, and he tightened his arms even more. "Just helping my girlfriend celebrate her first night in her new house."

Now they had Annabelle's full attention. "You landed the hottest Moo Daddy. Nice."

"Ha!" Thea's short, sharp laugh vibrated through her chest, and he dropped a kiss on top of her head, partly to keep up their story and partly to reward her for her bravery tonight.

He looked up to find Peter studying them with amused condescension. "New bet: the plant outlasts the boyfriend."

Several things happened at once. Annabelle shouted, "God, Dad!" while Carly's lips pressed together so hard they disappeared and Thea went absolutely rigid in his arms. That last fact was what led Aiden to lose his easygoing smile and let go of Thea so he could step forward to tell the older man exactly where he could stick his fucking bets. He'd gotten into this bargain in part to help out the sad little girl who'd cried silent tears on her swing set the day they buried her father. She deserved kindness, and if he needed to be the one to send that message, so fucking be it.

But Thea grabbed him and tugged him back before addressing Peter in the iciest tone he'd ever heard her use. "Unlike the plant, Aiden can feed and water himself, so I give him good odds for surviving my company." She squeezed his fingers and glared at her stepdad until he ducked his head and looked away with a muttered, "Of course. Sorry." Then she lifted her chin at her half sister. "Let's do a ladies' night soon, Belly."

"Cool." Sincerity warred with teenage boredom, but in the end it sounded like an invitation she'd be accepting.

"I'd love it if you could come too," she said, pivoting to Carly.

"That would be lovely." Carly folded her daughter into one more hug. "I'm so happy for you."

Approximately two seconds into their hug, Peter

clapped his hands. "Time to go, Johnsons. Belly has school in the morning."

He placed a beefy paw on Carly's shoulder, and she pulled away from Thea to rest her smaller hand on her husband's before following Annabelle out the door.

Peter, bringing up the rear, paused in front of Thea. "Big step, buying a house."

"Yep," she said shortly.

He chucked her under the chin and said gruffly, "Good for you, kiddo."

And with that, they were gone, leaving Thea to slump against the wall while Aiden tried to sort through what he'd just seen.

"Hey, *snookums*?" he finally asked.

"Yeah?" She looked up at him with big brown eyes, and something clenched low in his belly at the dazed expression he saw there.

"What the hell was all that?"

When her eyes dropped to the floor and her shoulders began to shake, he moved toward her in alarm, ready to pull her into a hug and dry her tears. Then she threw her head back and revealed that she was actually vibrating with laughter.

"*That* is why I moved out when I was eighteen and never looked back." She swiped at her eyes as her giggles subsided. Then the mirth on her face disappeared, and she wrapped her arms around her midsection, shrinking into herself.

Watching the sunny Thea Blackwell curl up in misery was too much for him, and he reached for her hand. "You know who'd be really proud of you?" Her eyes flew to his, and he twined his fingers through hers. "Your dad. So damn proud of the house *and* your independent streak."

She blinked a few times and cleared her throat. "Yeah, he would, wouldn't he?" Her throat worked as she swallowed hard, and then she nodded decisively toward the kitchen, where the paperwork waited on the counter. "Okay. Show me your big fancy schedule. Let's do this."

TWELVE

Thea stood outside the door to the Elephant and sucked in a steadying breath. There was no reason to be nervous, right? She'd pushed through this battered metal door a thousand times, and she'd been in the audience for more Moo Daddies shows than she could count. Tonight wouldn't be any different.

Ha. Lies. Tonight she was debuting as Aiden Murdoch's girlfriend in public. *Public* public, as opposed to his construction company or the home expo or a random hardware store. She was going to be the proud girlfriend watching her man bang the drums while never letting on that those were the only things he was banging right now.

Oh God, she'd never be able to pull this off.

"Ow! Hey!" Thea rubbed her elbow and glared at the brunette who'd just smacked into it.

"Sorry," the sylph called over her shoulder as she followed her friends into the building, leaving Thea's funny bone throbbing. It was a sign. She should go straight home and do a charcoal mask and forget this whole business.

But she couldn't do that. She'd promised Aiden. The bulk of his responsibility in their fake relationship was overhauling her house, and her main role was being his public arm candy. He was already hard at work on his end of the bargain, so now it was time for her to candy up and follow through on her end.

Chin up. Boobs out. Smile on.

With her self-confidence mantra echoing in her ears, she threw back her shoulders and sailed through the door, reminding herself that she was looking hot as hell in her smoky eye and slinky dress. Ordinarily the Brick Babes would be swarming the place when the Moo Daddies performed, but they hadn't been able to pull together an outing for the final show before Ana gave birth and Dave took a long paternity leave from performing. That meant Thea was flying solo tonight, and although Mabel had invited her to share a table, Thea didn't see her friend anywhere in the hot, crowded bar.

"Here you go."

She turned in surprise to see the raven-haired woman who'd jostled her outside. "It's an apology gin and tonic." She pressed a glass into Thea's hand. "I didn't mean to knock into you. Sorry!"

"Oh thanks. Alcohol equals forgiveness." Thea took a sip as her eyes roamed over the crowd, and the woman gave a knowing click of her tongue.

"Are you on the hunt tonight too?"

"Hunt?" She turned away from the stage where the band was finishing its setup to see that the woman's two friends had joined her. She was suddenly enveloped in feminine laughter and enticing floral scents.

"The Aiden hunt," the short-haired blonde said.

Thea took another long gulp of her drink before she was able to stammer out, "Ummm. Aiden hunt?"

The woman with a long brown braid pointed dramatically to the stage, where the man in question was bent over his drum kit and showing off an extremely impressive display of leg and ass in his broken-in jeans.

All four women watched in silence for a moment before the black-haired one sighed. "It's been forever since he took somebody home, and we're all suffering."

The blonde tucked a short curl behind her ear. "It's selfish really, to withhold all that goodness from the women of Beaucoeur."

"Bang Aiden Murdoch for clear skin!" the woman with the braid whooped.

The other two joined in the catcalling as Thea's mouth fell open.

"Sorry, I'm... Is this like a *game*?"

The glances the three women sent her were a mixture of pitying and amused, and the black-haired one spoke first. "I don't know, does scoring a night with the best ride in town sound like a game to you?"

"None of us have climbed on board the A-train yet, so the line forms here!" The braid shimmied and slapped the blonde a high five. Then she noticed Thea's stunned expression, and confusion clouded her pretty features. "Oh, are you not from around here? Aiden's a *legend*."

"No, I..." Thea couldn't seem to pull together a coherent thought. "I mean, he's a *person*. Aiden. He's not some... some *sex toy*."

The women exchanged a quick round of "who invited the prude" glances before the braid spoke. "Obviously he's a *person*. He's a person who's great for some hot sex where everybody goes home happy. If all the participants are having a good time, where's the harm?" She sipped her drink and gazed speculatively at Thea. "Wait, are you telling me you don't know a single woman who's banged Aiden Murdoch? Because that's statistically imp..."

The woman's words trailed off with a gulp as her friends' eyes widened comically, and Thea knew. She just *knew*.

"Hey there, *sugar bear*."

Her heart flip-flopped in her chest when Aiden's hand landed on her shoulder and spun her to face him. He was smiling as he bent to kiss her, but she felt the tension in his fingers, in his lips. And unlike every other for-show kiss they'd exchanged, this one felt forced and artificial. She responded as best as she could, but she knew in her heart that they both looked stiff as hell. And why wouldn't they? He'd busted her standing in the middle of a group of women who were talking about him like he was a prize haunch of beef at the Cavalier County Fair.

"Hi!" She smiled up at him and hoped the curve of her lips conveyed the embarrassment and apology rioting through her. Anger too. She hated the way those women had discussed him, as if he didn't have feelings or autonomy.

He merely looked at her blankly, so she reached for his hand and gave it a reassuring squeeze, holding her breath until he squeezed back. Then, to her delight, he tilted his chin and dragged his eyes down her body. "You look amazing. But you're braving the Elephant without a coat again?"

She grinned at the chance to show their small audience a different side of the man they thought they knew.

"I like to live dangerously." She tossed her hair dramatically, and he laughed and brought their entwined fingers to his mouth.

"Good thing I tossed a jacket into my truck just in case." He pressed a kiss to the back of her hand. "Can't have my girl getting cold."

"So thoughtful." She didn't have to fake the breathiness in her voice, and they shared a private smile, a real one this time. It made her brave enough to turn to the three women, who were sporting identical shocked faces. "As it turns out, I *do* know someone who's having sex with Aiden Murdoch."

She glanced up at him to see heat flare in his eyes, and without stopping to talk herself out of it, she grabbed the front of his T-shirt and pulled him down to kiss her again. There was nothing forced or awkward this time, and even though the kiss wasn't long, it was intense enough that one of the women muttered "Daaaaaamn" when they broke apart.

He brushed a thumb over her lower lip before slinging a casual arm around her shoulder. His body was back to its usual relaxed posture, and Thea breathed a silent sigh of relief that she'd apparently undone some of the damage that the women's gossip had caused.

"Mabel saved you a seat up front at the wives and girlfriends table," he said. "You ready?"

"Always," she purred, turning to wave at the three women. "Enjoy the show!"

Aiden placed a hand at the small of her back and guided her toward the stage. She was acutely aware of eyes following them as they weaved through the crowd to Mabel and Jake's table. Her friend's face lit up when

Aiden pulled out a chair and pressed a kiss to the side of her neck after she was seated.

"You two are the *cutest,*" Mabel squealed.

"She's cute enough for both of us." Aiden brushed a lock of hair behind Thea's ear, and she shivered at the whisper-light touch. "See you at the set break."

He turned and leaped gracefully onto the stage, where Dave was making last-minute adjustments to his guitar and fellow deejay Skip Stevens was strumming his bass. Once Aiden was seated behind his drum kit, Dave welcomed the crowd, and the band launched into the opening lick of "Seven Nation Army." The audience went nuts, and from there the Moo Daddies ripped through every high-energy song in their repertoire, hitting all their favorites before they lost their guitarist to daddy duty for several months.

Thea bopped away in her seat alongside Mabel while Jake limited his participation to the occasional jiggle of his knee. He only came to life when Dave pulled Mabel up on stage to sing a few songs, in accordance with Moo Daddy tradition and much to the delight of the audience.

"So you and Murdoch, huh?" Jake leaned forward to ask the question as Mabel adjusted the microphone and greeted the crowd.

"Me and Murdoch!" Thea replied brightly. Her gaze fell on Aiden, who was lit up in delight as his sticks flew across his drums. A tiny wave of regret washed over her at the big fat lie they were telling the world, but when he caught her looking and shot her a wink, everything receded. All she could see were his strong, lean forearms flexing as he pounded out a rhythm and his capable fingers curled around the sticks.

God, her fake boyfriend was hot.

At the end of Mabel's run of songs, the Moo Daddies took a break. Before Aiden was able to unfold himself from behind the drums, Jake had surged to his feet to sweep Mabel off into a secluded corner of the bar. Aiden exited the spotlight more slowly and dropped into the chair Jake had just vacated. "Having a good time?"

"I love watching you play!" Her compliment was immediate and sincere, and he grinned at her until a waitress interrupted to deposit a large glass in front of him.

"Wow, they really have your order down," Thea said.

"Ice water." He brought it to his lips. "The drummer isn't allowed to have alcohol on show nights. If I lose the beat, everything comes crashing to a halt."

He downed another long swallow while Thea watched his throat work. Just imagine if she were really his girlfriend. She could lean in close, press her nose against that hot skin, and inhale hard. She could brush her lips just under his jaw and enjoy the delicious scrape of stubble. The temptation this man's body offered was out of control, and she wished like hell she could give in and experience it all for herself.

That last thought had her pulling back and giving her head a sharp shake. God, she was no better than those other women who wanted him only for his body. Shame on her for forgetting he was so much more than a sexual thrill ride—and one she'd agreed she wouldn't be climbing on board.

"You okay, killer?"

Her eyes snapped to his face. "Y-yeah. Yes." She raised her glass in a salute. "Just wondering if you take requests."

"Depends on the request." He smiled lazily at her,

and everything below her waist gave an answering pulse at the invitation in his voice.

He was *not* making it easy to keep her thoughts pure.

"One Direction!" She blurted the first band name that popped into her head, then just rolled with it. "Let me live out my boy band fantasies through a bunch of grown-ass men."

He winced comically. "Dave's gonna veto that *hard*, but I'll do my best."

She laughed, and the temporary weirdness passed, leaving her able to chat with him like a normal person for the next ten minutes before Dave cruised by their table and shouted, "Adonis! Let's go!"

Aiden rolled his eyes at the nickname but dutifully drained his glass. Before he stood, he took her breath away by wrapping his hand around her neck and pulling her close for a quick kiss. Nothing showy. Just enough pressure to leave her pink and flustered. "Thanks for keeping me company." He murmured the words against her lips, then broke away and bounded up onto the stage as Mabel and Jake slipped back into their seats.

"You two are killing me with the lovey-dovey." Mabel slid a glance at her boyfriend. "We've got competition in the hottest-couple department, babe."

"No contest," Jake growled, and Thea turned toward the stage so they could suck face without an audience. Aiden had just finished conferring with Dave, and as he spun around to take his place at his drums, he shot her a quick set of finger guns that would've been dorky from any other guy but on him came off as unbearably sexy. Seriously, how did he *do* that?

"Friends!" Dave shouted into the mic, his round glasses reflecting the bright lights on the stage as he glanced around at the crowd. "Thanks again for coming out to our farewell-for-now show! We're kicking off this next set with a special request from our drummer's main squeeze."

All eyes in the room turned to Aiden, who pointed his sticks right at her with a wink, then launched into the opening riff of 1D's "What Makes You Beautiful" with a delicious quirk of his lips. Thea screamed in surprised delight and shimmied in her chair with a dopey grin on her face as the band threw itself into the performance.

The second half of the show flew by, and before she knew it, the band was performing its final encore. The raucous audience cheers gave way to a more general buzz as people either hit the bar or headed for the exits, ready to call it a night. Mabel and Jake said a swift goodbye, leaving Thea to make her way to the back of the stage, where Aiden was starting to pack up his equipment.

But a painfully pretty woman in a painfully tiny dress beat her there, gliding up to Aiden with a smile "Hey there, handsome. Got plans after this?"

Thea froze as fear wormed its way into her stomach. This was a test, and she was suddenly terrified he wouldn't pass. She started to edge away so she wouldn't have to watch whatever was about to go down, but he just smiled politely.

"I'm waiting for my girlfriend actually." His head swiveled around the room, and his eyes softened when they landed on her. "Oh, there you are, babe."

He held out his hand, and she lurched forward to take it, shame flooding her for doubting him.

"You were so great tonight!" she said, acutely aware that the rebuffed woman was looking at her with a distinct "Her? *Really*?" expression on her face. Thea's first instinct was to shrink into herself at the incredulous stare, but Aiden was smiling down at her as if she were the only person in the room, so she wrapped her arms around his neck and buried her fingers in his sweat-damp hair. "Ready to get out of here?"

"Absolutely," he murmured, bending his head to give her a quick, hard kiss.

When she finally pulled back, the "her?" woman was gone.

She giggled. Being the focus of his attention left her feeling buzzed in a way that a gin and tonic couldn't touch. "I know you picked me because I'm convenient, but this is turning out to be really fun," she whispered.

"Convenient?" He released her with a frown.

"Well yeah. I was conveniently nearby when you hatched this plan, and now here we are." She spoke quietly even though the noise of the bar patrons basically ensured that their conversation was private.

He dropped his hands to her shoulders and looked at her with zero mirth on his face. "Hey. Don't sell yourself short, okay?"

"O-okay." The intensity in his eyes left her shaky, so she murmured her agreement rather than prolong the conversation.

Once the strange moment passed, it was all business as she helped him pack up the rest of his kit and carry it to his truck. By the time he'd slammed his tailgate shut on all his equipment, the parking lot had emptied quite a bit, although it was nothing like that cold, dark night when this had all started.

"Back at the scene of the crime, huh?" She looked around them with a nervous little laugh.

"Appears so," he said. "Still need a ride home?"

She nodded, feeling suddenly shy. They'd agreed that morning that she'd grab a Lyft to the bar so he could drive her home to keep up appearances. But that practical decision suddenly felt fraught with danger under the glow of the lights scattered throughout the lot.

"Here." He opened the door and gave her a hand up into the too-tall cab, and his observant thoughtfulness just ratcheted up her self-consciousness even more.

Chin up. Boobs out. Smile on.

Yeah, that mantra wasn't very useful in the cab of his truck, which smelled like sawdust and varnish and aftershave and was the *last* place she should be thinking about her boobs. When he slid into the driver's side and fired up the engine, her nerves took over, and her mouth engaged without her brain's permission.

"I started cleaning up the flower beds in the front yard since I had some time on my hands. Turns out I know remarkably little about plants for the daughter of a landscaper." Her inane comment only served to make her sad, and when she tried to laugh it off, what emerged was a watery little bleat. To his credit, Aiden immediately reached for her hand, and when their fingers met, the tightness in her chest eased a tiny bit.

"I still remember what your dad taught me about rosebush maintenance." He rubbed his thumb over the center of her palm. "I can help you do some pruning."

"That would be great."

"Guess I *do* have more to offer than just sex." He glanced at her as they idled at a stoplight, but his wry smile didn't quite reach his eyes.

Shit. He really had been bothered by those women's comments. Unexpected protectiveness surged in her chest, and she said fiercely, "Of course you do. I hate how those women talked about you before. I'm sorry I stood there and listened to it."

His jaw clenched as he accelerated through the intersection. "It's okay. They're not the only ones who think that."

"What do you mean?"

He sighed and gave an exaggerated wave at the dark neighborhood they were cruising past. "Everyone around here feels the same way."

Something in her chest pinched. "None of them know the first thing about you."

"Oh, I think they know plenty."

He fell silent, and after a moment she worked up the nerve to ask the obvious question. "So why then?" He raised his brows in a question, so she clarified. "If it bothers you what they think, why do you sleep around? Why no relationships ever?"

He shifted in his seat and didn't meet her eyes. "I don't talk about it much, but a woman broke my heart when I was a sophomore in college. An older woman, very sophisticated. I never got over it, and I guess I've been compensating for it ever since."

She gasped softly and reached for his hand, "Oh my God, that's—"

"Nah, I'm messing with you." He shot her another glance, this one full of teasing that banished his mournful tone. "There's really no big story. Sleeping around was fun in high school and easy in college, and when I graduated and moved back home, it just kind of stuck." He shrugged as he turned in to Prospect Point. "My parents bugged me about settling down for a few years, and I guess I started going out of my way to prove I wasn't cut out for it."

He pulled into her driveway and notched the truck into park, turning to face her. "Sometimes I think I did too good a job of convincing them."

The downward slant of his lips suggested that this sadness wasn't faked, but in a flash he blinked it away. All she wanted was to throw her arms around him and banish the loneliness pouring off of him, but that was far, far too dangerous in the quiet of his cab.

Instead, she changed the subject. "Okay, why the drums?" She gestured toward the truck bed, hoping his hobby would lighten the vibe a little bit. But if anything, his expression hardened even more.

"Another little rebellion against my parents' plan for my life. I took music lessons in college as a *what the hell* elective and kind of fell in love. But my dad convinced me it was pointless to keep going when the family business is nails and two-by-fours." His voice was casual, but restlessness tinged his words. "When Dave put together a cover band a few years ago, I thought, why not? It keeps me busy. Reminds me I'm more than a cog in the Murdoch machine."

"You're so much more than a cog." She let her head fall against the seat back as she studied the man sitting next to her, handsomer than anybody she'd ever dated for real or pretend.

His plain black T-shirt pulled tight across his broad shoulders and solid chest, and his fingers tapped out a rhythm on the steering wheel as if he was lost in the thought of making music. Her heart broke that too few people bothered to look past his playboy exterior to see what else he had to offer. Because he had *so much*. So much warmth and humor and thoughtfulness.

Danger.

She reached for the door handle and practically flung herself out of the truck and into the crisp chill of early March, throwing the brakes on this whole encounter. "Um, I should really get to bed. Thanks for the ride."

She didn't even wait for him to wish her good night, instead slamming the door and almost sprinting to the safety of her house. She'd been about two seconds away from kissing him for real, which would've been a catastrophic breach of their agreement. Once the hobbit door was safely shut and locked behind her, she exhaled hard.

Crisis averted. But for how long?

THIRTEEN

"Pardon me, Ms. Blackwell."

Thea spun around with her coffeepot in one hand and her travel mug in the other to address the Murdoch Construction employee tromping through the kitchen with an armful of drop-ceiling tiles.

"I told you, it's Thea," said as she finished pouring her coffee.

"Whatever you say, Ms. Blackwell."

He didn't pause on his way out the front door. Not that she expected anything different by now. The members of Aiden's crew who'd appeared on her doorstep like magic over the past week insisted on calling her Ms. and ma'am and generally treating her like porcelain when they came and went on their various tasks. It both amused and annoyed her.

Today's work seemed to be tossing grody carpet and stained ceiling tiles into the dumpster that had been delivered to her driveway as the first step of the renovation process. Aiden hadn't been kidding; fitting her renovation around other jobs and his packed schedule wasn't easy, but she was slowly seeing the house's tacky outer layer being peeled away to reveal its lovely bones underneath.

"Hello, girlfriend," said a warm voice behind her.

Flutters. Always flutters when Aiden was around. She took a moment to steady herself before turning to greet him. "Good morning!"

Then he shocked the hell out of her by wrapping an arm around her waist and pulling her in for a kiss.

The mint of his toothpaste and spice of his aftershave filled her senses as he pressed his lips against hers, soft and unhurried, as if they exchanged sweet kisses like this every morning. When he pulled away, he was smiling, which made her heart pound even harder against her ribs.

"Ben's outside," she whispered. "You don't have to do that."

He just shrugged and grabbed a mug from the counter behind her, moving to the coffeepot. Since she'd moved in, he'd become as much a fixture in the house as her bedroom set and her grandmother's dishes, coming and going as time permitted. It was far too easy to forget that this was all an act sometimes, particularly when he relaxed against the kitchen counter, all tall and lean in his flannel shirt over a Murdoch tee. Jokes and affectionate touches were second nature to him, and it made things feel too real sometimes. She was on a perpetual mission to remind herself that he was acting, she was acting, and this would all end.

Still, when she handed him the sugar bowl, knowing by now that he wanted his coffee sweet, their fingers brushed and his gaze traveled down her body.

"You look nice today."

"Thanks." Her voice came out bright and happy. *He* made her bright and happy.

She took a step back to get control of her racing pulse and brushed her hands along the front of her black swingy skirt, which she'd paired with heels and a pale yellow blouse that had ruffles marching up the front.

"It's getting warmer, but I'm still worried about exposing this much leg. The station thermostat is usually set to arctic." She frowned and tugged at the hem.

When she looked up, Aiden was watching her with an interested light in his eyes, but the expression disappeared when he cleared his throat.

"It's the perfect amount of leg." He lifted his mug to his lips. "I can't believe you haven't taken control of the thermostat through some kind of bloodless coup."

"Corporate might object." She rolled her shoulders to banish her annoyance at the faceless overlords in the Detroit HQ. "So anyway, when are you thinking of starting work in the kitchen?" Might as well redirect the conversation toward the reason Aiden was there.

"Right." He set his mug down. "It's on the revised schedule I emailed you last week. Next Friday I'll pull the old cabinets out because the new cabinets should be delivered by then."

"Oh yay! I'm excited to start organizing in here." Because the whole of her house was a work in progress, she'd kept everything but the bare essentials packed away since the move-in. As fun as the progress was, it was getting tough to live out of partially unpacked boxes.

"Hope you're okay with takeout for a while. It's gonna get messy."

"That's cool." She flipped her hair over her shoulder with a supermodel-ish toss of her head and said huskily, "I was born messy."

The corners of his eyes crinkled as he smiled. "I

believe it. Just give me a few more weeks now that the shag carpet is gone and the last of the drop ceiling goes today. It'll be in such good shape you'll be tempted to flip it for a nice little profit."

"I would *never*." She dropped the vamp act and slammed her hands on her hips in outrage. "Don't even joke! This is my home now."

"Sorry, sorry, sorry." He held up his hands. "I know you're committed. Now that it's warming up, we'll start working on the outside too." He turned to the sink, where he rinsed and scrubbed his coffee mug before setting it on a dish towel to dry.

She watched him in amusement. "Sorry. My contractor hasn't installed the new dishwasher yet."

"God, he's lazy. Good thing I can run my own mug under some water." He dried his hands and watched as she pulled on her jacket. "I'll walk you out. Protect my guys from your wrath."

"What wrath?" As they headed down the driveway, she gave a wide berth to the dumpster blocking access to the garage. No sense risking rust stains on her blouse.

He moved to walk between her and the corroded metal exterior. "Oh, was that a different short brunette I saw yelling at the plumbers for parking on her lawn last week? If that wasn't you, it was your hotheaded twin."

"Everything is thawing! I don't want them to turn my yard into a mud pit!" She'd reached her car, which she was parking on the street as construction was ongoing.

"Hothead," Aiden muttered fondly while her stomach pitched and rolled over how damn cute he was when he smiled at her like that. There was no way he understood just how devastating he was to the unsuspecting women around him or he'd muzzle that smile in the interest of female sanity.

And in the interest of her own sanity, she needed to quit smiling at him on the front lawn of her beautiful new home. "I have to go. Try not to let the house fall into a giant sinkhole today."

"Small sinkholes only! Got it!" Aiden called as she climbed into her car.

She was still laughing as she pulled away from the curb, but after such a flirty start, her day had nowhere to go but down. It wasn't one single thing that she could pinpoint that started the crappy avalanche. It was a billion small ones.

It turned out to be too cold in the office for a skirt after all, so she spent all day goose-bumpy.

Her email password had to be reset, which required an hour on hold with the Lowell Consolidated IT department in the Detroit headquarters.

Her Bluetooth headset hadn't charged overnight, so she had to wait on hold on the corded phone rather than multitasking by organizing the supply closet or cleaning the copy machine innards with an old toothbrush or literally anything to help her pass the time as IT decided whether she was worthy of her own email.

The delivery guy got her lunch order wrong, and she ended up with a sandwich that seemed to be mostly onions rather than the chicken salad wrap she'd been looking forward to.

And everybody seemed to be out of the office, so she did nothing but send calls to voice mail for the ad reps and the deejays. Even Mabel was gone before noon, which made the day drag even more than normal. Usually she could count on girl talk to make the clock tick forward a little more quickly. The deejay on air right now was Skip, who was friendly but didn't usually leave the booth during his shift, so there was no hope of entertainment on that front.

The final straw came when her email was finally up and running again and she found a reply in there from Brandon. The boss from hell unequivocally denied her request to digitize all the office forms into fillable PDFs. No explanation, just a terse "don't bother."

She slammed her palms on the desk with a little scream of frustration. It had been a good idea, and it wouldn't have cost the company anything. She could've streamlined the forms, cleaned up the questions they didn't use anymore for ad sales and new music requests and whatnot. But noooooo, Brandon clearly wanted her to stay in her lane, her lane being phones and faxes. Her brain was going to rot in her head thanks to corporate bureaucracy.

By four p.m. she'd been reduced to staring dully at the parking lot security footage. Brandon had insisted on cameras and a locked entrance for the safety of the employees, but absolutely nothing was stirring today, not even the ground squirrels that lived in the grass beyond the edge of the lot.

"Bored!" She wilted over the edge of her chair and wailed the word to an uncaring universe.

Her phone buzzed. The universe had heard her and sent a rescue! She snatched the device from her purse to find a photo of a beaming Mabel holding a tiny, red-faced infant. The message read *Welcome to the world, Lucille Marie!*

She set the phone down to glance along the empty station hallways. Is *that* where everybody was? Ana had gone into labor, and nobody had given her a heads-up. Which... fine. Ana hadn't been due for another two weeks, so this must've been unexpected, and cell reception in Beaucoeur's hospital was notoriously spotty. Still, it hurt to be reminded that she was ever so slightly outside their circle of friends.

She shook her head. God, she was being a brat. Babies were chaotic, and she shouldn't have expected anything different. Swallowing her disappointment, she typed back: *Tell them congrats! She's perfect!*

Mabel: *She is, even though they didn't name this one Mabel either.*

She was smiling as she pulled up the number for a local florist and ordered a celebratory bouquet to be sent to the new parents from their friends at the Brick. But after that was done, all she wanted to do was put her head down on her desk and cry.

What was *wrong* with her? She pressed a hand to her stomach to try to diagnose it. Frustration at feeling trapped in her job? Jealousy over Dave and Ana expanding their family, which obviously included Mabel as a cherished member? Sadness that her mom and Belly had cancelled their planned ladies' night on Saturday because Peter had surprised them with a weekend getaway to Chicago?

Of course, on top of all that was Aiden, who was so effortlessly charming that she was starting to forget that everything was fake. If his smiles were dangerous, his casual touches were lethal. She almost needed to drop him off at a bar so he could get his flirt on with somebody else, if only so he'd get it out of his system and quit turning it on her. Of course, that was equally depressing; she trusted him not to break their "nobody else" deal, but she also didn't love remembering that he'd been the town's biggest player before and would undoubtedly be that guy again shortly after their deal was over. She needed to keep her head on straight when it came to their relationship. Their nonrelationship.

Peter didn't know it, but that plant actually was going to outlast them. God, he was going to gloat when that happened even though a dignified breakup was exactly what she and Aiden had planned. It was enough to make her want to set that damn thing on fire, but she wasn't a fan of harming innocent foliage.

Still, all of it—Aiden, her mom, the plant, new baby Chilton, her cold legs, the unchallenging job—left her thoroughly demoralized by the end of the day. When the clock hit five, she wasted no time in powering down her computer, snatching her purse, and getting the hell out of the station. But once she was home, her mood didn't lift as she'd hoped. Aiden or one of his guys had gotten her gutters under control and had started doing whatever grout repairs they deemed necessary, and the inside was starting to take shape too. The lighting throughout the downstairs was far less murky than it had been, no doubt due to some kind of light bulb magic on Aiden's part. She could see every area that was being improved: the sanding underway on the living room floor, the walls newly stripped of their ugly wallpaper, the exposed ceiling beams in the master bedroom waiting to be stained. It was all coming together faster than she'd ever expected.

And that was a major part of her problem. The brightest spot in her life right now was her new house, but that was entirely wrapped up in the man who was reno-vating it. Once he was done, he'd be gone and she'd be left with walls full of memories.

That preemptive melancholy tangled with all the bad-work mojo from earlier and clumped together in a hard ball of mad in her stomach. She wandered to the kitchen and, lacking any better ideas, grabbed a fresh bottle of wine from the pantry. She poured herself a glass and stared glumly at her closed laptop.

Maybe she could spend the night clicking through shelter listings and rescue sites, bookmarking every pair of sad doggie eyes and sad doggie sob stories that tugged at her heart. How many dogs could her new house hold? Six at least, probably. She'd be the new lady on the block with a fake boyfriend, a job she hated, a sucky stepdad, and six dogs.

Cool. Very cool.

She sipped her wine and veered ever closer to self-pity territory, but recognizing an imminent downward spiral, she grabbed her phone and hit the first number on speed dial. When Faith answered, she demanded, "Tell me you're free for drinks tonight."

"Can't." In the background, a raucous chorus of voices spoke over one another and almost drowned Faith out. "I'm waiting for the District 18 school board meeting to start. They're voting on funding proposals tonight."

And since Faith's nonprofit depended on those funds, she'd want to be there of course. Thea was so hard up for company that she almost offered to join her for the meeting, but she wasn't quite that desperate. Also, she was half a bottle into the wine already.

Then another idea popped into her head. "You know what I'm gonna do? I'm gonna get a start on tearing out these kitchen cabinets."

"Wait," Faith said. "You're doing *what*?"

"Demolition time!"

"Whoa, are you sure?" Faith sounded alarmed, but Thea didn't care.

She had to do something to purge the dark energy bunching in her limbs and clenching her stomach. Tearing out some ugly 1970s cabinetry was exactly what she needed.

"Yeah, I'm good, actually. This is what I'm doing tonight. Thanks for listening, Faithy." She hit End and tossed her phone down, then picked it back up and powered it down. She was done talking for the day.

Was she worried about Aiden's fingerprints all over her new house? Then she'd better be the one who did some of this work herself. She'd leave her own imprint.

She drained her glass and marched upstairs to change into work clothes. Once she was back in the kitchen, she tied her hair back with a bandanna and got to work.

FOURTEEN

Aiden pulled into Thea's driveway and turned off his truck. Faith had called him twenty minutes ago in a state of mild panic to ask if it was safe for Thea to start pulling out the cabinets alone tonight. He'd assured her it was, then bolted out the door as soon as he hung up.

He walked to the back of his truck to grab the necessary supplies before heading up her sidewalk. Lights blazed from the front window, and from the front porch he could hear music thundering through the house. The sound of the doorbell hadn't finished echoing through the house when the music snapped off and Thea appeared, holding a screwdriver in one hand and a wineglass in another.

Her mouth dropped open in surprise. "What are you doing here?"

"Hello, ma'am." He pretended to tip a hat at her. "We've received complaints of unauthorized home repairs happening after hours and sent a crew to inspect it."

Her forehead creased and then immediately smoothed. "Faith called you," she said flatly.

"Faith called me," he confirmed. "I'm just here to make sure you don't accidentally knock your house down."

She heaved an impatient breath. "Fine. Come in. Work during your off hours. See if I care."

He hid a smile and stepped over the threshold. He'd seen nervous Thea, chatterbox Thea, excited Thea, charming Thea. Grumpy Thea was new and kind of fun.

"Why does Faith even have your number?" She wheeled around and brandished the screwdriver at him. "You know what? Don't answer that."

He followed her into the kitchen. She was wearing a thin white tank top under baggy denim overalls, and god*damn* it looked good on her. He tried hard not to notice that she wasn't wearing a bra, but her small breasts pressed against the tight fabric of her shirt were impossible to ignore.

He swallowed hard and dragged both his thoughts and his eyes away from her body to refocus on why he was there. "Okay, killer, let's see what you've got going on."

She'd unscrewed three of the cabinet doors so far, and a fourth hung by just one hinge.

"Good start," he said. "Did you kill the power along this wall?"

"Yep."

"You're a natural." Their agreed-upon timetable floated through his head, and he couldn't help but point out, "You know this wasn't supposed to happen until next week."

She rolled her eyes. "You and your schedules."

"Your new cabinets haven't been delivered yet! I'm trying to save you from inconvenience."

She sent him the world's greatest "you have insulted my intelligence, sir" look, and he hid his smile at her adorable irritation.

"Okay then. Hope you enjoy having no kitchen for a week. Why don't you keep removing doors, and I'll come behind you and unscrew them from the wall."

She scowled. "This isn't nearly as destructive as I thought it would be."

"Safety first." He pulled a pair of goggles out of his back pocket and settled them on her nose, then put on a pair of his own. Then he looked inside the first doorless cabinet. "Actually, you may get your wish. These are glued to the wall. You know what that means?"

Her face lit up. "Time to smash?"

"Time to *carefully* smash. Let's get rid of what we can through civilized means first."

"Ugh, fine."

He grabbed a second screwdriver for himself, and they got to work removing doors and shelves, but after a point all that was left were the old, ugly cabinets themselves refusing to give up their grip on the wall.

"Time to pound shit," he announced. "Be right back."

He jogged out to his truck and grabbed two sledgehammers. When he got back, Thea was doing that curled-in-on-herself thing that he'd seen after her stepdad's visit, which was so much more alarming than her earlier grumpiness.

Good thing he had the perfect remedy for shitty feelings.

"Go to town." He handed her a sledgehammer. "Try not to destroy the walls."

"Nice!" Her face brightened, and she squared up to the cabinet on the far end. But her first swing was too tentative and glanced off the side without making an impact.

"Here." He hefted his own hammer. "Like this, see? Swing at the waist so the power comes from your whole body."

He turned, swung, and struck the cabinet with a satisfying *thunk* that sent chunks of old, brittle wood tumbling to the ground.

She watched him closely, then mimicked his stance and swing. The sledgehammer hit the cabinet this time, but it barely nicked the front edge. "Dammit!"

Her growl was ferocious, and again, he hid a chuckle. She might use that hammer on him if she knew how cute he was finding her irritation.

"Okay, good start. But again, you've got to swing from here." He hesitated for a beat, then moved behind her and set his hands lightly on the curve of her hips just below her waist. "Use your body weight to propel the hammer forward."

She glared over her shoulder. "What are you saying about my body weight?"

His fingers tightened, and he drew her back against him for a fraction of a second, suddenly reminded of that morning when he'd kissed her without a second thought. It hadn't occurred to him to wonder if they had an audience. He'd just done it on autopilot. His fault for going without sex for as long as he had and for enjoying her company as much as he did. Those two things were a dangerous combination.

Still, his hands lifted to smooth down the satiny skin of her exposed shoulders. "You're a tiny, delicate flower, so it's going to be harder for you to give your swing enough force. But I believe in you. Give it another go."

He moved his hands back to her hips—the better to feel her windup and not because he enjoyed the warmth of her skin of course. And this time when she swung, she knocked a large chunk of cabinet free. She hooted and swung the hammer over her head in triumph, almost clocking him in the process.

He dodged, and she winced. "Sorry. I'll try not to murder you with construction equipment tonight."

"Appreciated," he said. "I'll loosen what I can with the crowbar, and you keep knocking the rest free. Sound good?"

She nodded, and soon enough the only sound was the thunk of the sledgehammer and the crack of the wood separating from the wall. Demolition was punishing work, but Thea held her own, swinging and connecting over and over as she excised the ugly from her house.

After forty minutes without speaking much—forty minutes in which Aiden surreptitiously watched Thea's body twist and sway as she worked—they'd stripped the kitchen wall bare. He set his crowbar down and brushed debris from the front of his damp shirt. "Nice work."

She turned to him with a bright smile. "We did that!"

"Sure did," he said, thrilled to see her sparkle back. "As good as any member of my crew could've done."

She ducked her head and waved off his praise, wincing a little as she rolled her neck and stretched out her arms. She'd be sore tomorrow, for sure. His first instinct was to stand behind her and massage the soreness out of her muscles, but touching her like that screamed danger. Fuck, she looked good though. Sweat darkened her formerly clean tank top, the skin on her neck and chest glistened with perspiration, and her hair stuck in damp tendrils to her cheeks. She pushed the safety goggles onto her head again and swiped a dusty arm across her brow, and all he could think about was a shower. A joint shower. Imagine the hot water running over their bodies, washing away the sweat and grime, easing their aching muscles, pinkening Thea's skin...

Goddammit. Every time he was around her these days, touching her was all he could think about. Maybe he should've remembered his abstinence bender before he agreed to spend hours and hours with a smart, funny woman who always smelled nice. A woman he'd made a no-sex bargain with.

The only shower he'd be taking tonight was a cold one on his own.

Still, he wasn't ready to walk away from the reason for his visit tonight. He might not be allowed to touch her the way he wanted, but he could at least try to make sure she was okay. "So. Want to talk about it?"

Just like that, her gaze zipped away from him, and the joy she'd found in destruction fell from her face.

"Talk about what?" She pivoted and yanked open the refrigerator, disappearing briefly into its depths. She emerged with two bottles of water, handed one to him, and dropped into one of the chairs at her kitchen table with a glare. "The fact that you want everybody to think you're some cool, laid-back guy but you're actually super rigid and unwilling to deviate from your precious schedules?"

His arm jolted to a halt as he lifted the bottle to his lips, startled that she'd evaluated him so precisely in one short sentence. But the fact that she was insightful as hell wasn't what they needed to address tonight.

"No deflecting with observations about me." He pointed his water bottle at what they'd just done in the kitchen. "Maybe that was just a random nighttime home-improvement streak, but I'm asking if maybe it was something else."

She worried the corner of the water bottle label instead of answering. "Did you know I've never dated anyone for longer than four months?"

Okay, he'd definitely missed a step somewhere. "Um, no?"

She twisted off the cap and took a swig. "Remember how fast Mom and I moved away from your neighborhood?"

He nodded and took the seat next to her, still not following this conversational track.

"Some people aren't built to be alone, I guess." She ripped a strip of label off the bottle. "So Mom married the first guy who came along."

Ah. Okay. "And did she regret it?"

Thea shrugged. "I sure did. But she says she's happy. And she loves Annabelle." Her stepdad's fucking spite plant sat in the center of the table, and she poked her finger into the pot, then dumped the rest of her water into the soil. "Next time I see her, she's going to ask me if I can afford the property taxes on this place, mark my words. He'll have gotten into her head."

Aiden's irritation flared. Those people should be delighted that Thea had managed to make her dream come true. But that didn't fully explain her previous comment. "And the boyfriend thing?"

"Yeah well, if you watched your mom become a completely different person because she married somebody she knew for five months, you'd be choosy too." One corner of her mouth twisted down. "Somewhere along the line, I got kind of used to moving on before things got serious because God forbid I end up stuck with someone who makes me miserable."

Aiden rubbed his knuckles along his jaw, reconciling what he knew about her habits with this new information. "Makes sense."

"Oh, is that also the reason you've never settled down with some nice girl?" She raised a challenging brow at him, and he rewarded the return of her sass with a grin.

"Hardly. My parents have a great marriage. I just prefer to embrace my Peter Pan syndrome."

She rolled her eyes. "Lord, grant me the confidence of a mediocre white man."

"Hey! Ain't nothing mediocre here." He gestured down at his sweaty shirt to cover his discomfort at discussing his relationship history. When they'd discussed it before, it hadn't felt so... personal.

She made a *pshht* sound. "Please. You're magnificent and you know it."

He'd never been called magnificent before. Had to admit, he liked it.

She blushed and looked down, her teeth worrying the corner of her lip, before saying briskly, "*Anyway,* I can now add kitchen demolition to my list of skills."

"Hell yes you can." They exchanged high fives, then a thought struck him. "Same deal with the jobs?"

"What do you mean?" She snagged their empty water bottles and got up to toss them in the recycling bin.

"Is that why you run through careers the way some people run through songs on a workout mix?"

When she turned to face him, she was frowning. "I guess I've never really thought about it like that. But yeah. Maybe. People start to rely on me at the job, and I get the itch to move on." She shifted from foot to foot. "I'm... not happy working at the station."

Her voice was a barely audible whisper, and he crossed to where she stood in front of the sink. "Oh yeah? Is this how it usually goes for you?"

She glanced toward the dark stillness of the river, clearly uneasy with the subject. "Yeah. I've got my favorite temp agency's number on speed dial for when I wake up some morning and just need to make a change." She blew out a breath and shot him a smile that didn't quite reach her eyes. "Guess I haven't found the job that makes me want to settle down yet."

Haven't found the job or haven't found the man? The question almost slipped out, and he was suddenly more curious than he should be about the guys she'd dated in the past and how they'd failed to satisfy her. Weeks ago he'd pegged her as a "marry me" girl. She apparently would disagree, but he wasn't convinced he'd been wrong. Then again, how many men were worthy of her quick wits and sunny nature?

Just as he was about to lose his damn mind and start saying things that a fake boyfriend really shouldn't be saying, she yawned and sagged against the counter. "I think it's time for bed."

Fair enough. If this was a heavy conversation for him, it would be massive for her. "Okay if I leave my stuff here for the night? I'll be back tomorrow to take out the countertop and finish cleaning all this up."

"Ha. I messed up your schedule for a second day," she crowed.

He good-naturedly grumbled as they ambled to the front door, but he paused before saying good night. Part of him wanted to tell her to ignore her mom's mistakes and her stepdad's shittiness and trust that she'd find the right guy someday. But another part of him—a loud, annoying part—didn't want her to start picturing some other guy in this house, at least not while he was still here doing work. He wanted to have her to himself for a little longer.

"Thanks for tonight," she said. "I feel better."

"Hitting things with a hammer'll do that for you." He took a step toward her until he could see the specks of dust in her hair from the destruction in the kitchen. "You've got..." He brushed away the traces of their work, then let his hands drift to her cheek, her neck.

When his fingers kept moving downward, all thoughts of plans and schedules and agreements flew from his head, which gave him permission to do something he'd been wanting to do all night: he slid his hands into the gap between her overalls and the bottom of her shirt, resting his fingers gently on her hips where they dipped in to her waist. He'd been tortured by flashes of her skin as she moved, and now he gave in to the overwhelming desire to touch.

Her breathing hitched as his thumbs brushed across her warm skin and came perilously close to slipping under the hem of her tank top. She closed her eyes and swayed forward, and for one dizzying moment, he leaned in too. Nobody was around to put on a show for. He wanted to kiss her because he wanted to kiss *her*.

And fuck, that's why he shouldn't. Because if he kissed her right now, he'd be tempted not to stop. This thing between them was changing by the day, in his mind at least, but that wasn't what they'd agreed to. He'd promised no sex, and right now he wasn't sure he could stick to that if he didn't put some distance between them. With immense effort, he took a step back, his hands falling to his sides, and when her eyes fluttered open, he couldn't read her expression. Relief? Disappointment?

He cleared his throat and took another step toward the door. "Sleep well, killer. I'll see you tomorrow."

He let himself out the door and kept his windows rolled down for his drive home, hoping the April air would cool his blood enough to let him sleep that night.

FIFTEEN

"Aiden? Boyfriend? *Cutie patootie?*"

Thea's voice echoed through the warehouse portion of Murdoch Construction, and she located the man she was looking for by the grumbled "Jesus Christ" coming from the back corner.

"What, you don't like cutie patootie?" she asked when she found him among a pile of sinks and PVC pipes.

"Worst one yet." But he smiled when he said it, and the sight of him, gorgeous and grinning, knocked her breath from her lungs and filled her with a surge of joy.

"You love it." She poked at his ribs, and he laughingly grabbed her finger to stave off a second jab. "So I've presented myself over the lunch hour, as requested. What's up?"

"Right. Follow me." He linked his fingers with hers and led her to a different section of the warehouse where a large hump of something was covered in cardboard and bubble wrap.

"What do you think?"

She looked again at the packing material. "You… shouldn't have?"

He laughed as he pulled a utility knife from his back pocket and cut through the wrapping with swift efficiency. It parted to reveal a minimalist slate-gray cabinet with clean lines and no frills.

"Oooh, they're here!" she cried. "And they're beautiful!"

"They are pretty nice." He ran a thumb along the closest edge. "These are going to transform your kitchen."

"I can't wait." She glanced up at him, almost bashful all of a sudden. "I don't tell you enough how much I appreciate everything you're doing for me."

He waved it off. "Probably as much as I appreciate what you're doing for me."

"Please. Spending time with you is no hardship." The opposite. She liked it way too much.

"I dunno. I'm sure it's tough, pretending to keep me satisfied at night." He winked, and her insides reacted as if he'd dipped her into a pot of boiling water.

The memory of his hands on her hips the night they'd destroyed her kitchen had haunted her all weekend, but the only satisfaction she could find these days was battery operated. And wasn't that the ultimate irony? Hours alone with the player of Beaucoeur, and all her orgasms were courtesy of her vibrator. A shame when Aiden had such long, lovely fingers *right there.*

Her head lolled to the side as she watched him bundling up the packing material, and she lost herself in the fantasy of what he could do with those babies. If only she wasn't, well, *her.* In all the time they'd spent together, she sometimes *almost* thought she was picking up a vibe from him. The way he leaned close. The way he watched her talk. The way his fingers flirted with the hem of her shirt on demolition night. But if he was actually interested in her like that, he'd have said so or done something by now. It's not like he was shy around women, for God's sake. But he always pulled away just when things were about to get interesting, probably because he remembered who he was with.

She was pathetic. The limits of their deal were clear, and she might as well go around in a potato sack and a chastity belt for all it mattered to him. She *had* to slam the brakes on her runaway thoughts.

Best to put on a brave face. She patted her new cabinets and bent down to whisper, "You're coming home with me soon."

"Okay, weirdo."

She allowed herself to enjoy the laugh lines around his eyes before she hiked her purse up her shoulder. "Well, if that's it, I should probably—"

"Oh, I'm not done with you yet."

Heat. Immediate heat in her nethers. What would it be like to have him say that to her *for real*, in whatever voice he reserved for naked play with the women he actually saw as sexual objects? She'd combust on the spot. The images flashing through her mind left her incapable of anything more than bobbing along in his wake as he led her to his office. He opened the door and ushered her inside, where she was greeted by a whimper that turned into a series of yips.

"What...?" She squinted at the little brown lump of *something* plopped on a coat laid in the corner of Aiden's office. Then the lump shifted and changed shape until its angles resolved itself into four legs and a snout. "Is that a *dog*?"

"Surprise," Aiden said sheepishly.

The dog quivered and wagged its tail, the action causing its whole body to shake. She immediately crossed the room and dropped to her knees, and the dog took a hesitant step in her direction. "Where'd he come from?"

"She, I think."

"Hi, girl," she crooned, holding out a hand to be sniffed.

The dog brushed the tips of Thea's fingers with her cold black nose before she gave her knuckles a tentative, tickly lick.

"One of the guys found her on a job site in rural Cavalier County, and I immediately thought of you."

"Me?" For a horrified moment, she thought he was comparing her appearance to the bedraggled, skittish creature in front of her, and she wanted to cry for both her and the dog.

"Yeah, a couple of weeks ago you mentioned you wanted a dog, and this one fell in my lap." He plunged his hand in his hair, looking almost nervous. "If you weren't serious though, I can find another home for her. I just thought..."

"I love her," Thea breathed.

The dog's eyes peered out at her from under a tangled clump of fur, two shiny little buttons looking warily out at a world she wasn't quite sure she trusted. Thea knew the feeling.

"Do you think she has an owner somewhere?"

"She's friendly enough." Aiden moved to crouch next to her and scratched behind the dog's floppy ear. "But she definitely looks like a stray."

"We need to get you cleaned up, poor hungry lady."

He gestured to a pair of bowls against the wall. "I

picked up some food for her and left her in here with plenty of water, but yeah, she's going to need a whole checkup."

She snuck a glance at him, taking in the little smile on his face as he brushed his fingers over the dog's knobby spine, and affection swelled in her chest as she watched how gentle he was with the frightened little thing.

Oh God, she needed to be careful. Those were *feelings*, and she couldn't afford to develop those for Aiden. Better to focus all her attention on the creature in the room who needed her most. She grabbed her phone and dialed a number.

"Hi, is Kylie working today? Yeah, thanks." Aiden looked at her curiously, so she put her hand over the speaker to whisper, "*Calling in a favor.*"

Five minutes later, Aiden loaded her and the dog into his truck to drive them to the veterinary clinic where her friend worked as a tech. The dog huddled on her lap and burrowed her head under Thea's elbow while she gently stroked the dog's sides where her ribs were visible under the coarse fur.

"I'm going to take such good care of you," she whispered to the dog.

Aiden glanced over. "She's lucky she's got you now."

She blinked back tears at his words, unexpectedly moved by his faith in her to care for this small, vulnerable creature. "Thanks." She curled protectively around the quivering dog until they arrived at the clinic on the north side of Beaucoeur, where she explained the situation to the woman at the front desk, who immediately whisked them into an exam room to await the arrival of her friend Kylie.

"You're lucky it's kind of a slow afternoon," the tawny

blonde said when she joined them. She moved efficiently through weighing the dog, looking into her ears, and listening to her heart. "Do you want me to see if she's microchipped?"

"Yes, please," Thea said.

Kylie waved the scanning wand over the dog. "Nothing. My guess is she was dumped by a crappy owner, or she's been a stray her whole life." She rested a gentle hand on the dog's back. "Question is, what do you want to do with her?"

"Keep her!" The words burst from Thea's throat, and she'd never felt more sure about anything in her life. "I want to keep her."

A grin split Kylie's freckled face. "Then we'd better get her cleaned up. Let me see what our groomer's schedule looks like." She breezed out of the room and was back moments later. "She'll squeeze her in around her other appointments this afternoon. Nothing fancy, just a bath and a trim to get her ready to send home. Is that okay?"

At Thea's nod, Kylie scooped the dog into her arms. "Great. Should take a couple of hours. We'll call when she's ready to go. In the meantime, we'll give her vaccinations, worm her, and check for heartworms."

"Thank you!" Thea called after her.

As they headed to the exit, Aiden asked, "Did I miss your stint as a vet tech or something?"

"Not all my friends are from old jobs, I'll have you know." Then she tipped her head in acknowledgement. "But okay, yeah, I met her during my not-so-illustrious time at the zoo."

"Right, the zoo. Where you learned how to feed lions and muck out the lemur cages, right?"

"I wish. That would've been better than soothing angry guests." Funny that with Aiden, her checkered job history didn't feel like something to be ashamed of. He made her experiences seem worthwhile, like they all contributed to who she was. After years of apologizing for her work hopscotch, it was a novel experience.

He dropped her off at her car outside his building after extracting a promise that she'd let him pick her up when Kylie called to say the dog was ready. "We're in this together," was his last word on the subject.

Four hours later they were back at the vet's to claim what looked like an entirely new dog. Thea gasped in delight.

"She did clean up well, didn't she?" Kylie said proudly. "We even dug up a fancy collar for her."

The dog had emerged from her grooming session with a light brown, slightly curly coat and a pointy little snout that twitched as she sniffed around the room. She was still painfully thin, and she wore a hot-pink rhinestone collar around her neck that was absolutely ludicrous and absolutely perfect for her somber face.

"Look at you, beautiful Blue!"

"Blue?" Aiden asked.

She scooped the dog into her arms and buried her face in the soft, clean fur to hide her blush. "Short for Blueprint? I just figured since you found her on a construction site. And I know you live to make sketches of all your projects."

His delighted smile eased her embarrassment at such a sentimental, Aiden-centric name. "Blueprint. I like it." He reached out to ruffle the dog's fur, and for a scary second the three of them felt like...

No. Those feelings—those *family* feelings—had no

place here. Zero. She didn't do family feelings, and neither did he. She squashed them and turned to her friend. "Thanks, Kye. I owe you."

"Happy to help." She handed over a clinic-branded leash. "Call me. Let's do drinks sometime."

Aiden held open the door for her, and after they'd paid at the counter, they came face-to-face with an older couple who'd just entered with a miniature poodle on a leash.

Aiden stopped short, and his hand shot out to claim hers, linking their fingers in a death grip. "Mr. and Mrs. Santiago. Hello."

The stiffness in his tone surprised her, but she threw herself into good-girlfriend mode without batting an eye, softening into his side ever so slightly and letting her lips curve into a pleasant smile.

"Hello." The gray-haired man spoke curtly, his gaze darting to Thea and then down to Blue, who was in the middle of sniffing the poodle's butt.

"This is my girlfriend Thea Blackwell. Thea, this is Tony and Isla Santiago. They own Santiago's Pharmacy. Murdoch Construction's in the middle of a big renovation project there." He spoke carefully, with none of the relaxed confidence she was used to, and a glance at the Santiagos showed identical grim sets of their mouths.

Huh. No idea what this was all about, but the tension radiating from all three of them made her want to crawl out of her own skin. "Nice to meet you," she said, flipping through her mental index of people she knew. "Let's see, Santiago... Are you related to Millie?"

If anything, that made the vibe so much worse. Aiden twitched, Isla frowned, and Tony's mustache quivered in outrage. "That's our daughter," he bit out, eyes cutting to Aiden.

Shit shit shit. It didn't take a genius to figure out where the awkwardness stemmed from. Time to do some serious tap dancing to smooth over whatever sexual indiscretion Aiden had committed with their darling little girl.

She took a tiny step forward to ever so slightly interpose herself between Aiden and the frowning couple. "Oh, that's so great! Millie and I were in the same graduating class. She was the smartest girl in algebra. How's she doing? Last I heard she was studying engineering, right?"

At the mention of Millie's smarts, the Santiagos melted before her eyes. "She finished her PhD last year and went to work for Saratoga." Isla beamed.

"Did she really? That's amazing! Is she designing medical equipment for them, or is she more on the manufacturing side?"

Now Tony came to life. "Manufacturing. Very hands-on."

"Well of course! Do you remember our senior year science fair? She built a working semiconductor that put my golf ball model of the solar system to shame. I always knew she'd get out there and change the world. And is she still dating that medical student?"

She held her breath, praying she was correctly remembering the conversation she and Millie had the last time they'd bumped into each other at a bar on Thanksgiving Eve a year or two ago.

She'd guessed right.

"He's a doctor now. An internist," Isla said. "They're engaged."

"That's wonderful!" Thea clapped a hand over her heart. "You must be so proud."

Both Santiagos nodded immediately, and Thea did an imaginary victory dance for a job well done.

"Please tell her I said hi and to look me up when she's in town next." Then she turned to Aiden, who was staring at her with an incredulous expression on his face. "But right now I think we need to get our girl home and fed, don't you, hon?"

As if on cue, Blue looked up at them with an adorable little whine that made the whole group laugh.

"Absolutely," he said, smiling down at her. He dipped his chin toward the Santiagos. "Good to see you both."

They headed toward the exit, but Tony's voice stopped them. "Wait."

Aiden's hand tensed in hers as he turned back around.

"I was sorry to hear about your father's health issues. How's he doing?"

He tensed even more, and she dropped his hand to slide an arm around his waist. Not for the Santiagos' sake but because he looked like he could use the comfort.

Although he kept his eyes on Tony, he dropped his arm over her shoulder and hugged her to his side. "He's getting the best treatment we can find for him, and we're hoping for good results."

"I'm glad. Give him our best," Tony said. After a beat, he added, "Drop by the store sometime if you'd like to see how the work is progressing."

The tension in Aiden's body dropped, and he nodded. "I will. Thank you, sir."

After they said their goodbyes and stepped through the exit, Aiden stopped dead on the sidewalk, gathered her close, and dropped a fast, firm kiss on her lips. "God, you're good. Do you even know how good you are?"

"How good am I?" The words sounded shaky as they escaped her lips, but what else could she do under that hot, admiring gaze?

"So fucking good, killer." He kissed her again, not in an overtly passionate way but with a comfortable, proprietary press of his lips against hers that Thea enjoyed way, way too much. "I'll fill you in on the way home."

SIXTEEN

"Thea? Blue?"

Aiden's steps echoed on the newly exposed wooden floor in the living room as he moved to the kitchen. The glow of the late April sun filled the room, but there was no sign of the woman he was looking for, or her dog.

"Thea?" This time he raised his voice, and an answering "up here" floated down the staircase.

He bounded up the steps and into the master bedroom, but that was empty too. "I'm here to take final measurements for the cabinet install, *sugar lips*."

"Oh yay!"

The balcony. Her voice was coming from the balcony. His breath froze in his lungs as he sprinted to the sliding door and found her on her knees, trying to coax Blue away from the railing in the far corner.

She tossed a look over her shoulder. "This little lady got out and refuses to—"

Her words ended in a squeak when he stormed onto the balcony and scooped her up, cuddling her close to his chest where his heart was flailing against his ribs. Her arms wrapped around his neck as he carried her across the wooden boards in two long strides.

Once they were safely inside, he turned and gave a sharp whistle. "Blueprint!"

At his stern command, the dog trotted inside and sat on her haunches, her tail lashing back and forth against the floor and her tongue lolling happily. He kicked the door shut with his heel and wrapped a hand around the back of Thea's neck, pressing her face to shoulder.

"I told you it's not safe!" He was shouting, but fuck, she might've just taken a decade off his life.

She pushed back to look at him, pointing toward the balcony. "And I told you Blue got out, and I—"

"It could've collapsed," he rasped. "It's a twenty-foot drop. You could've been hurt. You could've..."

The thought of losing her was too much for him to put into words, and with fear and adrenaline tangling in his chest, he poured it all out on her the only way he knew how. With her body still cradled against him, he lowered his head and kissed her.

Kissed her? Hell, he devoured her, biting at her lips until she opened for him, sweeping her mouth with his tongue until she squirmed in his arms. He swung her so her legs wrapped around his waist, and he banded one arm around her lower back while his other hand tangled in her hair, pulling enough to tilt her chin upward.

"Don't do that again."

Her brown eyes blazed. "If I do, will you kiss me like that again?"

He growled and spun around so her back met the wall, using it as leverage to flatten her body against his while her legs tightened around him. Her chest rose and fell as she pulled air into her lungs, and that's when he realized he was so far beyond the boundaries of their agreement that he couldn't see the line anymore.

"I'll kiss you any way you want as long as you don't go out there until I've fixed it."

To show her how serious he was, he gripped the bottom of her T-shirt and yanked it up. She raised her arms to assist, and he gave a helpless grunt when he saw that she wasn't wearing a bra. The sight stopped him in his tracks. Given the choice over the years—and he'd generally been blessed with a multitude of choices—he'd always favored curvy, well-endowed women. But now he was cursing himself for missing out on this all his life. Thea was sleek and lean all over, from the slopes of her collarbones to her flat stomach to her perfect breasts. They were apricots tipped with dusky-pink nipples, and he bet he could fit all of her into his mouth. He swallowed hard at the thought and raised a hand to the soft slope of her shoulder. Her heated eyes followed his movement.

"I'm—" His voice cracked, and he cleared his throat to try again. "I have to touch you. Is that okay?"

A wicked little smile drifted across her face. "I told you weeks ago, you don't have to ask for permission."

"This is gonna be pretty fucking different than what we've been doing," he warned her in a dark voice.

When she arched her back toward him in invitation, he exhaled hard and ran a finger across her solar plexus and down to one hardening nipple, smiling when a shiver rippled along her perfect skin. Bending, he swiped his tongue along the path that his finger had just taken, and her shivers turned into a shudder.

Unable to hold back any longer, he placed an open-mouthed kiss over her left breast and found that yes, he could fit all that tender flesh into his mouth. So he did, circling his tongue over the nipple while sucking on her skin, scraping it lightly with his teeth. Her chest heaved as she gasped for breath, and her fingers crept up to tangle in his hair as he kissed his way to her right breast and repeated the action.

He gripped her hips and pulled her down tight where his dick was straining in his jeans, sneaking a look at her face. Her eyes were screwed shut, face twisted with pleasure. He trailed his fingers down her stomach and settled them between her legs, gratified by the heat he found there. He pressed the heel of his hand against the seam of her leggings and twisted once, twice, three times until they were both moaning.

"Aiden," she whispered. "Now. Please."

"But you haven't—"

His hand kept up its motion between her legs, but she whimpered in her impatience. "I've waited long enough."

He didn't have to be told twice. He pivoted and all but tossed her on the bed, then stripped off his shirt, shoes, jeans.

"Condom. Nightstand."

He obeyed her command, then gripped the waist of her leggings and dragged them off her to join his clothes on the floor. Her silky blue underwear followed, and she fell backward on the bed, legs spread in welcome.

"My God, killer." He tore his eyes away from the beauty sprawled in front of him long enough to rip open the condom and slide it on with clumsy fingers. He couldn't remember the last time he'd felt this rushed, this raw and eager. When he stretched over her body, her hands gripped his shoulders.

"*Now*," she urged, and he settled between her legs,

pausing to enjoy the heat of her mouth on his as he guided himself into her.

Every coherent thought stuttered to a halt as he plunged into her tight warmth. Her legs wrapped around his waist and her fingers dug into the muscles of his arms, and he was sure he'd never felt anything hotter than this woman's sweet pussy.

"God, yes." She thrust up against him. "Harder."

Her assertiveness hit him like an electrical prod to the nerves, and all the sensations heightened: her hot little breasts brushing against his chest, those strong legs wrapped around him, her nails branding his back with streaks of pleasurable fire. And all the while commands spilled from those soft lips, urging him to claim her, take her, *fuck her*.

He was on the brink of losing himself in the arms of someone he liked. Someone he *more* than liked.

Too much. It was too much. It bowled him over, and his balls started to tighten.

"Oh God, you... you're...," he stuttered out. "I'm going to..."

And then he was coming, spilling inside her, feeling every delicious pulse from his scalp to his heels until he was nothing but a boneless husk of a man slumped against the woman who'd just shattered his equilibrium.

Several moments passed before he was able to think clearly, let alone speak. When he finally caught his breath, he rolled off her and grabbed a tissue from the box on the nightstand to wrap the condom in.

"I'm sorry," he gasped out. "You didn't finish. I was too fast. Your body... I just..."

His cock twitched as he relived the deliciousness of

the past few minutes, and he reached for her waist to pull her to him. "Your turn now—"

But she slithered out of his grasp and leaped from the bed, snatching her shirt from the floor. "No, that's okay," she said, her voice thick. "That was— That was fun, but you should go."

Wait, what? "Not okay. I want to do for you what you just did for me." He gave her his best lopsided smile, the one that worked on women in bars and servers at restaurants and old ladies in line at the grocery store.

It didn't work on Thea though. Her expression remained stony, and his smile faded as he sat up. "Hey, I'm really sorry." And Christ, he was. Both sorry and embarrassed. He pushed his hair off his forehead. "I swear, I'm not usually such a fast finisher. It's just that you—"

"Yeah, I get it." She held her shirt in front of her like a shield. "You don't have to spell it out."

Aiden was starting to feel like she'd fucked all the smarts out of him because he had no idea why she was upset. He slid across the mattress to sit on the edge of the bed in front of her, which put them almost at eye level. He reached out and rested his hands on her hips, giving her plenty of chance to back away. She stayed put, but she also stayed tense, so he spoke gently. "I'm sex-dumb right now, so talk slowly to me. What's going on here? Don't kick me out because I got off too fast."

A tear leaked from the corner of her eye, and she directed her gaze to the ceiling. "Please stop saying that," she whispered. "Please just go."

She wouldn't look at him. Why wouldn't she look at him? He surged out of bed and stood in front of her, naked and desperate to understand what he'd done to cause her tears.

"Talk to me, killer. What did I do?"

"Are you really going to make me say it?" Her voice trembled, then she snapped her head up and met his gaze, defiance sparking in her eyes. "Fine. You've made it super clear over the years that I'm not the type of woman you'd ever choose to take home." She gestured to her chest, the movement angry. "I just didn't think you'd want to rush through sex to get it over with. I thought—"

"Rush through sex?" He barked out a laugh. "Are you kidding?"

Hurt bled into her voice. "You don't have to make fun of me."

She turned away again, and he was horrified to see her dash impatiently at another tear. But at least he was starting to understand what was going on.

He wrapped his hands around her shoulders and turned her back to face him. "Are you telling me you think that I fucked you fast to get it over with because your breasts are a little smaller than the last woman I slept with?"

She pulled away from his hands now, trying to get free. "I said, don't make f—"

He hauled her against him and kissed her hard, teasing her lower lip with his tongue. She was stiff at first, but after a beat she gave a little sigh and let her rigid shoulders fall. Once she'd gone pliant in his arms, he broke their kiss and moved his hands up to cup her cheeks.

"Killer, I finished fast because you are so goddamn hot."

Thea snorted—actually snorted—and tried to pull

away again, and Aiden's anger flared. He should be back in that warm bed working her toward an orgasm, not standing naked on a drafty floor trying to convince this woman that she'd just rocked his world.

Actually no, fuck that. He *should* be getting dressed and walking the hell out of her bedroom. Nothing they'd just done was part of the plan they'd agreed to in February. None of it. She might have wanted to sleep with him in the moment—it's what women usually expected from him, after all—but now that she was back on solid ground, she'd realize he'd just erased all their agreed-upon lines in his relief that the balcony hadn't killed her.

Leaving was absolutely what he should do. But he didn't reach for his pants. Instead, he addressed her in a sharp tone, unaccountably anxious that she believe him. "Hey. Listen. I'm telling you the truth." His hands moved to rest on her shoulders again. "I think you're exquisite. Every inch of you is perfectly made. And I came faster than I have since I was fifteen because having sex with you was so good that I couldn't slow down."

His thumbs brushed her cheeks, and his eyes met hers, searching for some sign that she believed him, that she saw the truth of his words in her eyes. But doubt still caused her brow to furrow, so he grabbed her hand and guided it down to where his cock was hardening again at the thought of what they'd just done. Her eyes widened, and her fingers tightened fractionally around his length. He bit back a groan.

"See? I want you. Let me prove it to you."

This time he abandoned the lady-killer grin and just smiled at *her*, at Thea, hoping his expression reflected the genuine delight he found when they were together. Thea offered a small, tentative smile in return and let him pull the shirt out of her hands. Better still, she crawled back onto the bed and watched raptly as he followed her and kissed his way down her body before settling between her legs.

"Let me show you how perfect I think you are. Let me worship." He wrapped his hands around her thighs and nudged his shoulder under her knee, lowering his mouth to her. She bucked against him at the first light stroke of his tongue, and as he settled in to drive her wild with his mouth and fingers, he reached up to cup her breast with his free hand, teasing and stroking with his left hand while his right hand found every sensitive spot between her thighs.

He alternated suction and light strokes with his tongue, and her hips began to move against him in a rocking motion. When the leg slung over his shoulder tightened, he increased the pressure but not the pace, growling in satisfaction when her hand shot down to tangle in his hair.

"Aiden, God, yes." Her back arched off the mattress and her voice trailed off into a moan as he pushed two fingers inside her while the hand on her breast pinched and rolled her nipple. That did the trick, and she pitched over the edge of her orgasm, shuddering and gasping his name. He let her ride it out, then slowed his pace, reluctantly pulling away and crawling up to lie next to her. Her head lolled to the side, and her glazed eyes slowly regained their sharpness.

"Do you swear?" she asked breathlessly.

His brows snapped together in confusion, and pink stained her already flushed cheeks.

"That you find me attractive? That this wasn't some pity thing?"

Aiden kissed her softly. "Pity? Never." He moved his hand back down between her legs, and she whimpered and slammed her knees shut, blocking his fingers.

He propped himself up on his elbow and brushed a few dark strands of hair off her damp brow. "I'm telling you that I find you so attractive that I was hoping to make you come again. And then maybe me too, once you're thoroughly satisfied."

He searched her face and was dismayed to see her expression shutter.

"I can't," she bit out.

His hand stilled as he sorted out what she was saying. "Can't what?"

She flung an arm across her eyes. "Can't come a second time."

"Never have? Or never tried?"

"Never have." Her voice was tight and clipped and not at all the way a well-pleasured woman should sound.

He tugged her arm down. "I bet you can. I bet you'd like it," he coaxed. "I know I'd very much like to try."

His fingers hovered above her breast, and those eyes of hers just killed him, wide and nervous and hopeful. How was a woman who'd just come against his mouth still so skittish? Then to his absolute delight, he saw her make the decision to trust him.

She lifted her chin, her hair shifting against the crisp white pillowcase. "Try then. But no promises."

He kissed her, thrilled by her small bit of bravery.

"*I'm* promising."

SEVENTEEN

Thea wasn't sure she was going to survive the night.

First she'd been disappointed by the mediocre sex she'd had with the purported sex god. Then she'd convinced herself that the sex was mediocre because he wasn't attracted to her. Then he'd shouted at her that she was hot and tossed her onto the bed and drove her out of her mind with that mouth of his and those long fingers she'd been obsessing over for weeks.

And now here he was, stretched out next to her and practically begging to wring more pleasure from her body.

She was afraid she might pass out.

"Aiden, I don't know about this—"

"Shhhh." He stroked one hand across her brow as he trailed his other hand down her body. "Let me work, woman. Just concentrate on feeling good."

She tried to relax and do that, but all she could think was that she'd never come again so quickly. Not that any her old boyfriends had ever tried terribly hard, and oh God, why was she thinking about her exes when she had

Aiden freaking Murdoch working himself into a carpal tunnel brace trying to get her there again?

At that moment Aiden freaking Murdoch bit down on the spot where her neck met her shoulder and growled, "Stop thinking so much."

The sharp not-quite-pain made her cry out, and it jumped her body into hyperdrive. Her hips surged up to meet his seeking fingers, and her already sensitized flesh pulsed and tingled every time one of the calluses on his workman's hands scratched against her skin.

It didn't take long at all for her to say in wonder, "Oh my God, I'm close."

"That's more like it." His words tickled her neck, and he hummed in satisfaction as her orgasm pulsed around his fingers. He then kissed down to her breasts, his stubble rasping against her skin as his mouth pulled into a smile. "I think these were made just for me."

He cupped both her breasts, lifting them to his mouth, and her breath came in pants as he dipped his head between the two, sucking and biting gently. She was almost starting to believe that he was serious when he said he liked her body.

"Can we go again?" He looked up at her. "Give me another shot to impress you?"

No. Say no. Because she'd been right; Aiden was magnificent, and saying goodbye to him at the end of their fake relationship was already going to suck. But if she let herself sleep with him a second time, watched him come apart again while he was inside her body? Well, she didn't know how she'd make it through unscathed.

Then he brushed his thumbs over her nipples and smiled at her with those eye crinkles that had made her weak in the knees even before she'd known how good his tongue felt on all her sensitive spots. And so all she could do was nod, too overwhelmed with everything that had happened on this magical bed to speak.

Then all at once she found her voice. "Let me be on top." She wasn't sure where that request had come from, but out of nowhere she wanted control.

Aiden immediately rolled to his back and folded his arms behind his head with another scorching grin. "Be my guest."

She reached for another condom and rolled it onto him, then positioned herself and slowly worked him inside. His hands flew to her hips, and he hissed as he slid all the way home while she shifted to accommodate his full length.

"So big. My God," she murmured and was rewarded with a flare of his eyes and a tightening of his hands on her skin.

She slowly raised and lowered herself once, marveling at the hard heat of his cock, and Aiden let her set the pace at first. She luxuriated in the friction between them, bouncing and rocking and thrilling herself with the sounds their bodies made as they slapped together, with the delicious sensation of being filled. When he dug his fingers into her hips and dragged her down to grind against him, she moaned and arched her back, thrusting her breasts forward. He surged up to take one in his mouth, trapping her between a hand gripping the nape of her neck and his tongue torturing her nipple.

She felt every point of contact between them as if they were fiery brands searing her skin and stoking the tension coiling inside her even higher. They were both gasping now. Aiden's mouth was hot against her breast, and he slammed up into her over and over, increasing the pace as her hips moved in a frantic circle while she chased her release.

"Yes, Aiden, please *please,*" she begged, unable to organize her words into any coherence.

He pulled away from her nipple long enough to flick a naughty smile at her, then returned to continue laving her with his tongue. One of his hands slid out of her hair and down between their bodies to press against her clit, and she exploded, crying out and surging down onto his cock. He responded with a series of sharp upward thrusts that ended in his own climax. His hands, which had been so deliciously rough with her, now smoothed tenderly down her shoulders as she collapsed onto his chest, his thumbs drawing little circles in the sheen of sweat that covered her back. He kissed her brow, then her temple, as they caught their breath.

"Wow," she finally managed.

His chest moved underneath her as he huffed out a laugh. "Wow?"

She slapped a lazy hand along his flank. "Yes, wow. I guess I *can* do that more than once."

"Told you so."

"And I guess you *can* actually impress a woman in the sack." She grinned up at him, feeling bold enough to tease him now.

"Hey!" His voice was lazily satisfied, not offended. "It's your fault everything is so *wow.* I'm lucky I made it through a second round."

When her thigh muscles started to protest, she shifted to move off him, feeling a sharp little pang of loss as he slid from her body. After he'd dispensed with the condom, she tentatively laid her head on his chest, unsure of what happened next. No-strings sex wasn't usually her style, and she definitely had no idea how to handle no-strings sex with her fake boyfriend. Should she ask him to stay? Assume he was eager to leave? She didn't want to be clingy. Or pushy. Or presumptive.

His chest rumbled with laughter. "You're stiff as a sheet of drywall when you should be doing like I am and falling asleep. What's going on?"

If anything, her spine got even stiffer. "Honestly?"

"Always," he said drowsily.

She sighed. "Honestly, I was wondering what to do with you now."

She peeped up at his face. His eyes were closed, expression relaxed.

"You've already done everything with me, killer. I'm used up."

She batted a hand at his chest. "I know that! I mean... do you want to leave?"

"Do you *want* me to leave?" Now his eyes were open.

She didn't know how to answer that, and at her silence, he sat up, suddenly alert.

"Wait, *do* you want me to leave?"

She sat up too and twisted her fingers together anxiously. "No! But I don't want you to feel like you have to stay. I don't know what you usually..."

Her voice trailed off, and horror swamped her when his expression twisted into disappointment.

"You're wondering if I usually tiptoe out after sex?" His voice was unamused, all traces of relaxation gone.

"I didn't say that. I've just... I've never done this before, so..."

Aiden sagged back against the headboard, and suddenly the distance between them felt immense.

"You know, I haven't exactly done this before either."

Her brows shot up her forehead. "You're telling me you've never had a one-night stand?"

"*That's* what you think this is?" If anything, he got even angrier.

She immediately regretted starting the conversation in the first place, but he was already sliding out of bed and reaching for his clothes.

"What *I've* never done before is sleep with a woman I know and like and intend to keep spending time with." He jerked on his jeans. "So yeah, with other women, I'd generally leave afterward. With you, I was hoping you'd want me to stay."

Her mouth dropped open. "But I *do* want you to stay!"

He yanked his shirt on, yelling as soon as his head popped out the neck hole. "Then why the hell am I getting dressed?"

"I don't know!" she yelled back. "Get naked and get back in bed!"

They both glared at each other for a long moment before his furious expression dissolved into laughter.

"Wanting me naked again so soon? I should pick postsex fights with you more often." But he did as she asked and shucked his shirt and pants, chuckling to himself the whole time.

When he crawled back into bed and gathered her close, she let herself go limp. Exhaustion from the sex and the yelling pulled at her, and even though she should really haul herself to the bathroom to scrub off the day's makeup, all she could manage to do was let her head fall against his shoulder.

"This was a dumb thing to fight about," she muttered.

He kissed the top of her head. "The dumbest. You can make it up to me tomorrow."

Thea smiled at the thick promise in his voice, at the implication that he'd still be here in the morning. But she had no idea what any of this *meant*, so she fell back on a joke. "You bet. I'll brew you my finest cup of coffee."

He laughed and reached around to pinch her ass. "Can I convince you to serve it to me naked?"

She squeaked but didn't respond. Was she brave enough to parade in front of him naked in the bright light of day? She'd have to see how bold she felt when the sun came up.

Her eyes drifted shut, then popped back open. "Um. Was she there this whole time?"

She pointed, and Aiden looked to where Blue was snoring softly in a pointy heap in the far corner of the room.

"If she managed to sleep through all that, I'm impressed." He glanced over at her. "Are you a 'no dogs in the bed' kind of person?"

"It's only been two days, so the jury's still out."

He dropped a quick kiss on her mouth that left her breathless, then gave a soft whistle. "Blue!"

The dog's head jerked up and she leaped to her feet with a little *whuff*, then trotted to the bed. She hopped up, spun around three times, and curled around Thea's ankles with a contented sigh.

"My two ladies. That's more like it," he said, and Thea grinned to herself in the dark, knowing she was about to fall asleep with a man she'd be excited to wake up next to in the morning.

EIGHTEEN

"Good morning."

Aiden turned to the source of the raspy voice to find that Thea had emerged through the sunroom door to join him in the backyard, blinking sleepily. "Good morning. Bed catch on fire?"

"Har." She scrunched her face up against the morning sunlight and bundled her disheveled hair into a lopsided ponytail, then looked around the yard with a scowl.

"Geez, you're really *not* a morning person. Here." He handed over his half-full coffee mug and bent to scratch Blue's chin when the dog trotted over to them.

Without a word, she tossed the rest of the liquid down her throat. "Give me another three cups and I'll be able to have a conversation." She yawned. "Why are you standing under my bedroom window at eight o'clock on a Saturday morning?"

Because I woke up in your bedroom at seven thirty on a Saturday morning and had no idea how to feel about that or what comes next. His morning-afters with women were rare, so when he'd woken up in a strange bed to find Thea curled into a ball and tucked against his side, he'd escaped to the kitchen to make coffee.

They had to talk about it. No way around that. But tossing questions at the woman with bedhead didn't seem fair, so he instead gestured to the wooden slats running along the bottom of the balcony. "Just making my plans for the day."

She jerked her head toward the kitchen, and he followed her inside so they could both pour fresh cups. "I thought your plan was kitchen cabinets."

"It was." He settled next to her in the breakfast nook. "But if you and Blue are going to risk your necks on an unstable balcony, I'd better do that first."

"You'd change your plans for me? I'm flattered." She flattened a hand over her heart and fluttered her lashes at him, and his heart thumped at how pretty she was in the morning with her bare face and bare feet.

"Up to you. Which do you want done first?"

She turned to study the empty walls in her kitchen. "I feel like you're going to worry about that damn balcony until you fix it, so I can live with this mess a little longer."

"Cool." He'd left his binder on the kitchen table last night, so it was within arm's reach now. He grabbed it and started jotting notes on what supplies he needed for the balcony repairs.

"Aiden." Thea's small hand rested on his, and he immediately stilled at her serious tone. "We had sex last night."

He dropped the pen and wrapped his fingers around hers, his nerves unaccountably ratcheting up. "Yes. More than once."

"What do we do now?" She worried her bottom lip

with her teeth and looked at him expectantly, as if he had all the answers. Christ, he wished he did.

"I'll do whatever you want. Pretend it didn't happen. Carry on like normal. Hell, I'll"—he swallowed hard— "I'll end our deal early if you want. Finish the work on your house but no more obligation to be my girlfriend. Whatever makes you comfortable."

She yanked her hand away. "End it early? Pretend it didn't *happen*?" Apparently she was now awake enough to be outraged, which told him he was already screwing this conversation up somehow.

"Like I said, it's whatever you want." He tried to smile at her, but she only scowled back. "You specifically asked that our agreement not include sex, and I broke that part of the deal last night, so—"

"Wait." She held up her hand. "*I* asked for our agreement not to include sex?"

Her confusion stopped him short. "Didn't you?"

"I don't have perfect recall or anything, but I think I asked *if* it would include sex. That doesn't mean I wasn't *interested* in sex."

"Were you?"

She blushed. "Obviously."

"No, back then I mean." He didn't know why, but the idea that Thea might've been interested in him before last night reverberated through him like a cymbal crash.

"Um." She shifted in her chair and avoided meeting his eyes. "I have wondered from time to time what the whole Aiden Murdoch experience would be like."

"Oh yeah?" He crossed his arms and leaned back in his chair, no doubt failing miserably at hiding his intense curiosity. "And in the end, what was it like?"

She threw her hands up in exasperation. "You tell me!

I thought it was great, but you're being Mr. Chill this morning, so maybe *you* want to pretend it didn't happen."

"It *was* great," he said immediately, dropping the teasing grin. But knowing it was great wasn't the same as knowing how to move forward, so he opted for honesty. "I'm not sure how to do this."

"Not sure how to fake a relationship? Or not sure how to have sex with the same person more than once?" She quirked an eyebrow at him. "Or maybe you're not sure how to talk about your feelings."

"Nobody's talking about feelings. We're talking about sex." He snatched his mug to take a fortifying sip. "And that's not part of the agreement."

"I wish you'd stop calling it 'the agreement.' It makes me feel like a high-paid escort."

"Or maybe *I'm* the high-paid escort." He smoldered at her, and as he'd hoped, it made her giggle.

She perched her foot on the seat of her chair and wrapped her arm around her leg, propping her chin on her knee to study him. "We can't exactly unring that bell."

"True. But we can make sure it doesn't happen again."

"Probably smart." She looked down quickly, but he still caught the disappointment that floated across her face. This was exhausting. Maybe he should've stuck to the no-sex plan, no matter how great last night was.

He laughed softly. What the hell was wrong with him? Last night *was* great, and he wanted to do it again, and soon. She clearly did too. And hadn't he just been lamenting that his recent celibacy was making this fake relationship harder on him than it needed to be? So maybe the solution had just landed in his lap and given him an inconvenient erection.

"Or…" His voice trailed off enticingly.

"Or?" Her eyes snapped up to his, sharp and inter- ested. Fuck *yes*. He could make this work for both of them.

He relaxed back into his chair. "Neither of us does long-term relationships. Yours last longer than mine, but we're not in it for the long haul, right?" At her nod, he continued. "So we take this weekend to have as much sex as we want, knowing that neither of us is going to let any long-term feelings get in the way."

Her brow furrowed as she pulled her hair from its ponytail. His fingers itched to tousle those brown strands, but he forced himself to stay still.

"Only sex," she said slowly. "Only this weekend. And then we're back to being high-paid escorts for each other so we can fool the world into thinking that we're two functioning people capable of finding love."

He snapped and pointed at her in approval of her concise rundown. "That's exactly it. I'll keep convincing my dad's clients to take me seriously, *and* I get the novelty of sleeping with the same person many days in a row."

"Hmm. What do I get out of it again?"

Her stare was bold now, and he leaned forward and smiled wolfishly. "You get the house of your dreams and the novelty of having many orgasms in a row."

"I suppose it'll help sell our fake relationship better." She tossed her hair over her shoulder, and her threadbare T-shirt pulled against the hard points of her nipples.

He bit back a groan. God, she was responsive. And that's exactly why he needed to remind both of them about the parameters of this new stage of the plan.

"So we get it all out of our systems this weekend, and

then when I finish up in a few weeks, it's back to being friends."

"A few weeks?" Her mouth turned down at the corners.

"I thought you'd be glad to have all the work done." He pointed to the torn-up kitchen behind her. It bothered him that he'd deviated from his schedule and left her with bare walls for as long as he had.

She dismissed the kitchen with a wave of her hand. "Yeah, of course. It's just…" Another flash of white teeth against pink lips. Then she tipped her head and ran a hot gaze over his body. "In that case, we'd better use the time we still have left before Sunday."

He didn't bother to hide his delight that she'd just agreed to turn her body into his personal playground. "The things I'm going to do to you," he murmured.

With a pretty blush, she pointed toward the staircase. "Bedroom. I want those pants off in the next sixty seconds."

She didn't have to tell him twice.

THREE HOURS, three orgasms, and one trip to the lumberyard later, Aiden was balanced on a ladder, hammering a support beam into place under Thea's balcony.

"Do you mind if we have company during our sexca-pade weekend, *sweet cheeks*?"

He glanced down at where his sunglasses-wearing pretend girlfriend was stretched out on the lounge chair she'd dragged into the grass to watch him work. "Only if it's not your stepdad." He swiped at his sweaty brow.

She wrinkled her nose. "Ew. Of course it's not." She held up her phone. "Mabel texted to ask if she and Jake could stop by."

"Tell her they can only come if Mr. White-Collar's willing to get on a ladder and help me run a string line to check how level the center beam is."

"I offered to help you with that!"

"And I was the sexist asshole who said no to you dangling from a ladder."

She huffed, then brightened immediately. "Honestly, that's fine. The view's way better from down here anyway. You could charge clients more to work shirtless." She peered showily at him over the top of her sunglasses, then grabbed her phone to tap out a text. He turned back to his work with an amused shake of his head. Because this April was unseasonably hot and the backyard was in full sun during the afternoon, he'd ditched his shirt an hour ago. And he couldn't remember the last time he'd been this purely content. Sex with an enthusiastic woman, followed by hard physical work under the sun and the promise of another night in her bed. All the elements for a perfect day.

In short order, Beaucoeur's most popular morning-show host and her accountant boyfriend appeared around the side of the house, each brandishing a bottle of wine.

"I love your new place!" Mabel called, and Thea leaped up to hug her as if they didn't see each other at work every day.

"Thank you!" She gestured over her shoulder. "Don't mind my houseboy."

Mabel pushed her sunglasses on top of her hair and turned to eyeball him. "Looking good, Adonis."

"Gotta keep my tan even," he called back.

Before he knew it, the women had disappeared inside and Jake Carey wandered over to the balcony. Aiden didn't know Mabel's boyfriend all that well, although he'd helped distract her a few months ago when she was trying to pretend she wasn't desperately in love with the guy. Of course, that road went both ways; she'd also been helping him escape all the crap that had been building up at work with his dad and brother. But apparently spending time with Thea meant spending time with her friends, so he might as well make an effort.

"Hand me that drill?" He pointed to the ground, and Jake scooped it up and passed it to him, then knelt to study the metal post base he was installing on the concrete pier the center beam rested on.

"Ah. Keeps the wood from too much contact with water?"

"Yep," Aiden said. "You want in on this?"

"Yep."

As far as male friendship went, that was a good start, and by the time the women emerged from the house with a second lounge chair and a pitcher of margaritas, Aiden had dragged the second ladder off his truck and Jake was similarly shirtless and hard at work hammering in the diagonal braces.

"Oh my God," Thea breathed. "This is heaven. This is hot-guy heaven."

Mabel plopped the chair down and settled herself in it, crossing one ankle over the other and settling her sunglasses on her nose. "This is better than *Magic Mike*!" she called. "Can you guys do some body rolls?"

"No body rolls!" Jake shook his head.

"We're on ladders," Aiden called down to them. "Definitely an OSHA violation."

He and Jake shared a long-suffering glance from across the underside of the balcony that spoke volumes without saying a word: *the things we do for these women. And goddammit, how did those* Magic Mike *guys make it look so easy?*

The afternoon wore on to the soundtrack of Mabel and Thea's nonstop conversation, which was eventually joined by a third voice. Aiden glanced over his shoulder to see Faith Fox settling cross-legged in the grass and pouring herself a margarita, her wild blond hair barely contained by a straw hat.

"When the hell did Faith get here?" he asked Jake. By now they were almost side by side, applying a waterproof stain to the new lumber.

"No idea. They must have sent out some kind of lady Bat-Signal." Jake glanced down and called, "This is kinda weird, babe."

"Shut up and let us ogle," Mabel yelled back.

Faith added a piercing wolf whistle to the mix, and Thea laughed so hard she tumbled off her lounger.

"Oh God," Jake muttered. "Are you three drunk?"

"How dare you?" Thea struggled up from the ground. "We are merely tipsy. Aren't we, Blueprint?"

She scooped up the dog, who'd been frolicking around the group all afternoon, and pressed kisses all over her body with such fervor that Aiden's jealousy flared.

"Hey, anybody got a *stud finder* handy?" Faith's question prompted shrieks of laughter from the other two women, and Blue happily joined in with her high-pitched yips.

"Pizza!" Mabel yelled over the commotion. "I'm ordering, so you boys better wrap up and make yourselves decent."

Aiden's stomach chose that moment to growl loudly enough for the whole neighborhood to hear, so he and Jake clambered down the ladders and cleaned up as the women headed inside to debate which place to order from. When the food arrived, they crammed around Thea's kitchen table with paper plates and red Solo cups of margaritas.

"So Jake agrees with me," Aiden said as everyone grabbed slices. "You need a grill for your backyard."

"You do," Jake agreed. "Perfect spot for grilling back there."

"Oh, I don't grill. It's just so much *meat*." Thea gave a delicate little shudder that had Aiden roaring with laughter.

"I'll teach you to grill meat, woman." He grunted like a caveman and turned his pizza around, biting into the crust first.

"Ew. Why?" Thea asked.

He paused with the slice in his hand. "So I save all the cheesy goodness for the last bite, obviously."

"Weirdo." She rolled her eyes, but her voice was affectionate, and he took a deliberately huge bite of his crust in response.

"Please, most of us here are survivors of Beaucoeur High School cafeteria food," Faith said as she blotted grease from the top of her slice. "Nothing can shock us."

From there, the conversation drifted into embarrassing high school stories courtesy of him, Thea, and Faith while Mabel and Jake laughed themselves silly. During a lull in the conversation, Thea dropped her crumpled napkin on the plate in front of her, wrapped a hand around her cup, and snuggled against him with a happy sigh. He obliged by wrapping his arm around her and pulling her close. They might not be the real deal, but it still felt damn good to have her warm weight at his side during a lazy night with friends when everything was soft around the edges from tequila and the exhaustion of hard work. The pads of his fingers rested on her hip, where he lightly tapped the drumbeat to "Every Little Thing She Does Is Magic."

"Your nose is pink," he murmured into her ear. "You should've worn a hat today."

"You're not pink. You're nice and tan." She yawned and burrowed closer. "Lucky to tan so easily. Gonna kiss you all over later."

He just laughed softly and ran a hand over her hair. When he looked up, Mabel was watching them with a thrilled little smile while Faith looked shocked. And that answered a question he'd been curious about: Mabel apparently thought they were a real couple while Faith seemed to be in on the deception.

He met Faith's gaze over Thea's head, and her eyes narrowed fractionally. "I didn't expect to be such a fifth wheel tonight." Her voice carried a warning, but thankfully Mabel and Jake were too busy kissing to notice the undercurrent around them.

Thea's head popped up. "It's fine, Faithy. Remember how I always used to tag along with you and Leo in high school? That wasn't so bad."

Faith went absolutely rigid at Thea's words. "That was a long time ago," she bit out.

"Yeah." Thea sighed and melted back into his side. "You two were such a cool couple."

Her friend stood abruptly. "You know what? I should call it a night."

Mabel yawned so hard her jaw cracked. "Yep. It's at least two hours past my bedtime."

"Oh no, is it eight already?" Jake asked, earning himself a smack on the arm.

"I'm not *that* much of an old lady," she said primly before turning to Thea. "Are we on for yoga tomorrow?"

Thea was interrupted mid-giggle by a jaw-popping yawn. "I'm thinking not this week."

"You two do yoga?" Aiden was inexplicably tickled by the thought of tall, laid-back Mabel and tiny, bouncy Thea getting all blissed out on yoga together.

"God no," Mabel said. "We usually just get donuts."

"If we're lucky, we'll get Faith to join us someday." Thea looked pointedly at her friend, who merely shrugged.

"The only way I'm doing Sunday morning not-yoga donuts is if you show up at my house with a dozen strawberry fritters in a box. Otherwise I'm not making the effort."

"Rude!" Mabel announced, and their laughing conversation continued as they gathered up the empty pizza boxes and paper plates and shoved them all into the trash before they headed to the front door.

After they'd said their good-nights, designated driver Jake wrangled the two women into his Jeep with a promise to get Faith home safely.

"Best weekend ever," Thea said as she shut and locked the hobbit door.

He grinned at her. "You think so?"

"I do." She smiled back, her eyes liquid in the light of the hallway.

He stepped closer until his mouth was a fraction of an inch from hers. "Guess what?"

"What?" she whispered.

"It isn't quite over yet."

Without another word, he picked her up and slung her over his shoulder, taking the stairs two at a time to show her the perfect end to the perfect weekend.

NINETEEN

Thea was nothing but jangled nerves when she walked toward the Murdoch Construction building. She hadn't seen Aiden since he'd given her a heart-stoppingly sweet kiss goodbye on Sunday evening, and she hadn't heard from him beyond a quick text on Monday morning to let her know that one of his guys would get her cabinet installation underway that week.

It was Thursday now. Her kitchen was essentially done courtesy of a Murdoch employee named Danny who communicated exclusively in grunts. The slate-gray cabinets were gorgeous against the backsplash she'd chosen, and every time she saw them, she wanted to cry. *Aiden* was supposed to do that work. It was part of the renovation plan they'd agreed to, and Lord knew he always stuck to his plans. Except the past weekend, when he'd set his plan on fire and spent three days in her bed. And now he'd pulled a vanishing act.

Her fault for being surprised. *Of course* the past weekend would complicate things beyond what either of them had been prepared for. Then again, the absolute silence on his end was a bit much, and it left her confused and hurt and a little pissed.

She battled back her overly dramatic jitters as she stood in front of the big window showcasing a luxury bathroom setup that Murdoch Construction could install for a customer with a taste for marble. Aiden might not even be there, and she'd be able to get in and out without having to deal with... whatever was going on. She took a steadying breath and pushed through the front door, where all her Aiden angst fled when she took in the scene in front of her.

"Look, I don't know, okay? I'm trying to find it, but... *Unnngh.*" Trip was hunkered behind the front desk, bashing his pointer finger over and over on the computer keyboard but apparently not finding what he was looking for. "Can you just, I don't know, keep waiting until we call you about it?"

Every part of her curled in on itself at the worst display of customer service she'd ever seen.

"No. *No!*" He was shouting now, and since nobody else was around to do anything about it, she'd just have to step in because this was intolerable.

She walked into Trip's direct line of vision and snapped to get his attention. When he finally looked up, she gestured for him to hand the phone over to her. He hesitated, so she snapped again with more authority until he surrendered the handset.

She leaned over the counter, pressed it to her ear, and spoke in her warmest voice. "Hi there. I'm so sorry. I had to step away from my desk, and Trip's been covering for me. How can I help you?"

An agitated male voice spilled from the other line. "I

was just asking when my screen door would be in, but that idiot couldn't tell me a single useful thing."

"Oh, he's not so bad. You should see him with a paintbrush in his hand. His color-washing technique could make you cry, it's so good." Of course, she had no idea if Trip was competent at any parts of his job, but a cheerful demeanor as thick as Teflon worked wonders in customer service. "Now tell me your name, sir."

Soothing the grump on the other end of the line was far better than dreading what she'd say to Aiden when she saw him, so she jerked her head at Trip to vacate the phone area. He scrambled to comply as she lifted the phone cord to allow herself room to move around the counter and take his seat.

She was greeted with a spreadsheet on the screen that listed hundreds of names in no particular order. God, was this their management software? A twelve-year-old version of Excel? Yikes.

But she'd worked with worse. She entered the man's name into the search bar and located him buried deep in the list. "Gil McConnell? 2628 Whitewood Lane?" When he grunted his confirmation, she tabbed across his listing but found nothing informative about any orders being placed. "Okay, I'll tell you what. I'd like to check into this status so I don't give you any incorrect information. And I hate to see you wait on hold while I do that. Can I get the most recent update on that order status and call you right back, Mr. McConnell?"

"I've left two voice mails already." His voice was peevish, and the yappy dog trying to join the conversation in the background added to the general agitation.

"I am so sorry about that," she said smoothly. "It's

been wild around here. Were you at the Beaucoeur Home Expo a few weeks ago, by any chance?"

"No."

Geez, he wasn't giving her anything to work with, but she forced a smile into her voice and continued. "It was incredible! You should've seen some of the new innovations out there. Tile with LED lights in them. Showers that you control with voice commands. You turn it on and set the temperature with your voice! I tell you, Mr. McConnell, we live in the dang future."

"That so?" he asked, curiosity creeping into his voice. "I've never heard of anything like it."

"I had extreme bathroom envy, I tell ya." She grinned triumphantly at Trip, who was listening to her end of the conversation with his mouth open. "Anyway, I don't want to keep you on the phone any longer. I'm going to find out about the status of that door, and I'll call you back as soon as I do, okay?"

She confirmed his phone number, and Gil McConnell hung up a much more cheerful man than he'd been three minutes earlier.

"What the hell did I just watch?" Trip was looking at her like she'd just poured gasoline on the countertop and set it on fire.

"Customer service, hello," she said. "Now where do you guys keep your records? I'd like to call him back this afternoon."

Trip pointed behind her, and she swiveled to find three identical black filing cabinets. "No. No way. You guys keep physical records?" She was already up and moving to the drawer marked *M*, and after rifling through the alphabetical-ish files, she produced a folder with Mr. McConnell's name on it. "Okay, says here he finalized his product selection, but I don't see any record that it was ordered. Would it be in here if it was?"

"Far as I know." Trip peered over the counter at the papers in her hand and tapped his finger on the scrawled writing on the sheet. "That's Dad's handwriting. I'm guessing he forgot to tell Mom about it, and it fell through the cracks. *Shit*."

Thea smoothed her hand down the paper in thought. "Okay, we can salvage this." A memory from the home expo tickled her brain, and she swiveled back to the computer for a quick Google search that confirmed her recollection. "Do you trust me to try to make this work, or do you want to call him? Or wait for Aiden to get here and handle it?"

At his brother's name, Trip's face closed down entirely. "*No.* Just make the call."

Yikes. So that weirdness was still going on apparently. She blew out a breath, cracked her neck, and punched in the grump's number. As it rang, she told Trip, "You guys need a Bluetooth headset. This phone ties you down like an umbilical cor— Hi, Mr. McConnell! It's Thea from Murdoch Construction." She crossed her fingers for luck and held them up so Trip could see. "Okay, good news and bad news. The bad news is that we don't have your door in just yet. But the good news is that there's still time to change your order."

"Why would I want to change it?" he asked suspiciously.

"Would you believe, it's that silly home show again!" she chirped. "At the booth next to the magic shower, the Adriatic Window company had its new products on display, and I saw the cutest screen with a built-in doggy door that gives your pal the freedom to run in and out, and it's tied to a chip in his collar to make sure he's the only animal that can get through. Wouldn't that be great as things start to warm up this year? Give your best bud backyard access without having to get up and down all the time to open the door? And the chip means no possums get into the house, only your dog."

She held her breath and bared her teeth in a comically nervous smile as Trip looked on. She was gambling that she'd actually heard a dog in the background, that they lived in a house with a fenced-in backyard, and that the grump on the other end of the line loved that little beast enough to spring for a fancy door.

Thank God, he let out an interested exhale. "Computer-chip doggy screen door, you say?"

"Absolutely. Why don't I shoot you an email with options and you can take a look to see if you might prefer that model? We'd be able to make that change for you, no problem. And I'll also see if I can dig up a promotional video of that voice-control shower just for fun. Some things a man's got to see for himself."

Once he'd confirmed his email address, she made him promise to let them know right away which screen door he preferred. "And if you want to book us to install a shower you can control with a literal word, we'll be here!"

She ended the call and sagged into the chair with an exhale. "And *that's* how you do customer serv..." When she looked up, she discovered two pairs of hazel Murdoch eyes staring at her. Her pulse ratcheted up. "Um, hi *puddin'*. Been there long?"

"Long enough," Aiden said.

Her shoulders tensed. He looked *pissed*. Well hell. She'd bulldozed her way into his business when she had no right to, and he was probably counting all the ways she'd crossed all kinds of lines in their "agreement," whatever that meant anymore. She opened her mouth to apologize, but just then the phone rang. Horrific timing, that. She raised her brows at him in a question, and he gestured for her to go ahead with a sharp motion of his hand. After a quick exhale, she picked up the handset.

"Murdoch Construction, this is Thea. How can I help you?" She kept her eyes on her fake boyfriend's unreadable face as she listened to the caller. "That's a good question, ma'am. *Will* someone be here at seven a.m. on Thursday to accept delivery of a shipment from Calloway Granite Countertops?"

He nodded once, and she shot him a thumbs-up. "Absolutely. Please schedule delivery for that time, and I'll be sure to add it to the work calendar. Thanks!"

When she hung up, she asked, "Have you guys ever considered upgrading to some kind of online project-management system for the company? No offense, but searching through Excel sheets and physical files for dates and phone numbers is a literal nightmare."

Even though she'd just given them useful, actionable advice, Aiden continued to stare at her stone-faced. "We're not making any changes until we know what's happening in the long run."

She laughed, shooting for breezy and landing on nervous as hell. "Gotcha. It's not in the plan yet, so of course you're not ready to jump. I was just thinking that the most efficient places I've worked all had some kind of synced, app-based program." God, what was she *doing*? She and Aiden had spent an incredible weekend together and then he vanished, and here she was babbling about software.

Aiden turned to his brother. "Can I steal my girlfriend, or do you need her to keep doing your job for you?"

Her heart sank. His voice was as hard as the side of a mountain, and the brothers glared at one another until Trip pivoted to stomp around the counter.

"She's a hell of a lot better at it than I am," he grumbled. She moved to stand next to Aiden as Trip's suspicious eyes landed on them. "I don't buy it, by the way."

She laughed nervously and snaked an arm around Aiden's waist, shocked at the tension she felt in his back. "Don't buy what?"

"Any of this." He folded his arms over his chest, his jaw set. "For one thing, you're way too nice to be with him."

The urge to defend Aiden rose up hot and fast, even though he'd kind of been an asshole this week. "I'll have you know your brother is one of the nicest men I've ever met." She rested her hand on his chest and glanced up at Aiden to see his lips tighten, but she forged ahead anyway. "And I'm not nice. I'm bossy."

Aiden finally stirred to life. "Aaaand that's enough of that."

He took her hand and started heading down the hall, but she dug in her heels long enough to ask Trip, "You'll email Mr. McConnell? I left all the links up in the browser."

His grunt sounded vaguely affirmative, so she let Aiden tow her behind him. Once they were alone in his office, he slammed the door shut and stared at her long enough that she squirmed under his gaze.

"I'm sorry," she said at the same time that Aiden said, "I can't believe he—"

They both laughed weakly, and he spoke first. "*I'm*

sorry. He shouldn't have asked you to cover the phones for him. He knows that's his fucking job while Mom's away."

Wait, *that's* why he was mad? She waved a hand from her head and down her body. "Hello. Bossy, party of one. I basically ordered him to hand the phone over. I couldn't stand watching him butcher customer relations like that." She nervously twined her fingers together, worried that she'd made the situation between the two of them even worse. "I tend to take over when I shouldn't. I won't do it again."

"Are you kidding? You were great. If McConnell calls back to buy that shower, I'm giving you a finder's fee." He smiled at her for the first time since he'd entered the building, and everything inside her unclenched a little.

"Yes!" She gave a comical fist pump, then let her hand fall. "But why the hell would Trip say I'm too nice for you?"

"I wish I knew." Aiden's shoulders slumped as he jammed his hands in his pockets. "He's been a dick for months now. Between him and Dad, it's been..." His eyes fell on a framed photo on the wall, and Thea followed his gaze to see a photo of him, his brother, and his father posed in front of their trucks, each with a Murdoch license plate. "My mom's big idea for company branding a few years ago. I swear it's one of the last times I remember the three of us getting along."

His jaw bunched, and he looked so sad that Thea's heart squeezed. Last week at this time, she'd have rubbed his arm or maybe even pulled him into a hug, but she wasn't sure how he'd react to that now. Thanks to the past weekend, they now shared an intimate language all their own, one made up of sighs and gasped breaths and one-word commands. How was she supposed to come back to touches-for-show and kisses-for-an-audience after that?

"I'm sorry." She clasped her hands behind her back so she wouldn't be tempted to reach for him. The warm, laughing guy who'd melted seamlessly into her friend group on Saturday was nowhere to be found in this office, and for an absurd moment, she battled back tears. She'd known there was a chance she was risking triggering his fuck-and-run impulse by sleeping with him, and now here they were. He could barely look at her. Even though she knew damn well they had an expiration date, this unexpected distance pained her.

"Thanks." He sighed and dropped into one of the chairs in front of his desk. "My mom called on Monday. Asked if Trip and I could come this weekend for an update on Dad." He dug his thumb into his forehead like he was looking for a pressure point to release all his tension. "So I guess I'm driving to Chicago with Trip."

She cautiously took a seat next to him. "Sounds awkward."

"You have no idea." He finally looked at her. "It's why I sent you Danny. I was planning to finish your kitchen this weekend, but since I won't be able to, I thought you might appreciate having the damn thing done already."

Ah. Well, that explained why she'd had a worker in her house all week. "Thanks."

As gorgeous as the new cabinets were, she'd rather have lived with a torn-up kitchen for longer if it meant that she'd be able to hang around and hand Aiden tools when he finally had the time to do the work. But her own disappointment fled as stress brackets appeared around his mouth.

"I know we're not actually a couple, but I'm here if

you need me." Then she quirked a brow to lighten the mood. "And furthermore, fuck Trip. You're extremely nice."

He snorted. "Okay, let's not rehab my image *too* much. I like a little mystery."

She laughed along with him, although her heart still hurt at his disappearance this week.

"So what brings you by the office?"

"Oh right." She'd almost forgotten she actually did have a reason to be there. "Danny told me he'd leave a can of paint for me to do some touchups in the kitchen, so I was swinging by to grab it."

He looked toward the door. "I can get it and bring it over. If not tonight, then—"

"Hey. Don't worry about it," she said firmly. No need to turn herself into one of his volunteer charity projects. "I'll do it when I get a chance. I can paint."

He leaned his elbow on the back of his chair and rested his head on his fist. "Did I miss your job as painter somewhere down the line?"

"Believe it or not, I touched up my share of exhibits at the zoo. All my skills come from somewhere, baby."

He laughed and walked with her to the front desk, where sure enough, Danny had left a can of paint with her name taped to the top. Trip handed it over with a glare and nothing else, and Thea was glad to escape out the door with Aiden.

As he stood with her outside her car, he still didn't touch her, which she couldn't help but notice. In fact, he was radiating *keep your distance* in a way she wasn't used to from him. Even when they'd been casual friends, he'd always been approachable, but this was a whole damn wall he'd put up. It made her check her instinct to offer to ride along with him to Chicago, just so he'd have some-body in his corner. If he wanted her along on this family trip, he would've asked. And he definitely hadn't done that.

Their goodbyes were subdued, with Aiden barely brushing a kiss on her cheek before he headed back into his office. She drove home wondering if the problem was that he'd gotten her out of his system and was ready to move on to the next woman. It was inevitable; she just hadn't expected it to happen so soon. The thought hurt more than she'd expected, which was ridiculous. She'd always been the one to end things in the past; Aiden was just saving her the trouble.

So why did she have to blink away tears as she headed toward home?

TWENTY

The hollow shell of Aiden Murdoch sat in his truck outside his brother's house early on Saturday morning, waiting to get started on what was shaping up to be the worst day of the week. And that was saying something.

Everything had been off since he'd said goodbye to Thea on Sunday and returned home. What used to be his meticulously renovated haven now felt as inviting as a tomb; it simply didn't glow with the warmth and energy of Thea's princess house. Even in the middle of the chaos, with furniture and boxes stacked in whatever room wasn't being sanded or painted or improved in some way, her Tudor house with the round-topped door was bright and vital and welcoming. Not returning to it this week had been almost physically painful.

But he'd forced himself to stay away for one simple reason: he liked it too much. Liked being in her bed. Liked being included in her circle of friends. Liked being the one she shared secret smiles with and draped her hot little body across when she was worn out at the end of the day. And he had no idea how to deal with any of that.

He'd never been a boyfriend, had never felt that confusing mix of affection and lust and tenderness that Thea sparked in him.

Responsibility too. He closed his eyes and tilted his head back against his seat. He wanted to make things better for her. He wanted to be the one making her smile. Instead, she'd been as nervous at his office on Thursday as she'd been when they started this whole thing. It made him feel like shit. He'd wanted to pull her down on his lap and kiss the strain off her face, but that instinct had no place in their relationship, such as it was. He was only good for one thing, and that wasn't what Thea deserved. The whole damn town knew it. Hell, even his brother wasn't afraid to say it to his face: Thea should be with someone who could give her more than one weekend of sex that had no promise for the future.

That's why he'd thrown himself even more frantically into work this past week, combing through notes on their completed projects over the past six months and finding countless little tasks that his father had left unfinished. Small things that made the difference in a job done and a job well done. And his insistence that they go back and finish those stray jobs had led to blowup after blowup with his fucking brother, who argued that done was done.

"'Sup."

Ah, there was his fucking brother now, slamming the passenger door of the truck and yanking his seat belt across his chest.

"Morning," Aiden said. "I grabbed coffee." He gestured to the two take-out cups in the well between the seats, and Trip grunted and grabbed one. Aiden put the truck in drive but didn't pull away from the curb. "Ashley not coming?"

His brother's frowning face frowned even harder. "Nope."

"Okay then." Aiden had always thought Ashley got along great with her in-laws, but maybe not. He turned up the radio and pointed the truck north, bracing himself for an awkward drive with only the radio for company. They probably should've driven separately, but they'd reluctantly agreed on Friday that it didn't make sense to have two vehicles headed to the same place. So here they were, sipping their coffee and listening to the Brick and pointedly not speaking.

As one mostly silent hour turned to two and edged into three, traffic started to pick up, and the pockets of businesses and office buildings flanking the interstate grew thicker. By the time Aiden had found his exit to the UChicago Medicine neighborhood where his mom had rented an apartment and was weaving through the city's Saturday-morning traffic, looking for parking, his shoulders ached from tension. He should've asked Thea to come along. She'd have kept up a running conversation for the whole drive that had them all laughing.

"Looks like this is as close as we can get." He'd finally found an open on-street spot, and he and Trip left the truck to walk the handful of blocks to his parents' new building.

"God, that's depressing."

It was the first full sentence Trip had spoken in miles, and Aiden heard the sadness in his voice as they studied the tall, blocky building. So he made himself a little vulnerable too. "I'm dreading this. I don't want to see how much worse Dad's gotten."

Trip's eyes cut over to him, his broad face radiating nothing but apprehension. "Yeah. I fucking hate it." Then he laughed once, a pale echo of the uproarious guffaws Aiden remembered from their childhood. "But we'd better get in there. I bet Mom's pulling something out of the oven right now."

The observation made Aiden laugh too. "How does she always do it?"

"Mom magic."

Trip led the way into the lobby of the building, and they boarded the elevator for their parents' ninth-floor apartment. Aiden knocked on the door, which was as undecorated as the rest of the hall, and was reminded of Thea's joy over ditching rental life for home ownership.

He missed her. God, when had she become central enough that he missed her when she wasn't around?

"My boys!" Gloria threw the door open and pulled them into a hug that Aiden sank into. "You're here!" She waved her hand and pushed them toward the kitchen table. "I just pulled a breakfast casserole out of the oven. Sit and eat."

Aiden caught Trip's eye, and they exchanged quick, suppressed smiles as they followed her to the table.

"Thanks." Aiden accepted a plate with sliced melons positioned next to a wedge of egg, ham, and cheese giving off the most delicious breakfast-y steam. "Where's Dad?"

"Asleep. He had an appointment yesterday, and that always wears him out."

Speaking of worn out. Their mother's voice sounded tired, and she looked thinner than he remembered ever seeing her, although her smile was still as warm.

"You're worn out too," he said. "We should be here helping you. We should—"

"You absolutely should not." Steel entered her tone. "You're running the business, and I'm sure that's hard enough with your dad and me gone." Her eyes traveled to the window, which framed a square of bright blue Chicago sky. "Believe it or not, I like it here. We're close to a park, and I've found a nice group of retirees to walk with. Your dad comes with me on his good days. If not, we have home health care."

"Really? Dad joined a senior walking group?" Trip asked.

She tossed her head back in a laugh. "He grumbles the whole time. But Chicago's been... interesting. How often does someone like me retire and move to the city? We've met so many people." Her hopeful gaze turned toward Aiden. "Speaking of people, how's Thea?"

Trip scoffed before he could answer, and Aiden bristled immediately. "You got something to say?"

"Yeah. It's bullshit." He lifted his chin as if daring his brother to contradict him.

"Language!" But Gloria zeroed right back in on Aiden. "Why is it bullshit?"

"It's not," he said, praying this would end the subject. But Trip scoffed again, louder this time, and Aiden's temper flared. "What's your problem with Thea?"

"It's not with her, it's with *you*." He crossed his arms over his chest with a glare, and Aiden's overtaxed patience finally snapped.

"And what the *fuck* is your problem with *me*?" Aiden tossed his fork down and lurched to his feet, too furious with his brother to control his tone.

"Boys! Knock it off." Their mother's voice cracked through the apartment. She pointed a finger at her first-born. "You, sit down."

Aiden dropped to his seat but didn't look away from his brother's red, angry face.

"And you." Gloria addressed her second-born now. "Apologize."

"But I—"

"Apologize."

Trip's flush reddened, and he glared down at the remains of breakfast on his plate. "Sorry." He sounded exactly like the sulky twelve-year-old Aiden remembered.

"What is going on with you two?"

Aiden crumpled up his napkin, tempted to shove food into his mouth to keep from having to reply.

But his mom wasn't new to the parenting thing, because she leveled a hard look at him, then Trip. "I bribed you both with a perfectly good trough of food. Now spill."

Aiden sighed and pushed the plate away. "You'll have to ask him."

But Trip just glared down and said nothing.

"I don't know what happened." Gloria's gaze bounced between the two of them. "You used to be friends. Are you jealous of your brother, Trip? Is it the attention he gets from all those women?"

"Jesus," Aiden muttered.

Trip groaned loudly. "No! God! Look, it's—"

Whatever Trip was about to say ended with the sound of a shuffle-thump moving down the hall. "Gloria, where's my—"

Rudy entered the kitchen, and for a moment he stared blankly at the three people around the table. Then his face split into an enormous grin. "Boys! I didn't know you were coming!"

He moved forward, and Aiden and Trip both stood to hug him. If he'd thought his mother looked thinner, that was nothing compared to his dad, who seemed diminished somehow in his plaid shirt and khakis. But his jaw was clean-shaven, his hair was neatly brushed, and his face glowed with excitement at sitting down to breakfast with his family.

"Did I know they were coming?" he asked Gloria.

The corners of her mouth dropped, but she nodded firmly. "I mentioned it. But it's okay. They're here now."

"They're here now," he repeated.

Gloria stood to fill a plate and set it in front of him with a quick kiss on the head. He picked up his fork and asked, "How's the work on the Johnsons' going?" Then he set the fork down, and the lines in his forehead deepened. "No. Not the Johnsons. The... the pharmacy. The Santiagos."

Relief settled palpably over the table, and it felt like he, Trip, and their mom all exhaled in unison.

"It's good," Trip said. "We're close to wrapping up." He nodded toward Aiden. "They're even letting this guy come around now."

Trip met his eyes, and Aiden inclined his head slightly. *Here* was Trip's true apology.

Rudy just harrumphed. "Shouldn't have kept him from coming around in the first place. Ridiculous."

His throat tightened. "Thanks, Dad." He had to clear it before he could speak again. "But the work's looking great. Trip oversaw a whole redesign of their lighting for the work area."

That spun the conversation off in a new direction about light bulb frequency spectrum, which could captivate his dad and brother for days. While those two debated LEDs versus fluorescents, his mom pulled him aside.

"The treatment's going well so far," she said quietly.

"The clinical trial is just getting underway. The doctors working with him have been wonderful. They have him following a medication regime along with exercise and mental acuity games. He has more good days than bad up here."

"That's great, Mom." He gripped her hand as one layer of worry peeled off his soul.

She squeezed his hand back, her smile fading again. "The thing is, it's made us both reevaluate things. And it's time for us to officially step away from the company. You and Trip, the business is yours now. Permanently."

The words filtered through his brain, a truth he'd known was coming even as he dreaded hearing it. "Okay." He exhaled hard. "Okay."

"That means you two need to fix this." She looked meaningfully at where Trip was patiently listening to Rudy explain about blue light spectrum versus yellow light spectrum, a topic Trip was already well-versed in.

"I wish I knew how." He shrugged helplessly. "But we don't exactly talk about our feelings."

"Is it because you went to college and he didn't?" Gloria laced her fingers together, and the gesture reminded him of Thea. "He never enjoyed school, so I never pushed it on him, but maybe I should have. Or is it—"

"Mom." He cut her off. "I love you, but don't do this. We'll figure it out. We both want the business to succeed."

When they'd all finished their meal, Aiden and Trip cleaned up the dishes while their mother grabbed a huge pillbox and fished out a handful of meds for their father to swallow. Afterward, she pulled Trip out the door to walk with her to the Garden of the Phoenix, which had apparently become her favorite park in the city. Aiden recognized it for what it was: a ploy to let him talk shop with his dad as he prepared to officially take over the business Rudy had built from the ground up.

"Mom says you're both liking it here," Aiden said as the two of them settled into the small living room.

Unlike his parents' Beaucoeur home, this space was stark and uncluttered, with only one framed photo resting on a side table as decoration. It was the last church directory picture they'd taken together, when he and Trip were both teenagers who'd been crammed into suits and forced to smile awkwardly at the camera early on a long-ago Sunday morning. For some reason his mother loved it.

"Chicago's different," his dad grumbled. "But it's not all bad."

He looked closely at Rudy's face and saw focus and clarity in his eyes. Thank God for that at least. "Mom says you're officially retiring?"

Rudy worked his mouth back and forth before he spoke. "Yeah. It's time. You boys'll do fine." He glanced at the framed picture, and a fond smile ghosted across his features. "More than fine."

Aiden blinked. From his taciturn father, that was sky-high praise. "Do you want an update on any more of the jobs we have going?"

But Rudy just waved him off. "Nah. Perks of retirement. Not having to give a damn about cost overruns."

Aiden chuckled because yes, cost overruns had become the bane of his existence.

Then Rudy shocked the hell out of him by saying, "So you're seeing someone."

He stiffened. He had never, not once, discussed a woman with his father. In fact, his dad had made it clear years ago that he'd given up on his oldest son settling down, which pretty well closed the book on conversations about his personal life. Back then, Aiden had considered it yet more evidence that the whole world saw how fundamentally unsuited he was for anything deeper than sex. But now Rudy was opening the door for a relationship talk—and just when he felt the least prepared to handle it.

"I am," he said haltingly.

"And you like this girl?"

Yes. She's wonderful. She's funny and vibrant and adorable when she's nervous. She makes me laugh and she kisses like a dream. And I'm a coward who's been avoiding her for days.

The torrent of words stalled on his tongue. They were all true, and they terrified him. His entire adulthood proved that he wasn't the guy a woman like Thea could rely on. Yet at the same time, he missed her touch as much as he missed her laughter. But in the end, all he could bring himself to say was "I like her a lot."

And those five words were enough to conjure a paternal smile that filled the small apartment where his parents were carving out a new life for themselves.

"Good. That's good. Your mother and I know how happy you could make the right girl." His father looked at him and asked, "Do you make her happy?"

Aiden didn't even have to think about it. "I do." Or he had, anyway, last weekend. And he wanted to keep making her happy for far longer than that. He just wasn't sure he knew how.

TWENTY-ONE

Hours later, Aiden and Trip hugged their parents goodbye with a promise to call once they'd made it home safely, then boarded the elevator in silence. They didn't make it more than two floors before Trip sighed.

"We should've visited earlier."

Aiden glanced over at him, surprised that his brother was voluntarily making conversation. "We really should have. Let's try to come back soon. Maybe bring Ash next time?" He held his breath, unsure if he'd overstepped by bringing up a touchy subject. But Trip just nodded.

"Yeah. She'd probably love Mom's Phoenix park." He stared hard at the ground as he said it, as if the idea needed deep internal scrutiny of some sort. They didn't talk again until they were on the interstate heading south, and Aiden took advantage of the possible cessation of brotherly hostility to broach the subject of their parents' retirement.

"Did Mom talk to you about her and Dad's decision?"

Trip sagged back against the seat, his skull hitting the headrest. "She filled me in." His brother's voice held the same resignation that Aiden was grappling with. "I guess we all knew it was coming."

"Sooner than we ever expected though."

Trip offered him a half smile. "At least it won't be hard finding a replacement for Mom." When Aiden looked at him curiously, he said, "Your girlfriend, dude. She kicks ass at it. We should hire her full time."

Aiden almost swerved onto the shoulder as the idea took hold and expanded in his brain. How had he not seen it? Thea was cheerfully competent at everything he'd seen her do. She fixed fake kitchen displays and talked down pissed-off clients and God only knew what else was in her arsenal of skills and her magic purse. For thirty years, their mother had ruled the company with warmth and a firm hand, and Thea would be an amazing replacement to take them into the next thirty years.

One problem though.

"It's not that easy," Aiden said. "For one thing, we're not..."

Trip raised his brows. "Not really dating?"

Aiden's hands clenched around the steering wheel. "Fine. You're right."

"Shocker," Trip said flatly, but he didn't sound pissed this time, just amused.

It gave Aiden the push he needed to have an honest conversation with his brother about his personal life. "It started off as a way to help each other out, but now it's... complicated."

Trip gave a surprised grunt. "Complicated? Didn't think you did complicated."

"I don't," he snapped, rubbing a hand over his forehead. "So yeah, if she was just some woman, I'd say we should hire her in a heartbeat. But she's... I mean, we're not..."

They weren't actually dating. They weren't getting married. And that meant that once they were back to being friends, he'd have to see Thea every day at the job. Eventually he'd have to watch her leave work to go out with some other guy, maybe someday even go home to a family that didn't include him.

The idea was intolerable, and the more he thought about it, the heavier it settled on his chest. Because the truth was, he was *tired*. Tired of being the guy who was always alone. Not alone on Saturday nights, because that was easy enough for him to fix, but alone when it counted. Alone on lazy Sunday mornings. Alone at the family dinner table. The kind of alone that made him look at the amazing woman in his life and wonder if she could fill the hole in the center of his chest. That hole had grown bigger with each year that he told himself he didn't have any kind of forever to offer another person. Until Thea.

She made him want things he didn't think he was capable of. Things he'd insisted to his family he didn't want. Things that he'd shown the world he didn't care about. And once he'd shut down the idea of ever having those soft forever feelings, the world had responded by expecting nothing more of him. He'd drifted along, happy to comply, until Thea had shocked the hell out of him by making him question whether he could let himself want something other than the life he'd been living.

And that was fucking terrifying. No wonder he'd run in the other direction this week.

In the end, all that was way too much to say to Trip, so he stuck with a terse, "I'm not sure hiring Thea would be the best idea." He wasn't even sure she was speaking to him right now, to be honest. Only a complete asshole would blow her off all week because his insides were all tangled up every time he thought about her smile.

Trip grumbled, "Yeah, well, I don't think me answering phones is the best idea either."

"We agree on that."

His brother snorted in amusement, then sobered immediately and leaned forward to flip the air-conditioning vent open and closed a few times before blurting out, "Dammit, I'm sorry, okay?"

Aiden flicked a surprised glance at him. "For what?"

"I just"—he exhaled hard—"I owe you an apology. About everything. And I'm sorry."

Heavy silence descended on the truck cab until Aiden said, "Did Mom put you up to this?"

"Kind of." Trip had moved on to spinning his phone nervously between his fingers. "But she's right. We can't run the business with me making shitty comments about you all day."

Months of pent-up hurt and anger climbed up Aiden's throat, but he stuffed it down and asked as calmly as he could, "I've gotta know: what the hell did I do to make you so goddamn pissy all the time?"

Trip dropped his phone in his lap and hardened his jaw. For a second, he looked like he wasn't going to answer, but he finally unclenched enough to say, "It's Ash, all right? She... she wants me to be more like you."

"She *what*?" Aiden looked over at him in horror, grateful that they were finally past the worst of the Chicago congestion so he could focus on the conversation without fear of plowing into any stop-and-start traffic. He had no idea how marriage actually worked, but comparing your husband to your brother-in-law didn't seem like a great sign. "She doesn't, um…"

He was too appalled to even finish the sentence, but thankfully Trip gave an emphatic shake of his head.

"*No*. God no. She always says she married the hotter Murdoch brother."

Trip's face softened then, and the satisfied little smile that crossed his face belonged to a man who was thoroughly besotted with his woman. Aiden was starting to understand what that felt like. "Poor Ash," he quipped. "She's wrong, but I'm glad she loves you anyway."

That brought out a full-blown guffaw from his brother, and Aiden laughed right along with him before Trip sobered.

"No, it's not like that. But she says we're in a rut. Wishes we did more things." The tension was back in Trip's shoulders. "'Aiden's in a band, Aiden went on that trip to Jamaica. Aiden's always meeting up with his friends.' She wants me to be more *adventurous*."

"Huh." Aiden was at a loss. Trip had been stomping around pissed for months because his wife wanted more date nights? "I'm actually pretty boring when it comes right down to it."

"I know that, asshole," Trip said immediately, but there was no anger behind the words. "And yeah, we could probably go out more. But it… it wasn't just that." His hands clenched and released before he continued in a rush of words. "Things with Dad were getting shittier and shittier, and I knew you were gonna be the boss at work sooner rather than later, so when Ash started bringing you up at home too? It was just a whole fucking lot of the Adonis show, all right?"

Aiden glanced at him with dawning comprehension.

"Is that why you got in my face about all those clients not wanting to work with me?"

Trip ducked his head, looking embarrassed. "Yeah. I'm sorry about that too. I was just glad somebody else out there wasn't buying the hype."

"Trust me, there's no hype," Aiden said flatly. "And actually..." He drew in a deep breath and pushed out the next sentence in the interest of honesty. "I stay so busy because my life's pretty empty otherwise."

"Not anymore."

"What do you mean?"

Trip lifted his hand in an "isn't it obvious?" gesture. "Thea looks at you like you're the goddamn solution to every problem in the world, man."

She does? Aiden wanted to demand to hear more, but Trip wasn't done with his apology.

"Anyway, I'm sorry. Things at work have been... better. The guys appreciate your leadership. And honestly, I wouldn't want to do half the shit you put up with."

Aiden braved a smile. "Dealing with budgets and city permits not your dream job?"

"Nope, and neither is telling Pritchard that he can't wash his lucky hunting socks in the breakroom sink."

They both gagged at the memory of the unforgettable stench that had befouled the small room and sent every employee running for cover the previous week.

"So many challenges to running a business that I never even considered before the past two months," Aiden said mournfully.

"Better you than me," Trip said. "Anyway, Mom kicked my ass today, and she's right. We need to work together, and it's not fair for me to take my shit out on you."

A hard knot in Aiden's chest loosened at the sincerity in Trip's voice. He'd hated being at war with his brother. "Thanks. And I'm sorry too for ever implying that you were jealous that I was single." He forced himself to face a terrifying truth. "I'm actually a little jealous of you. You and Ash."

When Aiden looked over at his brother, he expected to see surprise on his face, but instead he saw a kind of speculative understanding.

And instead of letting his brother ask whatever question was brewing, he hit him with one of his own. "So, uh, what kind of things would Ash like to do, exactly?"

Trip groaned and tossed up his arms, almost knocking the truck's rearview mirror askew with his flailing. "I don't know! I have no idea. I thought about suggesting a cooking class or some shit, but I don't know if that's what she had in mind."

"If it helps, I'd never do a cooking class." Then he reconsidered. "Actually, that sounds like something Thea would want to do, so I guess I might." His next words were the best peace offering he could come up with. "Maybe we could double-date sometime? Cooking night with the Murdoch boys and their ladies?"

Trip lifted one shoulder. "Could be all right."

When he glanced over, Trip's lips were pulled into another small smile, so he was getting this right at least. Of course, he still had one problem. "I kind of blew Thea off all week."

"Dude." Trip sounded actually outraged. "Why?"

"We... well. Last weekend we finally, you know..."

Trip's mouth dropped. "You've been not-dating her for two months, and you guys hadn't boned yet?"

Talking about this felt disrespectful to Thea, yet he opened his mouth and said, "Correct. And it was great, man. It was fucking great. And I don't know what to do now."

"What do you mean, 'what to do now'?"

Aiden took one hand off the steering wheel to gesture helplessly. "How do you relationship people do it?"

"Do *what*?"

Trip sounded downright amused, so Aiden asked the question that had been rolling around his brain.

"Before, did you say Thea looks at me like...?"

"Like you're a fried pork tenderloin she wants to rip into." Trip tilted his head to study him. "Actually, no. Like you're the secret recipe for fried pork tenderloin that she covets and wants to keep for herself."

Huh. He'd never been so flattered to be compared to a greasy piece of meat before. Trip wasn't done though. "That's another reason I was pissed. Thea's nice. She doesn't deserve whatever you end up doing to her."

His stomach dropped. "She really doesn't." That was another thing the brothers agreed on, and didn't that make him feel like shit.

Then Trip said something so profound that it smacked him in the forehead like a two-by-four. "So don't."

"Don't?"

"Don't do it," his brother said. "Don't just fuck her and leave. Stick around. Be in a relationship."

A sharp wave of yearning hit him, but it was overlaid with an equally sharp pulse of fear. "How?" The question clawed its way out of his throat. "How could somebody like me make that work?"

This time when Trip laughed, there was no meanness to it at all. "If you're asking that question, you're probably on the right track." Then he mercifully changed the subject. "So I guess we'd better start making some plans for the business. Your favorite thing, huh?"

"I do love a plan," he agreed, but as they hashed out the distribution of responsibilities on the final hour of the drive, Aiden's mind refused to fully let go of thoughts of Thea. And after he dropped Trip off at his place, he didn't point his truck toward his empty house. Instead, he drove straight toward the person who was starting to feel more and more like home to him with every passing day.

TWENTY-TWO

The sound of the doorbell startled Thea enough that she jumped and smacked her head on the underside of the kitchen cabinet where she was organizing her serving bowls.

"This better not be another surprise Peter visit," she grumbled to Blue as she headed to the hobbit door, rubbing the tender spot at her hairline.

The sight that greeted her was far nicer than her step-dad: Aiden, one shoulder propped against the doorframe and an unfairly gorgeous smile on his face.

"Hi, killer."

Her arm fell to her side as Blue rushed up to dance around his feet with happy barks. "H-hi." How silly to lose her breath at the sight of him. She'd kissed every angle of his face, had run her tongue along the edge of that jaw. But seeing him rumpled and tired on her doorstep made her lungs tighten and her heart squeeze.

His brow creased when he noticed her forehead. "What happened?"

He stepped inside and nudged the door shut behind

him, wrapping one hand around her neck and smoothing the other over the emerging bump.

"Oh, um, kitchen accident. It's nothing." He needed to stop touching her. She couldn't think when he was touching her.

"It's not nothing." He steered her toward the kitchen, Blue's little paws padding across the newly finished floors in their wake.

"Yeah, sure, come on in." She didn't care that she sounded peevish. He'd disappeared this week and treated her like a virtual stranger when she'd talked to him at his office, and now here he was dropping ice cubes into a towel. *Her* ice cubes and *her* towel. She snatched the bundle from him, eyes narrowed the whole time. "Why are you here?"

Her testiness earned her a small smile. "I missed you."

If anything, the words rankled her even more. "It's not like you didn't know where to find me." She dropped the ice towel on the counter and resumed her cabinet-organization project, turning her back to her visitor.

"I know. It was hard to stay away."

That quiet confession held no hint of his previous teasing vibe, and she spun to face him. "Then why—"

"Because I wanted to be here so badly, and I didn't know how to deal with that." His voice was raw as he paced across the kitchen to stand in front of her. "Thank God, Trip talked some sense into me."

He kept moving closer until their bodies brushed, and when he gripped the counter on either side of her hips, she was caged by his arms. She should shove him away, should kick him right the hell of out her house. Instead, she couldn't tear her eyes away from his mouth.

"Okay. So you're here now." Her voice was thready

and low, in stark contrast to the frantic beating of her heart.

"Yep."

And then he kissed her. No warning, no finesse. Just the press of his lips and the slide of his tongue and his hands gripping her waist to lift her onto the countertop.

Immediate. Arousal. All it took was hearing one word and being bodily placed onto a hard surface, and her irritation fled. In its place was a wet heat blooming between her thighs and a tightening of her nipples against her shirt.

Her legs fell open, and Aiden slid his hands down to her hips, tightening his fingers to pull her forward until she was grinding against him.

His big hand moved to the nape of her neck, and he held her in place as he spoke. "I don't want just one weekend." He breathed the words into her ear as his lips worked their way from her jaw to her throat.

"But"—she gasped when his thumbs found the tips of her breasts and rubbed across her aching nipples—"that's not in the agreement."

"Fuck the agreement." He growled and lifted her from the countertop, and she obediently wrapped her legs around his waist. "That okay?"

"*So* okay." And she kissed him and kissed him as he navigated through her house and tumbled them both onto one of the loungers in the sunroom, now washed blue in the twilight.

"I just want to kiss you like this for hours."

He cupped her cheeks and tried to pull her face down to his, but she resisted, instead sliding down his body until she was positioned between his legs.

"Are you sure that's what you want?" Her finger

traced up and down the zipper of his jeans, and she was gratified to feel his cock jump underneath her light touch.

"I want whatever you want." His voice was pure gravel. "But I owe *you* the apology."

"You absolutely do." She yanked the button free, and he lifted his hips so she could push the denim down. "Better start talking."

His eyes followed her hands as they moved down his stomach to wrap around his cock. She stroked her tongue along the underside, base to tip, and he gave a hissed "Fuck."

"That"—she smirked up at him—"was not an apology."

His hips twitched forward, then he jerked again when she repeated the motion along the top of his cock. She reveled in the power she had to command his whole body with these small, soft touches.

"I'm sorry I disappeared," he gritted out. "I won't do it again."

"Mmm-hmm." She rewarded him with another long lick, but this time she ended it by swirling her tongue at the top while she curled her fingers around the base and squeezed.

He groaned, and the back of his head hit the cushion of the chair. "I'm sorry you felt neglected." His words emerged through clenched teeth. "I'll make it up to you."

"You absolutely will."

This time she took his full length into her mouth and lost herself in the sensations: the loose grip of his hands in her hair. The slide and retreat of his cock between her lips. The hollowing of her cheeks and the flutter of her tongue. The pulse between her legs that ached to be filled by him.

She glanced up and found his eyes closed, the tendons in his neck taut, and for a moment the hurt of the past week roared back. Was he with *her*, or was he in his own world where she was just another hookup, some anonymous woman in the lineup?

But almost as if he'd heard her thoughts, his eyes opened, and his bright gaze found hers. "Killer."

He breathed that ridiculous nickname with so much affection, with so much warmth in those hazel eyes, that for a moment she lost the rhythm of her hand and her tongue as she worked him. He took the opportunity to grab her shoulders and haul her up his body. His arms crushed her against him, and he thrust his tongue into her mouth, the delicious invasion mimicking what she was desperate to have him do to the rest of her.

"Clothes off," he murmured, pulling her shirt up and over her head.

Within half a minute, they were both naked and he'd produced a condom from his wallet. Without a word, Aiden spun her so her back was to his front, and he guided her down to straddle him until she was impaled on the full length of him as they both faced the silent river beyond.

She whimpered at the rightness of being so full of him, surrounded by him. Night had fallen, and the room was bathed in silvery light. She was the princess in her castle, and he was her glimmering prince, once remote and untouchable as the moon outside but now alive and responsive as quicksilver under her fingers.

She braced herself on the arms of the lounger and rocked against him as his clever fingers roamed over her front, brushing her nipples, circling her clit, stroking and teasing, pinching and soothing. He chanted her name as if it was something sacred, and her breath came in pants as her pleasure built and built. She circled her hips, the motion becoming jerky and uncoordinated when his fingers moved exactly where she needed them on her breast, between her legs. When his teeth grazed the back of her neck, the lightning bolt of her orgasm raced through her. After the spasms passed, he pulled her tight so her shoulder blades pressed against his chest, and she tipped her head backward to meet his mouth in a kiss as his thrusts quickened and he followed her over the precipice.

For a few long minutes, the only sound was the night-time chirps and whirs of the insects behind the window and their breaths winding down into relaxed drowsiness.

"Am I forgiven?"

She felt the words vibrate under his rib cage almost as much as she heard them emerge from his lips, and she turned her head to nuzzle into his neck. "I forgave you back in the kitchen."

"Scammer." He pinched her nipple lightly, and she shivered. "Let's head upstairs so I can keep apologizing."

THE NEXT MORNING, Thea woke up all tangled in Aiden. It was an experience she'd recommend to anyone —if she were willing to share him, which she definitely wasn't. She allowed herself the luxury of watching his relaxed face until he slowly stirred into wakefulness under her gaze.

He blinked as his eyes focused on her, then smiled drowsily. "Imagine if we were waking up under a skylight."

The words in his rough morning voice made her laugh. "You and your skylight obsession." She slid an arm around his waist and propped her chin on his chest so she could look up at him. "Want to tell me about yesterday?"

She held her breath, not sure if he'd share with her after he'd slammed a metaphorical door in her face earlier in the week. But to her delight, he spilled every detail of his trip: his dad's progress, his mom's tentative foray into big-city living, their decision to retire, even his brotherly reckoning.

"So I guess I'd better find us a good cooking class," she said when he was done.

"Yep. You'll like Ashley. Her only real flaw is marrying my brother."

She giggled and smacked his chest lightly. "So the other stuff you said yesterday. About the agreement."

"What would you say if we just... kept doing this?" He rolled to his side and smiled down at her. His hair was sleep-tousled, and stubble covered his jaw. He'd never looked more perfect.

"Me. Sleeping with *Aiden freaking Murdoch* on a regular basis." She tried the sentence on for size, but her words made him close his eyes in a wince.

"You know I'm just me, right? This whole persona you have in your head isn't actually a thing."

She tilted her head and smiled pityingly at him, amused that he didn't see himself the way she saw him. "Handsome? Check. Charismatic? Check. Sex god? Check. Nice and funny and supportive and good with dogs? All the checks."

A flush appeared on his cheekbones, and he brushed a thumb along the curve of her cheek. "Well, that explains some things I guess, because I'm sleeping with *Thea freaking Blackwell* on a regular basis. Cheerful? Check. Smart? Check. Competent and creative? Check. The sexiest woman I've ever been with and also very good with dogs? All the checks."

Did he really see her that way? After years of girl-next-door invisibility? Now she was the one blushing—and the one about to deliver bad news.

"Unfortunately, Thea freaking Blackwell needs to get dressed and head out. I promised Dave I'd come over and meet the new baby today." She sat up, feeling only a little self-conscious that she was naked with the sheet pooled in her lap. "Do you... maybe want to come along?"

"Sure," he said easily. "I need to pay homage to the child myself."

After a quick round of showers and coffee, Thea insisted they stop at a party store to pick up a dozen pink and white helium balloons to go along with the gifts she'd assembled, and then they were headed to the Chiltons' house.

"Are you much of a baby guy?" she asked as they drove.

"I have zero experience with babies." He drummed out a quick rhythm on the steering wheel. "You?"

"I appreciate babies, but they also make me nervous." When Belly was born, Peter had made it clear that he wasn't comfortable with Thea holding her new little sister, and she'd internalized that distrust. But oh, she loved babies' bright eyes and grasping fingers and impossibly soft skin. She smoothed her sweaty palms down the front of her dress and bit back a sigh at yet another example of her messed-up fear/longing response.

When they arrived at the Chilton house, he jumped out first and walked to her side to help her navigate the big step-down from the cab in her strappy sandals, and her heart throbbed at his thoughtfulness. She grabbed the huge gift bag from behind the seat, then shoved the bundle of balloons into his fist.

"I'd better not float away like the house from *Up*," he warned as they walked up the porch steps.

"I'd pay to see that."

They stood side by side before the front door, but neither made a move to knock.

"Are we supposed to ring the doorbell, or will that wake the baby?" she whispered.

He shrugged. "Newborn etiquette is a mystery to me."

"We're a terrible pair," she said with a laugh.

"Nah. We're a great team." He slid an arm around her waist, and something warm ignited in her chest when he grinned down at her. "You've got my back, and I've got yours. If things get pukey in there, we bail."

"Deal." She smiled back, overwhelmed at the idea that they'd become a team. But before she could analyze the big scary swirl of emotions the idea generated, Dave solved the knock/don't knock dilemma by throwing open the front door.

"Friends! Come on in." He looked exhausted and elated at the same time, and his Ramones T-shirt was covered in a number of mysterious stains. "Lucille just woke up from her nap."

They followed him inside, and it was immediately clear that although this was her first visit to the house, Aiden was a frequent visitor.

He tied the balloons to the staircase banister and wobbled one of the rungs on the railing. "I still need to fix this."

He spoke more to himself than to Dave, whose lids had drifted shut as he leaned against the wall in the hallway, yet the father of three immediately jostled into motion and said, "Sure." Thea couldn't tell if it was a response to what Aiden had just said, but Dave pushed his fingers under his glasses to rub his bloodshot eyes and said again, "Sure."

"Okay, buddy. Let's meet the kid." Aiden took Dave by the shoulders and steered him down the hall toward the family room, where a glowing Ana cradled a tiny scrap of humanity in her lap and the two other Chilton kids were busy pelting each other with Legos.

"Hi, guys!" Ana spoke softly, her hand cupping the baby's head. "This is Lucille."

Thea walked directly over to the baby, who was almost too small for her to contemplate. "She's beautiful!" She reached out a tentative finger and stroked it along the baby's soft cheek.

"She really is." Ana looked down at her daughter with such focused love that Thea might as well have ceased to exist for a moment. Then her friend looked up and offered her a tired, radiant smile. "It's good to see you. And *him*." She nodded meaningfully to where Aiden was crouched to examine the Lego structure that Zeke and Dara were building. "Who knew he had it in him?"

"Right?" she said. "I almost hate to disturb them, but I brought gifts."

At the word *gift*, two pairs of kiddie ears perked up, and they abandoned their plastic bricks to crowd around her. She handed over two wrapped packages, and the pair whooped as they opened their oversized sketchpads and marker sets.

"Okay, you two," Dave ordered. "Let's keep it quiet for your new sister."

He and Aiden herded the two oldest kids out of the room, leaving Thea with a big wrapped box of ruffle-butt baby clothes for the newborn. Ana patted a spot on the couch next to her.

"To be clear, I wasn't surprised to see Aiden talking to the kids; he does that all the time when he's here. I was surprised to see you two *together*." She cocked her head. "Funny that the guy with a different blonde every night settled down with a brunette."

"Heh, yeah." Thea shifted uncomfortably on the couch, both at the lie she was perpetuating with Ana and at the idea of Aiden gravitating back toward blondes again soon. "What a contrast, huh?"

"Oh. I didn't mean it like that." Ana rubbed a hand across her eyes. "Sorry, nuance escapes me when I'm only sleeping three hours at a time. What I mean is, I'm glad he realized what a catch you are."

Thea's lips started to shape a hasty denial, but she bit it back. Ana and Dave weren't in the loop on their arrangement, but at this point Thea herself wasn't quite sure what their arrangement looked like anymore.

While she was sorting through her confusing thoughts, Ana changed the subject. "How's the station doing while Dave's on paternity leave?"

From one unpleasant subject to another. "Fine. Mabel's a good solo host, but the station's kind of boring without Dave around."

The station was kind of boring, period. Not for the deejays of course; *their* jobs were dynamic and engaging. And the ad reps had endless meetings and copywriting tasks that always seemed fun. But answering the phones for people doing far more interesting things was definitely not her idea of exciting. Then again, she was a lady with a mortgage now, so she couldn't exactly go hopping from job to job. Her professional future stretched in front of her as one long slog of taking messages and watching other people do cool things.

"Would you mind?" Ana deposited the newborn into Thea's arms and stood. "I want to get a fresh bottle started."

"Um. Okay?" She nervously cradled the breakable little human in her arms, looking around the empty room for help. But it was just her and the kid. "Let's just be cool till they're back, little Lucille. Don't choke or cry or anything, all right?"

The baby blinked up at her, and Thea tentatively rocked her back and forth a fraction of an inch in each direction, holding her breath the whole time.

"Such a natural."

The gently amused voice pulled her attention away from Lucille's round little-old-man face. Aiden leaned against the doorway, watching her with a lopsided smile. Then he strolled across the room and sat down next to her, helping reposition the baby into a more comfortable position in her arms. Once that was done, he brushed his fingers over the downy black hair on top of Lucille's head with such gentleness that Thea's ovaries vibrated.

"I thought you didn't do babies," she said quietly.

"Don't have much experience," he said in an equally soft tone. "Didn't say I don't appreciate them."

Oh no. Aiden Murdoch liked *babies*. How was she supposed to survive this? It was enough to give a girl ideas, even if that girl had no interest in long-term relationships. But watching him with a baby, knowing that he preferred to eat his pizza crust first, recalling how his breath caught in his throat right before he came, it was too much intimacy for this fake/not-fake relationship. Things could spiral out of control if she didn't keep reminding herself that they had a mutually agreed-upon breakup looming just down the road and he had his player ways to get back to.

As Thea was being bombarded by inconvenient musings about the man on the couch next to her, Lucille proved that she'd inherited her father's comedic timing by widening her big dark eyes, opening her rosebud mouth, and spewing a thin white trickle of vomit all over Thea's hands and dress.

"Aggh!" she cried as Aiden threw back his head in laughter.

"What happened to teamwork?" she hissed.

His only answer was to pluck Lucille from her hands. He gingerly slung the baby over his shoulder. "I got this now that she's all puked out. You go ahead and—"

Then his eyes widened as another stream of vomit poured from the baby's mouth down his back, and now Thea was the one doubled over and laughing.

"Teamwork!" she wheezed.

When Ana returned with a bottle, Aiden swiftly handed over the baby, and they said goodbye to the Chiltons a short time later, leaving in a much stickier state than when they'd arrived.

"Looks like we both have some laundry to do," she said.

"Yep." He twisted to check out the damage to the back of his shirt as they headed to his truck. "I should probably head home since I'm technically still wearing yesterday's clothes."

"Mmmkay," she said as neutrally as possible.

"Or..." He held open the passenger door and gave her a boost.

"Or?" Her pulse picked up.

"Or we swing by my house so I can get a change of clothes, and I finish painting your bedroom while you lounge around naked and shout encouraging words."

She pretended to think about it. "Is this just a trick to get me to wash your clothes?"

"Obviously. I'm using you for laundry service."

She shrugged. "As long as we're on the same page. Let's do it."

TWENTY-THREE

"Okay, I'll admit it. I was wrong."

Aiden leaned forward and cupped a hand around his ear. "I'm sorry, what was that? I couldn't quite hear you over the gentle lapping of the water."

Thea scooted closer to him on the bench seat of Trip's boat to poke Aiden in the ribs. "I was wrong! Boating is *incredible*."

It was the Sunday of Memorial Day weekend and three weeks since he and Trip had made peace on the way back from Chicago and he and Thea had agreed to be an "us." He and Trip were getting along better than they had in months as they collaborated on new systems at the office, and the work on Thea's house was essentially done. Life was good, particularly with Thea sitting next to him, vibrant and laughing and thoroughly kissable.

He captured her hand and brought it to his mouth, nipping at the tip of her finger. "No, *you're* incredible."

She just laughed him off, but he meant every word. She was fucking phenomenal, reclined against the boat railing in nothing but cutoffs and a yellow polka-dot bikini top, aviator shades hiding her eyes, and her dark hair whipping around her face in the late May breeze. She turned and laughed at something Ashley said as Trip steered *the Hammerhead* in a lazy loop around the Illinois River.

"Hey, watch it!" she called up to Trip. "If you don't snorkel to the narwhal side, your starboard port's gonna mess up the rigging!"

His brother burst into a loud guffaw, and Aiden draped an arm around her shoulder. "I don't know how a woman as good at everything as you are is so bad at nautical terms."

She leaned back with her elbow on the railing. "I can't be good at *everything*."

"Bullshit!" Trip said good-naturedly. "Did Aiden tell you that Gil McConnell's hiring us to redo his bathroom?"

"For real? That's so great!" Then she tapped a finger to her chin. "But I do believe I was promised a finder's fee..."

Aiden hauled her onto his lap and kissed her thoroughly, loving the sun on his back and Thea snuggled against his front. And he loved it even more when she murmured against his lips, "Sorry, I accept cash only."

When they hit a wide section of the river a few miles outside of Beaucoeur, Trip killed the motor on his Catalina 34 and moved away from the helm to sit next to Ashley.

"Um, don't you need to, like, steer?" Thea asked nervously.

"Nah," Trip said. "If we had the sails out, the wind today might carry us all the way to Chicago before we could stop it, but without them we'll just drift. I'll flip on the motor if we get too far off course."

Ash draped her legs over her husband's lap. "This is a time-honored tradition. Find a wide part of the river, float along, and make out."

"*Don't make a boat-orgy joke, don't make a boat-orgy joke, don't make a boat-orgy joke*," Thea intoned under her breath to laughter all around.

"No, boat orgies happen on Thursdays," Trip said.

Thea threw back her head with a delighted snort, and in that moment, all the pieces of Aiden's heart snapped into place. Things at work were humming, his brother was making jokes, and Ashley and Thea had spent most of the afternoon chattering away like old friends. His fake girlfriend was apparently the glue he'd been needing to fit all these bits of his life together.

Now if he could just convince her to remove the "fake" part from her title. He'd been trying to show her how good a life together could be, and he hoped like hell the blissed-out expression on her face meant she was feeling it too.

"Okay, what's it gonna take to get you to come work with us?" Trip asked.

"These guys could use the help." Ashley looked up from the cooler, where she was rooting around for her preferred flavor of seltzer water. "I heard all about how amazing you were at the home show too."

Thea's laugh mingled with the warm May air to brush across Aiden's skin. "You're far too nice. I didn't do anything anybody else couldn't have done."

"Not true. You're great with customers," Aiden said.

"And you're a hell of a lot better than I am on the

phones," Trip added, but she just waved away their praise.

"You guys want somebody who'll stick around for the long haul, and that's not me."

The words echoed in Aiden's head—*that's not me*—as Thea turned her attention to Ashley. "You're a teacher, right?"

"Third grade. Buncha cute monsters." She snuggled against Trip's arm, a La Croix in one hand and a cookie in the other. "They're about to head out on summer break and forget at least a quarter of what they've learned this year."

"Oh!" Thea brightened. "My best friend, Faith, runs a tutoring program that could probably help. They work with kids over the summer to fight off brain drain. I'm sure she'd put together a packet you could send home with your students for summertime learning activities."

"Yes please," Ash said immediately and tilted her head toward the cabin where they'd stashed their phones. "Shall we go exchange some info? And when we do, can you also give me the recipe for those divine cookies?"

"Absolutely," Thea said as they disappeared belowdecks. "Dark chocolate and dried mango's a powerful combination."

Once the women's voices faded, the only sound was the slap of the water against the hull of the boat and the pounding of Aiden's heart in his ears. Surely Thea was making light of her checkered work history and not obliquely warning him about the shelf life of their relationship.

"When's the last time we were out on the water like this?"

At Trip's question, he shook off the frisson of unease gripping him. "Gotta be at least two summers ago, right?"

"At least." Trip ran his eyes over the grassy riverbank at the edge of the water. "We should make this a regular thing."

"We should."

"Oh, I checked out the website for that project-management software. Seems like not the worst idea. Thea's, I assume?"

Aiden laughed. "How'd you know?"

"Because I'm starting to think she *only* has good ideas." He lowered his voice. "Seriously, how can we get her to come work for us? She's exactly who we need to replace Mom."

"I'm not sure we can." The unease returned, and it must've shown in his expression because Trip's face darkened.

"Wait, you're not thinking of dumping her or some bullshit?"

"No!" Aiden's gaze zeroed in on his girl, laughing as she emerged from the cabin into the sunlight. "If anything, the opposite. But you heard her just now. I don't know how to make her stay."

"Be honest with her," Trip said, reaching for another cookie. "Lock that shit down, man. These chocolate mango thingies are the bomb."

Hours later, Trip docked the boat and they all piled off in a laughing group. Thea's face glowed pink from the sun, and her hair was a gorgeous tangle around her shoulders. She'd never looked more beautiful.

"This was so much fun! Thank you both!" she shouted at Trip and Ashley as they went their separate ways in the marina parking lot. Once they were in his truck, she saluted. "Where to now, commodore?"

He responded with his list of priorities for the rest of the night: "Your place. A shower. Some solid food. Sex until neither of us can move. And tomorrow after Belly's graduation party, I'll tackle the roses in the front yard."

Thea chirped, "Aye, aye," and that *this is so right* feeling surged in his heart again. Lee Blackwell had taught him how to care for roses, and now he'd use those lessons to tame the bushes the man had planted at the house that now belonged to his daughter. Aiden could barely put the immensity of that into words.

When they reached her house and headed inside hand in hand, he took in all the work they'd accomplished since her move in March. Exterior grout redone. Gutters cleaned and resecured. Gleaming, refinished wooden floors and walls stripped of their ugly paper and painted with warm neutrals that embraced her cozy furniture. Gorgeous modern kitchen. Non-life-threatening balcony. He'd helped her make this house a home, and to his shock, the only thing in the world he wanted was to have a permanent place in it.

"Shower first or eat first?" She started to head toward the kitchen, but he snagged her wrist and pulled her back to him.

"Sex first." He nipped her ear.

She shivered—*fuck*, he loved the way he could make her shiver—and lifted her arms to run her fingers through his hair. "I'm baked to a crisp."

"Not a problem from where I'm standing." He tilted his head, reveling in the scratch of her nails along his scalp.

Her fingers moved down the front of his shirt,

undoing each button she encountered until she slid it off his shoulders. "You're pretty crispy too." She pressed a kiss just below his ear. "This isn't a problem for me either."

In the end, they didn't make it out of the hallway, and he didn't even manage to get her all the way out of the bikini top that had been tormenting him all afternoon. How could he even think about stopping when she shimmied out of her cutoffs, turned to brace her hands against the wall, and looked over her shoulder at him with such blatant invitation? He was pressed against her moments later, plunging a hand into the neckline of her shirt and plucking her nipple through the stretchy swimsuit material. His other hand moved between her thighs, and he hissed when he found her already wet for him. He stroked one finger into her, then two, and she groaned and slid her hand between their bodies to creep down the front of his shorts so she could grip his dick. She squeezed and stroked him while his fingers moved over her clit and her breast, and they breathed together until he made her come and she made him come right back.

When their heartbeats had slowed afterward, he brushed her hair aside to kiss up her neck to her ear. "It's never been hotter than with you."

She tossed a wicked little smile over his shoulder. "Ditto. But now I have to let Blueprint out, and you have to feed me."

They straightened their clothes and headed into the kitchen, where she whistled for Blue to follow her into the backyard while he threw together a stack of sandwiches. They carried them upstairs to eat on the balcony after a quick trip through the shower. He stopped short when he saw that she'd added a second lounge chair.

"Expecting lots of company in the bedroom?" Of course what he was really asking was, *Is this for me?*

But she just laughed and said, "Blue needs someplace to sleep too."

As if on cue, the little dog hopped up onto the far lounger and curled into a ball. She'd filled out in the month and a half since Thea had taken her in, and her round little belly quivered as she exhaled once and immediately started snoring.

"Guess I'll just have to share yours," he said.

They snuggled side by side and fed each other bites of sandwich while they watched the fireflies start their flickering dance in the blue-black that had fallen over her yard. Her head was a heavy weight against his shoulder, and her eyes drooped lower and lower as he combed his fingers through the damp strands of her hair.

He thought she'd succumbed to sleep as easily as her dog had, but she surprised him by shifting closer to him and murmuring, "Promise that we'll actually stay friends after this ends."

His hand stilled. "Who says this is ending?"

"Mmm," she said sleepily, burrowing further into his chest. "The arrangement. The work on the house is all done."

His alarm from earlier in the day rushed back sharper than ever, but he forced his fingers back into motion. "And what if I want to change the arrangement?"

She drowsily rubbed her cheek against his chest. "Nah. You're the guy who doesn't do relationships, and I'm the girl who runs when things get serious. This was always just temporary."

"That's awfully pessimistic." The words barely escaped the tightness in his throat.

"Optimism's too scary. Better to be realistic." She tipped her head back to study him, her eyes heavy lidded. "I mean, do you love me?"

He jerked as if her words had electrified him, but before he could muster an answer, she relaxed back against him.

"Exactly. Neither of us is built for the long-term stuff." She yawned, her voice a tiny bit slurred as sleep pulled her under. "And that's why we've got an end date. Avoid the emotional fallout."

Those were the last words she spoke before her breathing evened out into the deep heaviness of sleep. Aiden, meanwhile, lay underneath her, unable to do more than wrap his arms around her and lose himself in the now-familiar scent of her hair.

What she'd said made sense. It's how he'd always lived. In any other circumstance, he'd be relieved to have exactly this kind of out. But as her warm breath feathered his neck, all he could do was stare into the darkness and think about how *not* panicked he was by her question of whether he loved her.

TWENTY-FOUR

Thea woke up in bed.

Normally that wasn't unusual, but she was almost entirely sure she'd fallen asleep on the balcony last night.

She stretched, luxuriating in the knowledge that a big strong man had apparently carried her inside and tucked her in and that this had happened at the end of one of the best days she could remember. Sailing was actually pretty great. Maybe her next job should be on a boat.

She pulled herself upright, squinting at the morning light assaulting her senses and crossing her fingers that Aiden had stayed the night and was in the kitchen getting the coffee started.

"I love you."

"Ahh!" She started at the words and swung her head to see him sitting on the chair adjacent to the bed, elbows on his knees and serious eyes fixed on her. "Sorry, what?"

"Thea, I love you." He said it again more forcefully, and her eyes darted around the room. Was this a dream? Had she not made it in from the lounge chair after all?

But no, why would her dream include a pile of bras and shoes tangled in the corner of her bedroom?

She scooted backward on the mattress until her back hit the headboard. "I don't get it."

He stood abruptly and paced in a tight circle around her bedroom. He wore only his boxer briefs, and the sight of his long, lean body was almost enough to distract her from whatever he was trying to say.

"Last night," he said. "You asked if I loved you. And I do. I *love* you, Thea."

She blinked as her sleep-groggy brain struggled to catch up. "Okay, you need to stop saying that for a second."

She rubbed her eyes with the heels of her hands, halfway expecting to wake herself up and find him gone. But when she pulled her hands away, he was still watching her with that laser-like focus.

"I want to be the guy on the second lounger with you." He moved to sit on the edge of the bed and gripped her hands.

"Sorry, I think I need coffee for this. Are you saying—"

"No more agreement. Be my girlfriend for real."

The words started pouring from his mouth faster and faster, and all she could do was press herself tighter against the headboard in an attempt to avoid the dizzying onslaught.

"Let's not end things. Come and work for us. You'd be the heart of the company. You'd keep us running the way you keep me running. I *need* you, killer."

"What? No." She blurted it out over the pounding of her heart in her chest, jerking away from his grip.

He frowned. "What do you mean, no?"

"I mean," she said, groping on the nightstand for an elastic to secure her tangled hair into a bun, "that I've been awake for five seconds and you've just dumped all this on me and I don't know what to say."

"Say yes." He reached for her hands again, but she dodged him and folded her arms over her chest.

"Say yes. Just like that." Her words dripped with skepticism.

"Yes. Just like that."

He smiled that confident Aiden smile that she usually adored, but today it felt like a trap. That smile was a snare, pulled taut and ready to tangle her up until she couldn't run away. "What am I saying yes to exactly?"

"To me." His smile dimmed as he started to notice that she wasn't falling in line with her new marching orders.

"To... what? Loving you? Working with you? Maybe even *marrying* you someday?" Her voice rose with each question, getting sharper and higher with each ludicrous suggestion.

"Yes! All of that!" He launched into motion again, and Blue trotted at his heels as he paced, her tongue lolling happily with every mincing step of her little paws. At least one woman in the room was excited by this surprise attack. "It's so simple when you think about it."

She laughed a little wildly. "You think all that is *simple?*"

"Okay, you're right." He stopped in his tracks, pressing his thumb to his temple. "I'm not a 'marry me' guy, or I didn't think I was. But"—he moved back to the edge of the bed—"that was before you."

Her brain was finally lurching fully to life, and with each passing moment, the weight of what he was saying settled heavy on her heart. What was he doing? Why was he doing this?

"No." She shook her head, wishing she could shake off his words as easily. "This was supposed to be safe. Easy."

"Easy." He repeated the word in a flat tone.

Now she was the one up and moving, pacing from the bed to the closet and back again. "This wasn't supposed to be about feelings, remember? You're the guy who doesn't do love. You're..."

"Easy." His voice hardened.

Was he taking this personally? "Come on, I don't mean it like that."

He stared at her for a long moment, and she watched the hopeful expression on his face fade. "You're no different than the rest of them. I'm just the guy you fuck."

That last word, dripping with curdled bitterness, seemed to hang in the air between them for a moment before he bent to collect his clothes from where he'd shed them the night before, and she scrambled to set him straight.

"You're obviously not just the guy I fuck. You're..." God, how to explain it? "You've been this unobtainable *idea* for so long, so you were safe for me to fantasize about. But you weren't supposed to... to *love* me."

"And you want me to apologize for that?" He was shouting now, startling her with such an out-of-character outburst.

"Yes!" she sputtered.

"Right. Because I'm *easy*."

She watched him jam his legs into his shorts and yank his shirt over his head, getting madder the whole time. He was changing the rules and expecting her to jump in with no questions asked when he knew—*he knew*—about her commitment issues and exactly why she had them.

"Come on, you weren't being choosy. I was just the person standing closest to you when you needed a fake girlfriend, and you tossed me into the middle of your life. We've never even gone on a date! This isn't love—it's convenience."

His face reddened, but he didn't contradict her, and if anyone asked, she'd blame her frustration and embarrassment for what she said next.

"I don't know why you're getting so upset. I mean, we've joked about it before, but this all *started* because you're the guy who fucks and leaves."

His chest rose and fell before he spoke again. "And I can't change?"

"I didn't ask you to!" She was yelling now too, but he'd hit her with all this when she was unprepared for it. Straight out of sleep, and he was proposing some kind of lockstep future where she'd work with him and live with him and lose herself into his life and his family and his personality, and she wouldn't do it. She *would not,* no matter how precious he'd become to her. "This whole agreement was supposed to be *easy* because you're the guy who doesn't fall in love, and you especially don't fall in love with someone like me."

"Except I did!"

"Then stop it! Because I can't be in a relationship like that. I can't hand my whole life over to some guy just because he asks me to. I was counting on you to be the one to walk away!"

She thought he'd understood that. He'd known her dad, had memories with him that she didn't share, but he would never fully understand the way her mom's gradual disappearance into Peter's shadow had shaped her childhood. Had shaped her adulthood too. And now things were spinning wildly out of control, and she wasn't sure she could call it all back.

In the end, he was the one who calmed down first, lifting his chin to look down at her with something close to pity. "Bad news, *honey bunny*, but we're already in a relationship. That may not be how it started, but it's sure as hell what's happening now no matter how much you try to deny it."

"Well, sure. It's like you've said all along, we're friends." Even as she said it, she was aware of just how short that fell of describing what he actually was to her. But any other name for him was too terrifying to contemplate. And it didn't matter anyway because he was clearly confusing lust with other feelings. "Come on, you don't *love* me. You just like having sex with me."

He shook his head angrily. "How can you say that after yesterday? That was us being together because we wanted to be together. We didn't do that for some bullshit fake relationship. There is no fake relationship anymore. It's real."

She opened her mouth to correct him, but her throat locked up and prevented her from turning into a liar. They'd blown way past "doing it for public consumption" weeks ago, and he was right. Yesterday on the boat hadn't been about anything other than spending time with the man she...

No. She didn't love him. Love was the quicksand she'd avoided her whole life. But her resolve wavered when he stepped close and curled his hands loosely around her shoulders. "I didn't expect any of this either, but here we are. I love you."

Her heart and her head might be in turmoil, but her body still responded to all that damn magnetism. He cupped her jaw, and she let herself imagine what it would be like. Making it real, *really real*, with Aiden. Loving him. Working with him. Being with him forever.

Forever. The word expanded in her head and pushed out all other thoughts.

"No. I'm sorry, but I can't." She shrugged off his hands while her heart threw itself against her ribs over and over. She was working so damn hard to clamp down on the surge of emotions threatening to choke her that her next words emerged unguarded. "Look at it this way: I'm saving you from having to let me down easy when you're ready to get back to your Adonis ways."

He reeled back as if she'd struck him, the animation draining from his face. "You know what? You're right. This was..." He swallowed convulsively, his jaw bunching. "It was a mistake to bring this up."

His voice was wooden, and a cold wave of horror moved through her. But it was too late now; he was yanking on his shoes and moving toward the door. "The work on your house is done. Things are coming together at the office. It's as good a time as any to call it quits."

His voice betrayed no emotion, and neither did his eyes, and Thea had to choke back a sob. God, what was *wrong* with her? She was protecting herself like she always did, but this time it fucking *hurt*. Their mutually beneficial arrangement had spun wildly out of control, and her insides felt scooped out and hollow.

But it was done. She'd said what she had to, and he was leaving.

"At least let me give you the number for my temp agency." She barely recognized her own voice, ragged and small, but she could be his friend one last time. "They can send you someone to fill in until you can find a permanent hire."

His quiet laugh was deeply unamused. "Thanks."

He bent and stroked his hand down Blue's little back, then straightened and looked at her once more. She held her breath, terrified that he'd say something perfect. Something that would blow through the walls she'd tossed up for both of their sakes.

Instead, he shook his head. "See ya round, killer."

And he walked out of her room.

As his steps echoed down the stairs, she sank to the floor and wrapped her arms around her knees. Blue scampered over to climb into her lap and nuzzled her face with her cold little nose. She wrapped her arms around the dog's tiny body, grateful for her warmth.

She was right about this. She knew she was. Aiden would eventually be grateful for his narrow escape from domesticity. In fact, she bet business was about to get good again for the stacked blondes of Beaucoeur. And she'd just saved herself from the pain of being trapped in a relationship that had the potential to warp her into someone she didn't want to be. It was for the best for both of them.

So why did she burst into tears when she heard the slam of the hobbit door as Aiden walked out of her life?

TWENTY-FIVE

"Remember what I told you? Find the most unpleasant man in the group and direct all your pee at him. You'll know the one."

Blue yipped once and looked up with naked adoration on her little monkey face, her frantically wagging tail whacking Thea's ankle.

"Okay," she told the dog. "Here we go." With a big exhale, she pushed through the gate of her mom and Peter's backyard and headed straight for the lady of the hour, who was holding court in the center of the partygoers.

"Happy graduation, Belly!" She hugged her half sister, who squealed and hugged her back.

Belly glanced curiously over Thea's shoulder, and of course there was no Moo Daddies drummer to be found. But Thea *was. Not. Thinking. About. That. Today.* Today was about Belly, and the wretched state of her heart would just have to wait. She just needed to fake her way through the next hour or so and then fall apart at home.

Brave face on, big smile activated. Nobody would be the wiser.

Bless her heart, Annabelle didn't say a word about Aiden's absence, instead crouching to scratch Blue's ears. "Hello, pretty girl! Don't you look fetching today?"

Blue wriggled in delight, setting her rhinestone collar jingling. "She really is the best dog," Thea said. "So how does it feel to say buh-bye to Beaucoeur High?"

"Amazing." Annabelle, taller than Thea by a head and a half, slung an arm around her shoulder as they cased the backyard. "Okay, here's the lay of the land. My high school peeps are at the food table—don't worry, Mom had it catered—and Dad and his gross coworkers are hanging out by the grill." She wrinkled her nose. "It's not even on! I will never understand what it is with men and grills."

Thea's smile vanished. She had a brand-new grill sitting in her yard, and the guy who'd bought it for her wasn't going to be coming around anymore. "Yeah. Heh. Men and meat," she said weakly.

The new graduate didn't even notice her strained tone. "Anyway, the gift table's there, Mom's gossiping with the aunts inside, and most importantly, there's the drink station." She concluded by pointing one black-and-red manicured nail at a little bar cart tucked against the side of the house.

"Then that's where I shall be." Drink to forget, right? If so, she'd better start *right now*. "By the way, please tell me you're gonna ditch this shindig and spend at least part of tonight doing something outrageous with your friends."

"Pssht, of course. When I give the signal, execute Operation Distract Mom."

They exchanged the complicated fist-bump hand-shake they'd perfected when Belly was still using training wheels, and Thea couldn't help but smile as she crossed the yard to pour herself a glass of merlot. Peter was a pain in the ass, but she did love his daughter with all her heart.

Wine in one hand and Blue's leash in the other, she began making the rounds. Her eyes still throbbed from the tears she'd shed that morning, but she'd compensated with dramatic eyeliner and bright red lips. Hopefully nobody would notice the misery following her like a shadow. She stopped first at the gift table to deposit a wrapped box containing the high-end backpack Belly'd been coveting for months.

Then she moved on to greet Annabelle's teachers over the cheese tray, followed by the pack of tall girls her sister had played varsity volleyball with as they devoured a mound of pigs in a blanket. Every single one of the lanky eighteen-year-olds had uniformly straight, glossy hair and healthy, glowing skin. She had a decade more life experience than all of them, and she was being thoroughly shown up in the beauty department. If Aiden were here, he'd tease her about her inferiority complex—

Shit. No. Aiden wasn't here. She'd gotten exactly what she asked for that morning when she'd made it clear he had zero place in her life. She and Blue were flying solo, and it was *miserable*. But she forged onward, chatting with cousins, neighbors, and a big-eared, broad-smiling fellow graduate she suspected was more than a little head over heels for her sis. Good luck to them both.

After twenty minutes, she hit the *screw it* point and turned to brave Peter and his guffawing posse of fellow white male insurance agents. Not like the day could get worse, right? She crossed to the all-male cluster—still gathered around the massive silver grill—and greeted her stepdad with a perfunctory kiss on the cheek.

"Hi." She kept it short and waited for him to rain down hell about the fact that she was there without her boyfriend.

Instead, he surprised her by saying, "Good to see you. Fellas, this is my stepdaughter Thea. She works for the Brick radio station."

"Hello, gentlemen! What's new in insurance?" she said brightly to the half dozen ruddy-faced polo shirt wearers surrounding her. She'd mastered the art of doe-eyed obsequiousness over the course of her many jobs, and she knew this crowd would eat it up like she was driving a golf cart full of imported beer into their midst. "Isn't everyone so excited for Annabelle? She's going to love Northwestern."

"Hope so." Peter used a red-and-black HAPPY GRADUATION napkin to mop at his sweaty forehead. "It's going to cost us enough."

The men all nodded and harrumphed about tuition and highway robbery and student loans, leaving Thea free to glance down at Blue. *Now, girl. Do your dirty, sinful business on Peter's stupid tassel shoes.* That little bit of petty revenge might be the only bright spot in her weekend. But Blue just rolled to her back and waved her paws in the air in a blatant invitation for a belly rub. All the men ignored her friendly overture, the monsters, so Thea bent to do the honors.

"Gonna have to hold off on getting that boat, huh Pete?" one of the men asked.

Peter clapped a hand over his heart. "Bite your tongue. That Cat 34's got my name on it."

Thea glanced up sharply. "Oh! I was just out on a Cat 34 with my... friends."

The men all turned surprised faces to her, and as she stood, she dug through the recesses of her brain to recall any factoids Trip had offered about *the Hammerhead* the day before. "Its motor will absolutely get you where you need to go, but on a breezy afternoon, you won't find any better mode of transportation than those big, beautiful sails."

Although the memory brought nothing but pain, she offered the group a toothy smile and breathed a silent sigh of relief when they all muttered their approval of her sailing prowess. Peter's surprised gaze rested on her for a long moment, and she braced for some cutting comment about her getting her boat lingo all wrong.

But he just raised his beer bottle in salute. "I was in your neighborhood the other day. House is looking good."

She mustered a smile. "Thanks. I'd love to have you and Mom for dinner sometime soon."

"Let's schedule something," he said. "Landscaping could use some work though. Need the number of our gardener?"

Just like that, her equilibrium vanished, and she cut the conversation short and handed Blue off to Annabelle for a spot of sisterly dog-sitting so she could escape for a few minutes. She skirted the kitchen, where the family matriarchy was gathered to dissect the latest gossip, and headed to her old bedroom on the second floor. It no longer had a decor aesthetic straight out of Lisa Frank's trippiest nightmare, but it still had her old twin-size bed. She kicked off her flats and flopped onto the boring beige comforter, the bed frame creaking as it had for a decade. If she closed her eyes, it was just like being back in high school. Of course, back then she'd only imagined what it would be like to get to kiss Aiden Murdoch. Now she knew: it was incredible, and only a deeply damaged person would toss it aside lightly.

She curled onto her side and pulled her knees to her chest as if that would ease the ache in her heart. If only he hadn't taken her by surprise with his declarations of love. If only he'd eased her into it, given her the chance to get used to the idea that he truly felt things for her that went past friendly affection. If only...

If only you weren't a coward.

She curled even tighter into herself and fought back a sob.

"Honey?"

Her eyes flew open at her mother's voice, and she swiped at her tears before she sat up. "Hi, Mom."

"I was hoping to catch you before you left. I've got something for you."

Carly sat at the foot of the bed, and Thea took the opportunity to tap out a quick text to Annabelle: *Mom distraction is a go if you need it.* Belly was too good a kid to actually sneak out, but it was still the sister code.

She hit Send and reached out for the framed photo her mom was holding. The tears she'd been trying to suppress hit her in force when she recognized the two people in the center of the shot. "Is this...?"

"You and your dad. You'd just turned six."

She blinked to clear her eyes and studied the father and daughter duo standing on a front porch with an explosion of greenery off to one side. Her dad was crouched with his arm around her, his T-shirt and khaki shorts coated in dirt, and her knees showed a telltale layer of topsoil too. They were both squinting into the sun and beaming with identical smiles.

"Look closer at the background," Carly said.

She looked past the two figures front and center and almost dropped the frame when she recognized the round-topped door they were posed in front of. "My house!"

"He was doing a landscape refresh when you and I stopped by to bring him lunch. You insisted on helping him with some planting. The homeowner came out to watch and said it was one of the sweetest things she'd ever seen."

Thea brushed her fingers over the glass covering her dad's broad grin as a tear tracked down her cheek. "I think I remember that day."

"I hope you do. It was a good day." Now her mom was the one barely holding back tears. "He loved that house. He used to tell me he imagined you living in one just like it someday."

"You knew about my princess house?" Thea's voice emerged thick from her throat.

"Of course. Your dad and I shared everything." Carly tipped her head back, the soft line of her jaw working as she swallowed hard. "I was looking through old photos for Annabelle's graduation announcement and stumbled across it. What are the odds, huh?"

Thea hugged the frame to her chest, almost too overcome for words. "I love it. Thank you."

Her mom patted her knee, then said the worst possible thing in the world. "Aiden's not with you today?"

Her stricken expression must have been answer enough because Carly's face fell. "Oh. I see."

"Another one bites the dust, right?" Thea didn't even

have the strength to put any heat behind it. No breakup had ever hurt like this one had.

"Honey, no. I'd never joke about that." Her lips thinned. "And Peter's not going to joke about it anymore either, not after Annabelle and I yelled at him all the way home from your new house."

"You did?" She couldn't help the little spurt of joy at the thought of those two sticking up for her.

"Of course. You've always brushed him off before, but you seemed really upset that night. So we let him have it."

Thea closed her eyes and let herself imagine that scene for a few seconds. "I'm sorry I missed that."

"And I'm sorry it didn't work out with Aiden. He was always the nicest boy."

She sighed. "He really, really is."

Silence fell over the bedroom, punctuated by the party chatter barely audible from the yard.

When her mother spoke again, her voice was halting. "I... know what you really think about my marriage to Peter."

"I doubt that very much," Thea said flatly.

"You think I was scared to be on my own, so I married the first man who came along."

Well. Maybe her mom *did* have some decent insights.

"Well, you're right. And you're wrong." Carly twisted the wedding band on her finger. "I was *terrified* to raise a daughter alone after your dad died. But then I fell in love with Peter, and yes, it was a big change for all of us, but I've never regretted marrying him."

Thea wasn't able to mask her expression quickly enough, and her mom burst out laughing. "Really! For one thing, he gave me Annabelle. And I know he's opinionated, but those opinions are almost always meant to keep the people he loves safe and healthy. And that includes you."

"His love language is tactlessness?" She and her mom laughed softly together, but then again, how often had Peter fussed at her about upgrading Juniper to a safer car? She'd always assumed it was because he was image-conscious, but maybe he'd actually been concerned about things like side airbags and crumple zones. Too bad he didn't know how to be concerned in a less abrasive way.

"Everybody shows love differently," Carly said quietly.

And like that, Thea's mind got stuck on the idea of Aiden's love language. He'd taken her by surprise that morning with an out-and-out declaration, but hadn't he been telling her what he was feeling all along? He'd yelled at her about going onto the balcony. He'd trusted her with a dog. He'd begged her to take a key role in his family company. He changed his plans for her, for God's sake, turning something fake into something very, very real. Maybe all that had been his way of saying he loved her. And if she'd cherished every one of those moments, along with countless others she'd shared with him, did that mean she'd fallen in love right back?

"You grew up to be so strong. You stand on your own two feet, and I love that about you. But there's one more thing to think about, sweetie," Carly said. "Your dad and I got married after knowing each other for three weeks."

"You did?"

Her mom nodded, a secretive little smile on her lips. "Three incredible weeks. And we just knew." She picked up the picture frame and smiled down at her husband. "There's no right way to fall in love. And yes, there's no guarantee that it'll last. But what a tragedy not to find out."

Her words knocked the breath from Thea's lungs, and Carly leaned forward to press a kiss to her daughter's forehead. "I'd better go see if Annabelle's managed to sneak out with her friends yet. See you down there."

"Yeah," Thea said faintly. "See you down there."

But she didn't leave her room right away. She stared at the twenty-three-year-old photo of her, her dad, and her princess house, and she wondered if there was any way she could undo the mistakes of the past.

TWENTY-SIX

"Look sharp, gentlemen! Soft hands on deck!"

Aiden gritted his teeth at the shouted greeting but immediately replaced it with his usual grin as he joined the three-man crew in a kitchen swathed in tarps and plastic sheeting.

"Hardly. Ladies dig calluses." He addressed the loud-mouth in the group. "Speaking of, your daughter still dating that firefighter, Mendez?"

Ben Mendez's eyes narrowed. "You stay the hell away from my little girl, desk jockey."

Aiden raised his hands—sporting his many honestly earned calluses, fuck them very much—and said innocently, "Just asking." That earned an over-the-top relieved sigh from Mendez, which he ignored as he turned to Gene Fitzsimmons. "Figured you could use a hand on the wall teardown today."

He also figured if he spent another day chained to his desk, he'd lose his mind.

Fitz merely nodded, his dour face immobile. "Plenty of sledgehammers to go around."

Leaving Mendez to chip away at the old tile with an assist from the kid they'd hired last week, he and Fitz approached the massive wall running the length of the kitchen to separate it from the living and dining rooms. He gave a low whistle. "This is it, huh?"

"Yep." Fitz didn't have to tell him how much work it would take to knock that beast down.

This time Aiden's grin was genuine. "Let's do it."

Mendez's barbs had hit home; now that he was officially running Murdoch Construction, he wasn't much more than a pencil pusher, and compared to telling yet another client about the benefits of granite counters or figuring out why the hell his phone wouldn't sync to the master calendar on their new management software, knocking down a wall was so much simpler. A safe way to channel the anger that had been dogging his heels since he'd stormed out of Thea's house two weeks ago. So he pulled on a pair of work gloves, settled safety goggles over his eyes, grabbed a hammer, and got to work.

Swing, slam, repeat. He fell into the rhythm like he was rediscovering an old friend. The brainless, brutal work was the only good part of his June so far. Even better, Fitz wasn't a talker, and even if he was, the radio was turned all the way up. Nobody was asking for an updated timetable or a delivery date or an estimated total. And thank *fuck*, nobody was hitting him with sympathetic eyes about the fact that his girlfriend wasn't coming around anymore. Instead, he swung his sledgehammer and worked out his frustration through the magic of *swing, slam, repeat* until his Murdoch Construction T-shirt clung to his sweaty chest and his back and arm muscles screamed for mercy.

"I think that'll do it," Fitz announced after a solid sixty minutes of grunting and drywall dust.

Aiden pushed his safety glasses on top of his head, absurdly pleased at the job he'd just done.

The older man turned to Aiden and clapped him on the back. "See? You're not as useless as they all say. You can still do a man's job."

From the kitchen, Mendez and the new kid chortled, and Aiden deadpanned, "My delicate hands. I think I got a splinter." Then he made a show of pulling out his phone. "Would you look at the time? I've got to get back to my pansy-ass office. Guess that leaves you guys with the cleanup."

More laughter. More backslapping. But as he stepped through the front door, Fitz followed him out and walked with him to his truck with a serious look on his leathery face.

"Just wanted to let you know you're doing a good job, son. Some of the guys were worried about the transition, but you and Trip are keeping things going."

All Aiden could manage was a single nod of his head. His dad was likely never going to be in a position to see how his sons were running the family business, but praise from the longest-serving Murdoch employee was a strong second place to that paternal approval.

The older man fell silent, and Aiden's neck tightened as he waited for whatever complaint or problem was about to roll his way. Instead, Fitz's eyes searched his face for a long moment before he said gently, "I've got a granddaughter. Nice girl. You let me know when you're ready to get back out there, yeah?"

The clearheaded bliss of destruction faded. "Thanks."

He managed a semblance of a grin. "That's... Thanks. I'll let you know."

He sure as hell wasn't ready to move on with someone else, but unexpected emotion clogged his throat at the realization that Fitz considered him a worthy potential partner for a family member. Fitz clapped him on the back with a beefy paw and headed back into the house, leaving Aiden to trudge down the driveway to his truck. Once he was safely shut away inside, he dropped his veneer of normalcy and let himself sag into the husk of depression and anger that he'd become. He'd thrown himself into work both to keep the company humming and to bury any inconvenient shock waves of pain from his wounded, limping heart, but he still dragged around most days like the broken idiot that he was.

His muscles exhausted, his heart sore, and his brain empty, he drove to Murdoch Construction on autopilot. He parked and headed into the building where a sour-faced temp greeted him when he walked past the lobby.

"Mrs. Park dropped this off for you." She waved a paint-sample card covered in sticky notes.

"Thanks. And did—"

The stony-faced brunette held up an imperious finger to silence him when the phone rang. "Murdoch Construction," she said snippily, and he didn't have the heart to stick around to hear the rest of the conversation.

From the quiet of his office, he added details to the new software about Lin and Mary Park's color choices for their master bedroom and imagined a world where the front desk was staffed by someone warm and welcoming and goofy and beautiful. Instead, they were on their second temp this month as the company rotated through the available workers, and he was going to bed alone.

This would be the perfect night to pick a woman up at a bar and get his head on straight. He could probably use a couple of nights like that, frankly, and a couple of women. But none of that appealed to him. Not the bar scene, not the empty sex, and certainly not random women. Just a few months ago, he'd worried that he'd backslide into his womanizing ways, but it turned out the cure to that was falling in love. All he wanted was Thea, who'd burst in with her noisy sunshine and shown him that his life could be bigger and more joyful than he ever imagined.

Thea, whom he hadn't heard a word from.

"Shit." The word sighed out of his lungs, and he slammed his laptop closed. What had he done with his time before Thea? Surely it had been something more fulfilling than listening to the clock in his office tick down the seconds of his interminable life.

He reached for his phone to text Daniel, but hitting the gym and working his body until he couldn't move didn't sound all that appealing, especially because his shoulder had been throbbing since the wall teardown that morning. Plus Daniel was likely to either gloat over his heartbreak or offer way too much sympathy, and neither option sounded particularly appealing.

For similar reasons, he rejected calling Trip and Ash to see if they wanted to grab dinner or seeing if he could swing by the Chilton house to keep Dave company on daddy duty. He'd be terrible company for anybody, so he might as well drag his sorry ass home the way he'd been doing all month.

Of course, nothing improved once he was parked on his couch with his feet on the coffee table. Instead, he glared around his living room, irrationally angry at the boring gray walls and copper light fixture. He'd done all the work himself, and he hated every part of it because it wasn't Thea's house. Maybe it was time to list this house and start looking for another one to flip. Anything —fuck, *anything*—to keep his hands busy and his brain occupied and his body too tired to long for Thea's touch.

He hadn't gotten any further than plopping his computer on his lap and pulling up a browser to start looking at local real estate listings when a pounding started up on his front door. He wasn't expecting anyone, but that didn't stop him from tossing his computer aside and flipping on the outdoor lights. He pulled open the door to find Faith Fox on his doorstep.

"What the hell did you do to my best friend?" She pushed past him into his house, shoving a bottle of whiskey into his chest as she stormed by.

Without missing a beat, he cracked it open, took a long pull, and asked, "What the hell did your best friend do to *me*?"

Faith whipped around and ran judgmental eyes down his body. "Clearly you broke each other. When was the last time you shaved?"

He scratched his jaw self-consciously, grimacing when his fingers rasped along several days' worth of stubble.

"And when was the last time you did something other than drink your dinner?"

He curled the whiskey into his chest, and she rolled her eyes. "Good God. Where's your kitchen?"

Feeling distinctly sulky, he pointed the way, and she charged ahead. By the time he joined her, she'd located a loaf of bread and a jar of peanut butter.

"Sit." She pointed to the kitchen island, and he did as instructed with a grumble.

"How do you even know where I live?"

"Like it was hard," she scoffed. "I know people who know people."

She slid a plate in front of him with a sandwich that she'd cut into four triangles as if he was a child. He picked up the first wedge and crammed it into his mouth, mechanically chewing and swallowing. It landed in his hollow stomach, and dammit, she'd been right. He'd spent most of the time since he'd slammed out of Thea's house at work, and when he was home, most of his self-care was of the alcohol variety.

"Thanks," he mumbled as he ate, and as soon as his sandwich was gone, she whisked away the empty plate and dumped it in his sink.

"I didn't do it for *you*." She crossed her arms over her chest and leaned against the counter to glare at him.

"Were you this mean in high school?"

"No," she snapped.

That tracked, at least. She'd been in Thea's class, but surely he'd remember a freshman girl with white-blond hair storming around the hallways and scaring the shit out of everybody.

She stared him down for a long moment, then the starch leaked out of her spine and she steepled her fingers, inhaled deeply, and spoke in a slow, patient voice. "Sorry. Okay. Let's have a conversation."

"Must we?" Now that he had a layer of food in his stomach, he reached for the whiskey again, but she moved it out of his reach and rummaged through his cabinets. She pulled down two rocks glasses etched with the Murdoch Construction logo, a companywide gift from his mom a few Christmases ago, and poured a finger for each of them.

"We can at least be civilized." She handed his drink over. "Now. Explain to me why the nicest person I know has spent the past two weeks in tears while refusing to explain why."

He brought the glass to his lips and drained the contents, but the burn in his throat didn't make the answers flow any easier.

"I had a damn plan," he finally said.

"Yeah. The fake relationship. I warned her that shit would blow up in your faces." She held up her glass in a smug salute and sipped.

"Not that plan. *That* plan went great, thank you very much." He reached for the bottle to pour another round, and when she slid it out of reach, he gestured impatiently. "You're the one who barged into my house. You want me to talk, you keep pouring."

She raised her brows but uncapped the bottle and tilted it into his glass.

"The fake relationship was great. Best relationship of my life actually." He stared down at the amber liquid. "I wanted to make it real. She didn't. The end."

"And that was your whole damn plan? 'Make it real'?"

"Well, yeah." He pushed the glass away with the liquid untouched. Whiskey wasn't going to magically fix this. "The plan was to just... stay together. We make a great team." He rolled his head from side to side to stretch out the muscles he'd strained during his wall-removal session earlier.

"*Wow.* Is that how you tried to sell it to her?"

"No. I asked her to come work with me at Murdoch Construction too. And..." Was he really going to spill everything to this person he barely knew? Then again, it wasn't like he had anything else left to lose. "I told her I love her, okay? And not only did she not say it back, but it clearly pissed her off. So yeah. That's what your best friend did to me."

If he was expecting sympathy, he'd missed the stud with his drill because Faith's eyes widened in horror. "You offered her a *permanent job*? My dude, do you even *know* her?"

"Yes," he snapped. "I know her really fucking well. Enough that I thought..."

"Thought that she loved you too." Faith's voice gentled, and she tilted her head to swallow her last mouthful of whiskey, a purr rolling through her throat as the liquid hit her tongue. A year ago, he'd have asked her to stick around for another drink to see how the night might progress. She was tall and blond and thick in all the interesting places. But even if she hadn't been Thea's best friend, the thought held no appeal for him anymore.

"She made me think I could be more than my reputation," he said softly, staring into his glass. "And the more I opened myself up to the idea, the more I realized that my parents, my brother, my friends, they all believed I could be the guy in the relationship. *I* even let myself believe it. But in the end, she didn't."

He pressed his fingers to his eyes, pushing back against the searing emptiness as he considered his life without her. Once he'd wrestled himself under control, he glanced up to find Faith watching him with a pitying expression. But the instant his eyes met hers, her jaw hardened, and she set her glass down on the polished concrete countertop with a click.

"Here's the thing. I'm not here to spill her secrets or

give you some kind of pep talk. I only came here to kick your ass if it needed kicking, but you're just... kind of pathetic actually." She swept her gaze over him, clearly confident in her ability to throw down against a guy who'd strained his rotator cuff working a sledgehammer earlier in the day. "And it sounds like you were arrogant enough that you kicked your own ass the last time the two of you talked. So I guess you and I are good."

"*Arrogant?*" He'd been a lot of things in that last conversation, but arrogant?

She looked at him incredulously. "Um, yes. Did you think declaring your love was enough to cut through twenty years of Thea's relationship aversion and abandonment fears?"

His jaw worked back and forth as he considered her words. "I assumed..."

The words died in his throat. Oh, had he assumed. He'd assumed *all over* the place. Assumed that Thea loved him back. Assumed she wanted him, wanted to *be* with him for the long term. Assumed the privilege of his company would be enough to get her over her lifelong fear of commitment. But in the end, whatever misplaced hero worship Thea had for him at the beginning of the deal hadn't matured into anything approaching the overwhelming love he felt for her. And he'd selfishly only considered the ways the relationship would make *his* life better.

"Now you're getting it." Faith set her empty glass in the sink next to his plate. "Okay then. You can keep the rest of the bottle." She turned and left the kitchen as briskly as she'd entered it fifteen minutes earlier.

"Wait!" He followed her to the door. "That's it?"

"Yeah," she said impatiently as she rooted through her

bag for her keys. "I'm not your fairy godmother. I'm not here to fix things for you." And with that, she was gone.

"You're a shitty fairy godmother," he muttered, wandering back to the kitchen. He replaced the cap on the whiskey bottle and stashed it with the rest of his liquor collection as he turned Faith's words over in his head.

He'd fallen in love with a funny, beautiful woman who made him *want*. A future, a family. A life with her. And when she didn't love him back, he'd gotten pissed at her for filling his head with those dreams. But that wasn't Thea's fault; she hadn't asked him for any of those things. She'd just been so perfect for him that the dreams grew on their own.

Thick helplessness churned in his stomach. How was he supposed to stuff those dreams away now that they'd hatched? With a sigh, he shuffled to the sink to start washing the dishes Faith had left behind. Then a thought hit him with such clarity that he almost dropped one of the etched glasses.

Faith had asked what he'd done to her best friend. Said Thea'd done nothing but cry since their breakup. Surely she wouldn't be that upset if she didn't have some sort of feelings for him too.

That was enough to keep the embers of his dream alive. He'd just have to figure out a new plan.

TWENTY-SEVEN

Thea knocked on her boss's partially open door and stuck her head in. "Hey, do you have a—"

Her words died on her lips at the sight of Brandon Lowell with his elbows on his desk and head in his hands as a furious, tinny voice poured from the cell phone in front of him. When he looked up, the expression in his sharp blue eyes was the bleakest she'd ever seen.

"What can I do for you?" he asked tiredly, smoothing down his blond hair where his fingers had left it uncharacteristically mussed.

"Yeah, um, I can come back." She started to edge out the door, but he pointed a commanding finger at the guest chair.

"No need. It's just my two-minute hate."

She dropped into the seat. "Come again?"

"Every day that I'm on the road, my father calls to let me know the many ways I've disappointed him."

"Whoa." And she thought Peter was bad.

Brandon gave a terse smile of acknowledgment. "The bad news is, it's usually longer than two minutes. The good news is, I can mute myself and multitask while he's shouting it out."

At that moment, the angry voice picked up steam, and Thea distinctly heard "fucking disappointment" and "squandering my legacy."

"That isn't even on speaker. That's just his voice." Brandon sighed. "Anyway, what can I do for you?"

"No, seriously, we don't have to do this now. It isn't—"

"Talk," he ordered over the rise and fall of the man on the phone.

Okay then. Thea pressed her hands on the top of her thighs, breathed out hard, and said, "I'm quitting." Then she burst into tears.

Brandon looked at her in silence for a beat before he unmuted his phone and cut off the tirade on the other end with a firm, "Sir, I have a meeting to get to. I'll be back at headquarters on Monday." He ended the call, stood, and pulled off his suit coat, rolling first one sleeve and then the other. "You. Me. The Elephant."

Thea dried her eyes with a tissue she fished from her purse and followed him out the door even though it was only ten a.m. on Friday and she had hours of phone-answering she was supposed to be doing. But Brandon apparently didn't care because he hustled her out the door and into his sedan for the quick drive to the Elephant. Once they were settled at the long mosaic bar, he insisted they wait until they were halfway through their first drinks before he approached anything resembling a serious conversation.

"All right." He set his old-fashioned down on the glass bar top. "What are you quitting, exactly?"

"I don't know. The station job? The Brick Babes?

Ever feeling happiness or joy ever again?" She drained the rest of her mojito in one long gulp.

He nodded and brushed a thumb over his chin. "Okay. The station's no problem. You're a great receptionist, but we can deal if today's your last day." He sipped, swallowed, continued. "The Brick Babes? Also no problem. That's a volunteer gig, and you can bail anytime. Again, we'll miss you, but I get it. As for that last bit—"

"Oh God, ignore that. Sorry." She stabbed her straw to the bottom of her glass, embarrassed beyond belief that she'd gotten emotional in front of the heir to the Lowell Consolidated media empire. Brandon's family owned more than a dozen radio stations across the country, so he probably dealt with a handful of other Theas every day who all had their own crises as they kept the wheels turning at the Paducah hot country station or the Pahrump Top 40 or whatever.

But he didn't seem terribly bothered as he gestured at Tammy the bartender, who got to work mixing a second old-fashioned. "Another mojito?"

"I shouldn't."

"You were sobbing in my office twenty minutes ago."

Thea glumly tapped her empty glass on top of the bar, and Tammy tossed her long braid over her shoulder. "I gotcha, doll."

After their alcohol had been replenished, Brandon swiveled on his stool to face her. "Have you ever noticed that I visit the Beaucoeur station pretty frequently?"

"Of course," she said immediately. "Mabel complains about it all the time."

That pulled a smile from him. "Ever wonder why?"

"I assume it has something to do with your terrible dad." She raised a brow and met his eyes levelly. Last month she'd have flushed and apologized, but the part of her that worried about what other people thought of her seemed to have withered and blown away when Aiden left.

To his credit, Brandon simply raised a brow of his own and saluted her with his glass. "My terrible dad is why I drink and why I'm divorced and why I haven't seen my dog in three months." His eyes went unfocused for a second, then returned to hers. "But that raging narcissistic asshole actually isn't the reason I'm a frequent flyer into the Beaucoeur Regional Airport. I hit this station about twice a month, which is roughly twice the number of visits I pay to most of our other properties in a given year."

Thea nodded as she listened, unsure where he was headed but happy to hear him out since he seemed to want to talk and she was definitely in the market for a distraction.

"The Brick was my first solo station acquisition. I feel responsible for its success in a way that I don't with the others. It's something I'm helping build, and I like being part of that." He sipped his drink, then added, "Plus Mabel's hate keeps me strong."

She almost sprayed a mouthful of mojito across the bar. "Don't let her hear you say that."

He just waved an airy hand. "Please. She thrives on having a nemesis. Anyway, you're a woman with good ideas. Your PDF forms for one, even though Lowell Senior doesn't want to make any dramatic changes this year." He rolled his eyes, sipped his drink, and continued. "And don't think I don't know how you've been slowly reorganizing the supply closets to be more efficient despite Lowell HR frowning on unauthorized actions like that. You get shut down left and right because of bureaucracy, and every time I can sense you vibrating in irritation from eight hours away. You're somebody who needs autonomy and variety on the job, I think, and the Brick doesn't give you that."

"How did you…?"

"I'm a people person." He glanced over at Tammy and winked, and although his bored rich-kid affect and icy frat-boy beauty were out in full force, the seen-it-all bartender merely rolled her eyes.

"Best not let my wife catch you flirting," Tammy said coolly. "Joanne's a jealous woman."

"Flirting rescinded," he said with an easy grin before turning back to Thea. "Anyway yes, chase your professional dreams, wherever they lead you. With my blessing, not that you need it."

"Thanks," she said drily. As if it were that easy.

"So where are you headed next?"

She poked at the mint in her glass, the sharp scent tickling her nose but providing zero clarity. "I don't know."

"You're quitting without another job lined up? In *this* economy?"

She shot him a faint smile and then just… blurted out everything. "I had a job offer two weeks ago from the guy I was pretending to date so he could smooth out some problems at work and I could buy my dream house, but he went and fell in love with me and I basically pelted him with rocks until he ran off, and I've regretted it every day since because I love him too but was in no way prepared to say it back to him at the time. So I don't *think* I have a job waiting for me, but I do know that I can't keep doing what I'm doing at the Brick because my soul is slowly dying. No offense."

Brandon's eyes had gotten wider as she spoke, and when she fell silent, he gave a low whistle. "Gotta be honest, you're much more interesting than I gave you credit for." He cocked his head and studied her face. "You said you're in love with the guy?"

She nodded miserably, and he shrugged.

"Too bad. Then again, you technically *are* still my employee."

"Wait, are you...?" But he was already moving on before she could suss out if he was hitting on her or not.

"Do you want the job your guy offered?"

"I do. I think I'd really love it actually." Public interaction. Problem solving. Projects. Advice. Organization. And best of all, the freedom to make it all her own.

"Okay, then go get it."

She snorted. "And how am I going to do that exactly? I haven't talked to Aiden in two weeks. I'm not sure he'd take my call even if I tried."

"Two words." Brandon leaned close. "Assumptive close."

He spoke as if that answered everything, but Thea just stared blankly at him over the rim of her glass. "How does that help me?"

"Go in like it's a done deal. Assume the job's still yours. Assume the guy still loves you. Show up like he's going to thank you for being there."

"Just like that?"

"Just like that."

She'd never be able to pull off anything so bold, would she? But Brandon made it sound so reasonable, and she couldn't imagine living the rest of her life without at least trying to tell Aiden how wrong she'd been to reject him.

Hope started to unfurl in her chest. "Go big or go home, right?"

"Exactly. Go get your job. Go get your man." He pulled his car keys from his pocket and dropped them on the bar in front of her. "It's a rental. Don't wreck it."

"How will you get back to the office?"

He waved her off as he glanced around the Elephant, which was starting to fill up with a lunch crowd. "Oh, don't you worry. Unlike you, I'm not in love with anybody, and I see plenty of pretty young things just dying to be chatted up by an out-of-town businessman." He emptied his drink and waved the empty glass at Tammy. "If I strike out, there's always Uber."

She stood and slung her purse over her shoulder. "You know, you might just be the most memorable boss I've ever had."

"Why, thank you." He sounded genuinely appreciative as he flashed his bright white smile, although she hadn't exactly given him a compliment. Then he said, "If things don't work out with the job, let me know and we'll take you back in a heartbeat."

She snatched up the keys, suddenly eager to get started on her new plan. "No offense, but I hope I never see you again."

"Some taken," he said with a faint smile. "Now get out of here. I want your desk cleaned out by the end of the day."

"Th-thank you," she said, overwhelmed and a little giddy. She left him to his hunting grounds and drove back to the Brick with a head full of plans and a heart full of hope.

TWENTY-EIGHT

Aiden was starting to get pissed.

Voices from the lobby had been floating in through his closed office door all morning, but now the conversation had ratcheted up to full-blown waves of laughter. What could possibly be so goddamn funny out there this early on a Monday?

The temp agency must've sent a different person this morning because last week's receptionist hadn't spoken above a whisper and definitely wasn't suited to a workplace filled with a bunch of rowdy hammer jockeys. But he couldn't say for sure because he'd parked his truck in the back and headed straight to his office to avoid the hassle of small talk and basic human pleasantries.

He was shit at basic human pleasantries these days.

He ground his teeth at another roar of laughter from the front room of the lobby area and grimly turned his attention back to the stack of résumés in front of him. One of the people on these pages might be the perfect replacement for his mom, and once that person was hired, he could execute the next step of his plan to win Thea back.

Step One: hire a receptionist to show her that he didn't love her because of what she could bring to his company. Step Two:...

Okay, he didn't have a step two yet, but it probably involved apologies and moving slow. He was willing to take things as slowly as she wanted. Start from scratch with a real first date and a real first kiss.

No, fuck that. Kissing Thea had been real long before his brain had figured out what his heart was telling him. He missed her with a ferocity that threatened to overwhelm him sometimes. But he couldn't start figuring out how to win her back until he found someone good to run the office, so he forced himself to turn back to the papers on his desk. He'd just started skimming the work history on the top sheet when another commotion exploded in the lobby. This one sounded far less hilarious than the last few outbursts. In fact, some of the voices sounded downright urgent.

He set the résumé down and cocked his head, bracing himself for a summons to deal with whatever crisis had just occurred. But nobody came knocking on his door. Everything was quiet. *Suspiciously* quiet. Since he'd taken over for his dad, he'd learned that quiet wasn't necessarily a good thing.

"Goddammit." He growled the word as he stalked to his door and threw it open to see the new kid they'd hired last month hurrying toward the bathrooms with— Shit, was that blood on his shirt?

"Trevor! What's happening?"

The kid jumped at the sound of his voice and looked down at the red spatters on his hand. "Samuelson got himself with a nail gun."

"Got himself?" Fuck. "Where is he?"

The kid jerked his head toward the back room, but before Aiden went to check it out, he asked, "You okay?"

"I'm fine. It's not my b-blood. It's just..." Trevor's already pale face blanched even further, and he turned and bolted toward the restroom. Jesus, what kind of carnage was waiting for him back there? He charged down the hall and burst through the workroom door to find... everything under control.

"Benny, did you find the clean towels? Let's get Jesse's station cleaned up." The woman in the center of the controlled chaos pointed to the workbench in the corner of the room, and time seemed to slow down as Aiden's heart expanded to fill his chest.

Thea. Focused, calm, and the most beautiful sight he'd ever seen. When she turned, her gaze barely paused on him as she turned to another of his employees. "Did you find the first aid kit?"

"Yes, ma'am." The grizzled workplace vet handed the case over, and Thea gently rested her hand on Samuelson's back. "I'd like to get this cleaned up a little to see what we've got, okay?"

"I'm fine," Samuelson said through gritted teeth. "Don't fuss."

Aiden opened his mouth to forcefully remind the guy that company policy dictated all injuries be checked out immediately, but Thea didn't give him the chance.

"Come on," she coaxed in a firm, playful voice. "We can do it in the ladies' room. Haven't you always wanted to see what's through that mysterious door?"

Despite the bright red stain seeping through the cloth wrapped around his hand, Samuelson managed to laugh, and Thea guided him toward the restroom, the first aid kit under one arm.

When they walked past Aiden, she shot him a nervous smile. "Um, surprise?"

Then she hustled past him with her patient, leaving him rooted in place as the two of them pushed through the door to the hall. Ordinarily he'd insist on being part of the examination, but Samuelson always put on a tough-guy front with the guys, so it might be smart to give Thea a chance to take a look without him feeling the need to posture for anyone. Plus, the instant Aiden was face-to-face with her, he was going to have a hard time not falling to his knees and begging her to never leave. Instead, he helped Mendez clean up the area where Samuelson had been working, hiding his shudder at the tacky blood covering the workbench. Then he braved the restroom.

"How's it going?"

Thea looked up from the gauze she was wrapping around Samuelson's hand. "He'll survive, but he should get it checked out at prompt care. Human hands have tons of nerves and things, so a doctor needs to look at it." She held up her own and wiggled her fingers to demonstrate. "Gotta keep you nimble," she told Samuelson before addressing Aiden again. "Can you find someone to drive him to the hospital?"

It was so damn nice to hear her sweet voice again that for a split second he didn't move. But Samuelson's grimace of pain spurred him into motion. "I'll pull my truck to the front." No need to make the poor guy walk past the scene of the accident in the back.

In the lobby, Trip pushed through the workroom door and skidded to a halt when they spotted each other. "What the hell did I miss?"

"Samuelson nail-gunned his hand. I'm going to take him to get it checked out. Also, Thea's here."

Trip blinked once. "Okay, how about I take Samuelson to get checked out and you stay and talk to Thea?"

Aiden didn't waste a second objecting. "Good plan. Thanks."

A few minutes later, Trip had loaded the injured man into his truck with a promise to report back, and Aiden was left loitering outside the ladies' room with his hands jammed into his jeans pockets, waiting for Thea to emerge.

When she finally did, he pushed himself off the wall. "So you're the new temp who's had my guys laughing all morning, huh?"

As *give me a second chance* lines went, that one sucked balls, but he was so damn grateful to see her again that his woman-wooing skills flew from his head. Thankfully, she rolled with it, giving a self-conscious curtsy before twining her fingers together. "Yep! Just um... you know. Trying something new."

"Impressive performance so far. Did I miss a stretch when you worked as a paramedic or something?"

She relaxed as he spoke, her hands landing on her hips and her lips curling into a familiar Thea grin. "Former nanny, remember? I did a first aid course for that one."

"Thank God. You were a billion times calmer than anybody else would've been."

She lifted her chin. "I'm super-temp. Speaking of, I should..." She jerked her thumb toward the front desk, and Aiden's first instinct was to tell her that the phone and client requests and the whole damn business could go to hell.

But he knew a little bit about the woman he loved,

and he knew she'd want to do the job she was here to do. So he nodded instead of begging her to stay and talk to him in the hallway for the rest of time.

Still, he reached out and caught her wrist as she walked past. "Don't leave for the day without stopping by my office, okay?"

He didn't miss the hitch in her breathing or the nervous swipe of her tongue over her lower lip. "Okay."

The rest of the day proceeded at the slowest pace Aiden had ever endured. The minutes dragged. The hours crawled. Trip texted that Samuelson's hand was going to be fine. Laughter ebbed and flowed from the lobby area again, and Aiden was murderously envious of every person in this building who got to enjoy Thea's smiles. But he kept his distance for fear that he'd lose all control and throw her over his shoulder so he could find out what she was doing here.

Finally—fucking finally!—the day ticked to a close, and there was a soft knock on his door. Thea stuck her head into the office. "Is now a good time?"

"God yes." He shot to his feet and walked around the desk, fingers itching to touch her. But he stopped a few feet away. If she was here, it had to be for a reason, and he was absolutely not going to assume a damn thing this time. He'd spent all day trying to squash the hope bubbling up in his chest, but looking at her sweet face now, he couldn't hold back the words. "I meant what I said that morning."

Color washed over her cheeks, but she didn't look away. "Do you still? Mean it?"

He took a step closer, his voice dropping. "Are you asking if I still love you?"

Her breath hitched at the word, and she nodded, her big brown eyes locked on his.

"Yes. I do," he said. "And I want to date you."

She blinked. "What?"

"You said we'd never even gone on a date. You're right, and you deserve that." Another step brought him close enough that he could reach out and touch her, but he held himself back. "You deserve someone who sees you across a room and says, '*Her*. I want to get to know her better.' You deserve someone who'll pick you up at your front door and boost you up into his truck because it's too tall for your gorgeous legs."

Another step. Another few inches closer to the woman who was more important to him than anything in the world.

"You deserve someone who'll choose a quiet restaurant so he can hear everything you say over dinner. Because the things you say, Thea? The funny, smart, surprising things that come out of your mouth? I don't want to miss a single word."

She was blinking faster now as tears gathered at the corners of her eyes, and Aiden finally reached for her, cupping her face and blotting the moisture on her lashes with his thumbs.

"You deserve someone who'll drive you home and walk you to the door and kiss you good night. You deserve someone who'll leave you with a fast pulse and sweet dreams, who'll come back and take you out again, over and over, until he's shown you that he's worthy of your good, trusting heart." He leaned down, desperate to kiss her but reluctant to push. "You deserve *everything*, and I want to be the man who gives it all to you. I'll be patient. You made me believe I could offer someone a lifelong commitment. And now I want to date you and hold your hand and wait for you to believe you're worthy of that too. As long as it takes."

As he spoke, his hands slid down to caress the sides of her throat, then skimmed over her shoulders to fall by his sides as he waited in agony for her next words. Slowly, ever so slowly, her stunned expression shifted into a frown.

"No," she said. "I don't want that."

Pain lashed through him at her words, but before he could respond, she reached for his hand.

"I don't need any of that. I just need *you*." She tilted her head up to meet his eyes. "You overwhelm me. I didn't think it would be possible, but you make me want forever."

His palm met hers, small and soft in his grip. "Oh yeah? Forever?"

"I know. Such a long time." She shook her head helplessly. "But it turns out, loving you is actually really easy once you let yourself."

Joy. Total joy coursed through his veins at her words, and his whole body lit up. "You love me?"

"I do. So much," she said. "*Forever.*"

He studied her face, searching for any trace of doubt or fear, but her eyes were dreamy and her lips tipped up at the corners. This was what Thea looked like when she finally let herself believe in him, in *them*. He'd been sincere about every compliment he'd ever paid her, but time and again she'd brushed his words aside or laughed them off. Today though, he saw how she transformed when that belief sank into her bones. He never wanted her to lose that, so he did his part to drive the message home.

Sliding his arm around her waist, he pulled her close and said, "If I get to have any say in it, I'd choose to be with you forever too."

"You get some say in that, yes." She inhaled shakily and rested a hand on his chest. "So new plan: I'm choosing you. Work and home. My whole life. With my whole heart." Then a wicked little smile stretched across her face. "And I'm not just saying that because you still owe me a skylight in the bedroom."

"I'll get started on it tonight." He wrapped his other arm around her and lifted her up so she could wrap her legs around his waist and he could have unfettered access to her lips.

She looped her arms around his neck. "I might have a couple of things on my to-do list that are a little more important than that."

"Like what?"

"Me, for one," she said pertly, and he tightened his hold on her so he could open his office door, flick off the light, and carry her down the hall toward his truck so he could drive them straight home.

But they got a little delayed when he spun and pressed her against the wall so he could kiss her until they were both breathless.

"There's a lot more of that on my list," she said huskily when they pulled away. "But with a lot fewer clothes."

He groaned. "What am I going to do with you, killer?"

"Love me for the rest of our lives?" She looked up at him, and he had to kiss her again.

"Yep. That's the plan."

EPILOGUE

Nine years later

"Absolutely not!"

The two Murdochs froze as Thea stepped onto the front porch and slammed the hobbit door behind her.

"But Mom! I want to help!"

Thea turned her narrowed gaze on her husband. "A ladder? Really?"

Aiden shot her an apologetic smile. "A short ladder. With her dad standing right behind her."

She pressed a hand to her heart. "I swear, you two take ten years off my life every time you work around the house together. And *you*." She cast her eyes down at Blue, who was stretched on her belly and watching the pair with a doggy smile on her face. "We talked about this. You're supposed to bark for me when he lets the seven-year-old handle power tools."

Blue yipped and returned to her happy tongue-lolling

supervision of the installation of the Christmas decorations.

"It's a hammer." Aiden reached up to swing Leigh off the ladder. "A small hammer."

"I put the lights over the nails!" Leigh pointed to the strand of lights draped around the picture window in the front of the house, her face glowing with excitement, and Thea melted immediately. That girl had her father's charm to go along with his hazel eyes.

"You did an outstanding job," she said. "Think we'll be the best on the block again this year?"

"We'd better be, given our many years of combined home-improvement experience." Aiden pulled her tight against him, and she gladly slid into his embrace. The late-November air was too cold to be endured without the warmth of her handsome husband's body wrapped around her.

"Speaking of, I've got a line on a new venue for the company holiday party. Want any details before I book it?"

Aiden gave her the answer he'd used frequently during their nine years working together at Murdoch Construction. "Nah, I trust you."

"It'll be epic," she promised.

"When you're in charge, it always is." He noticed Leigh moving toward the rosebushes flanking the front porch and released Thea to crouch next to their daughter. "Remember what we talked about?"

"Grandpa planted these years before I was born, and if we're careful with them, they'll come back every year." She dutifully recited the information as Thea drifted over to join them.

"They don't look like much now, but they'll be beautiful again if we're just patient," Thea said.

"Patience." Leigh groaned.

"I know that's not your strong suit, baby doll," Aiden said, swinging her into his arms. "Let's get you inside and warmed up. We can be impatient together for dinner."

He walked up the porch steps with their daughter clinging to his neck, and Thea followed them. "Oh dear, did you two want dinner tonight? But you had dinner *last* night."

"And the night before that!" Leigh yelled as she and Aiden disappeared into the house.

"My demanding family," she said to Blue as the dog scampered into the warmth of the house, where photos of friends and family competed with Leigh's crayon drawings on the fridge and Peter's housewarming plant was a flourishing green fixture on the windowsill. Thea paused on the front porch to take in the work the pair had done that afternoon. Greenery decorated the railing, and the twinkle lights around the window glowed in the encroaching dark. A huge wreath hung in the center of the hobbit door, decorated with ribbons and pine cones and a plastic unicorn that Leigh had insisted on tucking right in the middle.

Before she joined her family inside, she leaned over to run her finger over one of the spindly branches of the rosebush, bare now but waiting to burst to life again in the spring. "Thanks for making my house so beautiful, Dad," she whispered.

The door creaked open, and she dashed away a tear as Aiden stepped into the wedge of light from the hallway.

"Are you with us?" He held out his hand, and she reached out and took it.

"Always."

Craving more Aiden and Thea?
Head here for a heart-stoppingly romantic bonus epilogue:
www.sarawhitney.com/lies

When Faith Fox comes face-to-face with the boy who almost destroyed her, he's all grown up and more dangerous to her heart than ever. **Tempting Fate** *is a sexy second-change romance. Preorder now, or sign up to be notified the instant it's available:*
http://www.sarawhitney.com/VIP

Dear reader,

2020 was a hard year.

pause while you laugh uncontrollably at what an understatement this is

But the thing is, hard years call for joy too. And more than anything, I hope that Thea and Aiden brought you a little bit of joy. If they did, I would love it if you'd share that. Drop me a line on my website. Leave a review at your retailer of choice. Tell a friend about the goofy, sexy book you read. Or just hold the warm glow of this happily-ever-after in your heart as you go about your business. Whatever works for you.

Speaking of joy, Tempting Lies wouldn't be the book it is without gallons and gallons of coffee, T. Swift's Folklore, and the support of my fantabulous friends. Yes, the year has been hard, but good people and good music and good booze and good laughs got me through it. I wish the same for you, reader.

I'm cooking up an epic second-chance romance for Faith Fox and the one who got away in Tempting Fate. Be sure to sign up for my mailing list so you'll know when it's available: **sarawhitney.com/newsletter**

Stay sassy, and stay in touch!

Sara Whitney

ALSO BY SARA WHITNEY

The Cinnamon Roll Alphas Series

Tempting Heat

Tempting Taste

Tempting Talk

Tempting Lies

Standalone novellas

Game On

Ghosted

Praise for Sara Whitney

Tempting Lies

"Sweet and funny and sexy all at once. I couldn't put this down." *Marianela Aybar, Mari Loves Books Blog*

"The right blend of sass and steam. Sara Whitney's smooth, upbeat prose is a delight to read. I devoured it fast. Too fast." *Elle Greco, author of the LA Rock Star Romance series*

"The roller-coaster ride the author takes us on getting to their happily ever after left me feeling slightly broken but so happy and hopeful." *Kristen Lewendon, Renaissance Dragon Book Blog*

"Thea and Aiden (loooooved these two together!) were unputdownable in so many moments, unforgettable in a lot of the others. If you love a fake relationship trope in romance, then you will adore this duo." *Briana, Renee Entress's Blog*

Tempting Talk

"A sweet, witty, and engaging story featuring likable, complex characters." *Laurie, Laurie Reads Romance*

"The interactions are hilarious, while the sparks are flying everywhere. I was all in cover to cover." *Jennifer Pierson, The Power of Three Readers*

"A fun, sweet and passionate romance. I loved these two, individually and together." *Valeen Robertson, Live Thru Books Blog*

Tempting Taste

"Sara Whitney has pulled together the most fun you'll have in a bakery with this one! I loved the cupcake-baking, cinnamon roll hero who looks like the God of Thunder. Hello to my new book boyfriend." *Christina Hovland, author of the Mile High Matched series*

"Sexy, sassy, and downright delicious! Whitney's pint-sized heroine and strong-but-silent hero make for the perfect pairing. Tempting Taste brims with her trademark wit, humor and warmth." *Kate Bateman, author of This Earl Of Mine*

"I love a broody hero, and Erik was amazing! Sweet, humorous and full of so much sexual tension." *Messy Bun Book Blog*

"A fun, sexy read full of humor and heart." *Sarah Hegger, author of Positively Pippa and Roughing*

Tempting Heat

"It made my heart squeeze and my cheeks flush. Finn and Tom are 100% guaranteed to make. you. swoon." *Blair Leigh, author of What Comes After*

"A brilliant read. I adored it from beginning to end." *Sandra, Jeanz Book Read & Review*

"The perfect amount of tension, smoldering heat, unexpected twists, and satisfying conclusion." *Sarah, Paranormal Peach Reviews*

"Seriously juicy, swoon-worthy, and light-hearted romance." *Jasmine, Reading with Jax*

ABOUT THE AUTHOR

 Sara Whitney writes sassy contemporary romance that's always sunny with a chance of sizzle. A multiple award-winning author, Sara worked as a print journalist and film critic before she earned her Ph.D. and landed in academia. She's a good pinball player, a great baker, and an expert at shouting her TV opinions to anyone who'll listen. Sara lives in Illinois surrounded by books, cats, and half-empty coffee cups. She loves hearing from readers, so drop her a line at sara@sarawhitney.com or find her on social media:

BB bookbub.com/profile/sara-whitney

f facebook.com/sarawhitneyauthor

g goodreads.com/SaraWhitney_

a amazon.com/author/sarawhitney

O instagram.com/sarawhitney_

🐦 twitter.com/sarawhitney_

Made in the USA
Las Vegas, NV
27 October 2021

33204487R00194